Hemlock

A Maeve Malloy Mystery

by Keenan Powell

Copyright Page

Hemlock Needle
A Maeve Malloy Mystery

First Edition | January 2019
Level Best Books
www.levelbestbooks.com

Trade Paperback ISBN: 978-1-947915-09-1
Also Available in e-book

Printed in the United States of America

To Dylan, Brady and Reilly

PROLOGUE

August 17, 2014
Kuskokwim River
Fancyboy Fish Camp

E sther Fancyboy draped another salmon carcass on a drying rack alongside a row of fish twisting in the breeze. Returning to the cutting table, she reached for another thirty-pound fish, chopped off its head and gutted it with a few flicks of her ulu. She tossed the head into a bucket, saving it for soup later. The guts went into another bucket for dog food. The scraps she dropped to two puppies panting near the table who caught them mid-air. Then she split the fish lengthwise, leaving the tail as a handle.

A river boat killed its motor and coasted up onto the beach a few yards away. The puppies trotted off to greet the boy and young man climbing out of the boat. Esther's seven-year-old son, Evan, fell to his knees, let the puppies lick his face, then he ran up the hill with the puppies racing after him, just as generations of Yup'ik children before him had. *This is good*, Esther thought as she reached into the bucket at her feet for another fish.

Gordi, Esther's nineteen-year-old cousin, dragged the boat up onto the beach, then climbed up to the cutting table. "Waqaa!" Gordi called.

"Waqaa, Gordi. You have grown."

He was tall, lean, and strong, his skin darkened by sun.

This was their first meeting this summer as, until yesterday, she had been in Anchorage where she and Evan now lived. She had taken two weeks off from her job, telling her boss that her aging mother needed help. He believed her.

Andrew Turner would not have understood what fish camp meant to Yup'iks. Being with her family, hauling in nets full of fish, living in a shed on the riverbank, cooking and eating outdoors, telling stories when the family gathered after a long day of hard work, the sunlight, the wind, the water. These were the things Yup'iks had shared for thousands of years passing their traditions on from one generation to the next. She was part of them. And they were part of her. And all this was Evan's birthright.

Gordi watched Evan crest the hill, the puppies behind him, as he stood before Esther. "This morning I got curious."

Esther cleaned another fish and carried it to the rack. She stood on tiptoe to drape each half of the fish over the cross beam leaving enough room for the sun and wind to whirl around them. In a few days, they would be dried, and could be packed away for the winter.

She returned to the table and picked up another fish. The puppies reappeared a respectful distance away and sat tentatively, their eyes trained on Esther.

"What did you do?" Esther said as she lifted the ulu. The puppies inched closer.

"I climbed on top of the water tank. I pushed the lid off."

Gordi was a second-year engineering student at University of Alaska, Fairbanks. He had always been fascinated with how things work. Even as a little boy, he could be found at the elbow of some man peeking into the engine of a snow machine or boat.

Esther tossed the fish head into a bucket. "What did you see?"

"Nothing."

The puppies scattered when the ulu fell from Esther's hand.

CHAPTER ONE

Monday, January 7, 2015
Russian Orthodox Christmas
Gathering Place, Alaskan Native Medical Center
Anchorage, Alaska

*W*here did Esther go?

Evan Fancyboy searched the crowd for his mother. He squatted against the wall, arms around legs, chin on knees. A chilled breeze swept across the linoleum floor. Someone must have opened a door. Tiny stars of frost stroked his face.

He tugged at the neck of his t-shirt. If only his grandmother would let him take off his parka, he wouldn't be so itchy.

Grandma Cora was sitting with the elders in the front row, watching the performers. Dancers in flowered kuspuks waved fur-trimmed fans. Old men sang and beat drums. Maybe she couldn't see him take off the parka. Maybe Esther would hold it for him.

Esther, his mother, had been late coming home from work. Evan knew his classmates in Anchorage called their mothers "mom," but Evan still called his mother by her first name like he had in the village. Now he and Grandma Cora lived with Esther in Anchorage, two plane rides away from St. Innocent's.

Evan had never left the village before that day last summer when he and Grandma Cora boarded the little Cessna. As they took off and circled over the river, his house, his school, and the village looked like toys. The plane kept going up, creaking, bending and bouncing in the wind, as beneath them waves of caribou ran across the tundra looking like ants.

Cora gripped the arms of her seat, looking scared, but Evan liked the bumps; they made his stomach feel funny. That night, they stayed in Bethel visiting relatives, then got on the big jet airplane that took them to Anchorage. Cora didn't like that either when she saw how far away the ground was. Evan was happy. He was going to live with his mother.

When they arrived in Anchorage, Evan found he didn't like the city. The noise. The big, smelly cars on the roads. Strange people going in different directions. But he was with Esther every day now. In the morning, he'd find her in the kitchen looking a little sleepy. She would give him her special smile, the one she gave only to him. He would watch her cook his breakfast and pack his school lunch. Every afternoon, she came home and the three of them, Cora, Esther, and Evan, ate dinner together. In the evening, Esther helped him with his homework, then kissed him goodnight. His heart was happy.

Tonight, just before they left for the Christmas party, Evan was watching Grandma Cora in the kitchen when he heard Esther's car pull into the driveway. The car door closed. A few seconds later, the front door opened. Cold air seeped into the kitchen before Esther walked in.

Grandma Cora stretched plastic wrap across a bowl of akutaq, Eskimo ice cream, and slid a look in Esther's direction. Esther pretended not to notice.

"Waqaa," Esther said as she had ruffled Evan's hair. She gave him that special smile, just barely turning up the corners of her mouth, as if she and Evan shared a secret. Her smile blossomed inside his chest.

Evan buried his face inside Esther's leather jacket. He liked how the cow hide felt cool to his face but smelled smoky, like it was still warm. Moose hide wasn't like that. Moose hide smelled like moose.

Esther peeled back the plastic wrap and dug a spoon into the akutaq.

"Ach, no seal oil," Grandma said.

Grandma watched Esther taste the shortening, sugar, and blueberries she had whipped by hand.

Esther slid the spoon into her mouth and pulled it out again. For a moment, she pretended she was thinking hard. Then she smiled at Grandma. Evan's heart filled again. "No one has seal oil in Anchorage," Esther said. "Your akutaq is the best. Everybody says that."

"They forget what akutaq should taste like," Grandma said, but she looked pleased.

Esther draped her long shiny black hair over her jacket and pulled her car keys from a pocket. "Time to go."

Grandma eyed her from head to toe. Black slacks, black sweater, high-heeled boots, short black leather coat. "Where's your parka? You look cold."

"I'll be fine," Esther said.

"You might be Eskimo, but you're no polar bear," Grandma said. Then she turned to Evan. "Where is your parka?"

Evan felt his heart race. His mind went blank.

"By the front door, where he dropped it." Esther went into the hallway and came back with the hooded coat. She held it up for Evan while he shoved his arms into the sleeves.

"His mittens?" Grandma asked.

Evan searched his pockets. He looked around the floor at his feet. He looked at Esther. Maybe she'd know where his mittens were.

Esther ruffled Evan's hair again. "Don't worry. I'll pick up another pair next time I'm out."

It was already dark during the drive to the Native hospital where the Starring ceremony would be held. Snow started coming down hard. Great fluffy flakes splattered on the windshield, one and two at a time, then so many Evan couldn't count them. The car slid through drifts piling up in the road.

They parked in the special elders' row closest to the

building because Grandma was with them. By the time they walked to the entrance, they were covered in snow. They stopped over grating just outside the door and stomped their boots.

"You look like a snowman," Esther said, laughing as she brushed at Evan's hair. She stood on her toes, surveyed the room and gave a small nod of her head. Then she leaned over Evan and said, "You go with Grandma Cora, there's someone I need to talk to."

Evan followed his grandmother across the large room to a table covered with platters of smoked salmon, dried reindeer meat, and cookies. While she pushed plates aside to make room for her bowl of akutaq, Evan looked for his mother. But he couldn't see where she went. The room was too crowded.

Starring was the Russian Orthodox Christmas celebration, held every seventh of January. Grandma said all the Russian Orthodox Native people gathered at the hospital to celebrate because it was the only place big enough. She hoped to see people from her own village and relatives from nearby villages. But people from all over Alaska celebrated there too, including people she did not know and did not want to know, traditional enemies from the old days.

"Don't take off your parka," Grandma said. "You'll lose it. Just like the mittens."

Where did Esther go?

As the room filled, Evan hunted for his mother through a growing forest of legs. When the people in front of him shifted, he could no longer see Grandma. Maybe she couldn't see him either. It was hard to tell with her. She always seemed to know what he was doing even when she wasn't looking.

At the front of the room, two tinsel stars the size of truck hubcaps were being spun in the air, each held by a big Yup'ik man. An orthodox priest led the audience in Russian Christmas carols. Evan tugged at his t-shirt, moist with sweat. Cool air filled the space he made.

The singers were singing, and the spinners were spinning.

Behind them was a Christmas tree decorated in blue ribbon and gold ornaments, the colors of the Alaska flag. In school, Evan had learned the flag had been designed by a Native boy just like Evan. But he was different from Evan because his mother had died, and that boy had grown up in an orphanage.

Another breeze swept across the floor.

Evan's eyes followed the frozen mist to its source. With her back to her son, Esther held the door handle. He couldn't see her face. She draped her hair down the black leather jacket and said something to a girlfriend.

Then she pulled the door open and walked into the blizzard.

CHAPTER TWO

M aeve Malloy settled on the edge of a damask chair in front of Arthur Nelson's desk, her fingers dancing across the upholstery as she watched him read. The receptionist withdrew quietly like a nurse afraid to disturb a dying patient.

The closing of the door muffled the law office clatter. The deferential feminine voices and machinery hum outside could barely be heard over the whispering of papers in Arthur's hand.

Something was wrong. Maeve could feel it. She could see it in the secretary's stolen glance as she bowed her head and turned away. She could tell by the way Arthur refused to look at her, pouring over the papers in his hand instead.

Maeve caught her ghost-like reflection in the windows behind Arthur's desk. Her shoulder-length auburn curls were weighted down by melting snow. Dark shadows hid her green eyes and accented her cheekbones, making her look skeletal. Her face looked thinner than she'd remembered. Her turtleneck and jeans hung on her loosely.

Maeve only wore a suit if she was going to court. Every other day, jeans and a turtleneck. Or, in the summer, jeans and a t-shirt. What's the point of living in Anchorage, Alaska, if you had to dress like you're going to work in LA? She didn't have court today, only this last-minute meeting Arthur had called so Alaska-casual it was.

Arthur turned another page. Sitting behind a massive mahogany desk in a high-backed leather chair, he looked imperial in an expensive gray suit, gray silk tie, and a thick head of neatly-trimmed silver hair. He had never been so aloof toward her before. She wondered if she should have worn a suit after all.

One of the most widely renowned trial attorneys on the West Coast, Arthur Peter Nelson had won multi-million-dollar lawsuits. He'd served as Alaska's attorney general. Now he was the senior partner of a large downtown Anchorage law firm representing well-heeled clients in business and property matters, the exact opposite of Maeve's little criminal defense practice, where her clients were lucky to have jobs. She represented people who didn't have the wherewithal to speak for themselves, didn't understand the legal system and would be squashed like road kill if they didn't have a champion.

Just over a year ago, Arthur had stepped forward to act as Maeve's mentor, professional penance demanded by the Alaska Bar Association after she finished an alcohol rehabilitation program.

After Arthur agreed to the mentorship, they had met regularly talking about law, talking life stories, talking sobriety. Maeve had come to see Arthur as more than a mentor. He was the first strong male figure who had taken an interest in her career. She trusted him, respected him, and yearned for his approval, which had been, until today, gently bestowed.

She didn't know why he had called her in. But it couldn't be good, given how the secretary behaved and Arthur's coolness.

Arthur signed the last paper and dropped it into the basket. He rocked back in his chair and looked at her like a doctor examining a patient.

"What are we going to do with you?"

"Pardon?"

"The bar complaint."

Maeve's heart flopped. "What bar complaint?"

"The Bar Association was kind enough to fax me a copy.

Take a look." He selected a sheaf of papers from his in-box and slid them across the desk.

The packet was a simple stack of white paper, black ink, stapled in the left-hand corner. An ordinary legal document, like the ones she handled every day. Maeve teetered on the edge of her chair, hands folded in her lap parochial-school style, as she examined the top page.

Arthur spun the document around and pushed it closer to Maeve. *In the Matter of Maeve Malloy,* she read. One paragraph in, Maeve knew what everyone else knew. Someone had accused of her of negligence.

Her mind fogged over. This couldn't really be happening. Not now. She'd done everything the bar had asked. She'd gone to rehab. She'd gone to AA meetings. She'd met with Arthur religiously. She hadn't missed a court hearing or a deadline, not that she ever had before, even when she was still drinking.

She'd just won the Olafson murder case, which she had taken only three weeks before trial. For that, Arthur dubbed her "the bulldog," commending her for digging out evidence no one else had seen.

Her clients loved her.

Still frozen over the pages on the desk, Maeve flicked her eyes to meet Arthur's. His face was hard. She couldn't bear to hold his gaze. She looked back down at the papers, unfocusing her sight so she wouldn't see the words. "That's why I went to rehab. The bar knows I went to rehab. So why this? Why now?"

"The bar knew you had a drinking problem and you were addressing it. Now they have an accusation of malpractice. There's no statute of limitations and no double jeopardy in bar proceedings. This is a very serious accusation, Maeve. I must caution you. While we're mounting your defense, it would be irresponsible to take new cases. You could be suspended from practice. Or worse."

Or worse. Disbarred.

Just like that. Law school, bar exam, didn't matter. All the good work she'd done, the people she'd saved, didn't matter.

The room was suddenly cold. The air crackled, not in a way that could be heard, but in a way that could only be felt. Everything looked flat, two-dimensional. Maeve's body felt as if it had been assembled incorrectly, her bones not quite fitting into the joints, the joints not quite bending the way they should. Beyond the floor to ceiling window, grey blocks of ice shifted across Cook Inlet, like an M.C. Escher painting in motion.

A phantom taste of beer crossed her tongue.

Before, after a bad day at work, or a good day were she to be honest, she'd grab a bottle out of the refrigerator, twist off the cap, and guzzle half of it before the fridge door drifted shut, her pledge of staying sober born of the shame of the night before dismissed. When the beer was gone, she'd start on the white wine. Then she'd finish off the night on her knees with her arms wrapped around the toilet, puking her guts up. Vomiting was cathartic. The next day, she'd arrive at work, zinging with the energy and, at the same time, shrouded with a vague guilt for what she never figured out. But by four p.m., she was ready to do it all over again.

None of that was an option for her anymore. She'd endure whatever would come. Sober. Awake. Painfully alert.

She pushed into the depth of the wing-back chair as numbness crept across her. She wanted to pull up her legs, wrap her arms around them and curl into a ball. On the other side of the desk, Arthur watched her over steepled fingers. The last thing she needed was her mentor thinking she was having a breakdown. So, instead of regressing right then and there as she wished so badly to do, Maeve pressed her feet into the floor and her palms together in her lap.

The only verbal response she could muster was unspeakable in polite company, so she remained silent.

"I've read the allegations which, frankly, come as a bit of a surprise," Arthur said. "You're the finest young attorney I know. I wouldn't have expected the behavior described in this complaint from you. Explain to me what happened."

Maeve took a deep breath, held it, and slowly exhaled

through pursed lips. The Mataafa case. The last case she had tried as an assistant public defender before going to rehab.

"That's the case I told you about a few months ago," Maeve said. "Right before the Olafson trial, I told you how the D.A. accused me of manufacturing evidence. He was talking about the Mataafa trial."

"Tell it to me again," Arthur said. "Slowly."

"Filippo Mataafa was accused of armed robbery of a liquor store. He produced a witness, Enrique Jones, who told me that Filippo had been with him all that night in a strip club, so there was no way Mataafa could have committed the robbery. Mataafa insisted on testifying and he insisted I put Jones on the stand. After the trial started, Tom found a witness who told him that Enrique was lying, that he hadn't been at the strip club that night."

"Tom Sinclair, your investigator?"

"He used to work with me at the P.D.'s. We worked this case together," Maeve said. "Right after finding the witness, Tom had to go out of town. He couldn't get hold of me and tell me about this new evidence. He left a note in the file, but I didn't see it. I put Mataafa and Jones on the stand. The jury must have thought the alibi was genuine. It was so unsavory, you know. Who admits they were paying for lap dances to get out of a robbery?"

"That's a crucial bit of evidence. Tom didn't try very hard to alert you."

"It's not his fault." Maeve had recounted the story to only one other person, her AA sponsor, and when she had, she'd hoped it was the last time she'd ever have to confess.

The story hung around her neck like the proverbial albatross, sometimes so heavy that she felt her head drawn down. When she unearthed it the last time, it felt like the sharp, jagged edges slashed her insides and left her aching.

"Tom called but I didn't hear the phone. He says he came by the house and knocked on the door. I didn't hear it, but I believe him. Tom doesn't lie. If he said it happened, it happened.

He wrote the note and stuck it inside the file, in the comments log, where I should have looked before the trial day started. We're trained to do that, look at that comments log whenever we open a file."

There, the story was out. Most of it, anyway.

"It's on me," Maeve said. "It's all on me. The jury delivered an acquittal. We were still in the courtroom, and the jury had just filed out. Mataafa and his friends were jumping up and down shouting, the judge was yelling at everyone to sit down and be quiet, when I saw Tom's note. It'd been there the whole time. It said 'alibi NG.' Alibi no good."

Arthur's eyebrow arched.

Maeve waited for the question, that one question Arthur, the experienced attorney, was bound to ask. The answer to that question felt like it was caught in her chest. She couldn't get it out on her own.

"Why didn't you see the note?" Arthur asked.

Maeve took in a deep breath, deliberately, slowly, buying time. Something caught in her throat, choking her. She coughed, and a disgusting wad slithered into the top of her throat. Being a lady, she swallowed it.

The other shoe was about to drop.

"Because I got drunk the night before."

Maeve paused as her response fell into place in Arthur's mind, then continued. "I was hungover and late to court that morning. I didn't look at the file."

A sudden lull in the secretaries' chatter amplified the funereal silence inside Arthur's office. Ambient sound seemed to roar with the throb of electricity, the winding up of furnace fans.

As the result of Jones's alibi, Filippo Mataafa had gone free. A few months ago, he had killed an innocent bystander in a drive-by shooting. He had been arrested and charged. That information was public knowledge. His alibi witness, Enrique Jones, was with him and had been charged with felony murder. That was public information too.

But what wasn't public information was that Jones had cut a deal. Not only did he agree to testify against Mataafa in the drive-by, he admitted to lying during Maeve's trial. Very few people knew that.

"Who made the complaint? I missed that." Maeve reached for the bar complaint. Before she could flip the top page, Arthur answered.

"Addison Royce, the public defender. Your former boss."

And ex-lover.

❦❦❦

Law Office of Maeve Malloy
Anchorage, Alaska

Maeve opened the door to her office. The empty receptionist's desk faced her. When she first opened shop, she'd bought it cheap from an attorney going out of business, figuring someday she'd have the money to fill it with an hard-working, loyal and extremely competent employee. She pulled off her heavy winter boots and tossed them over the desk into the pit between two banks of file cabinets.

"Where the hell have you been?" a man's voice called from the next room, her inner office. "You're late for your lesson."

The speaker was her investigator, the tall, sinewy Thomas Sinclair. He peered out the window as if searching for prey. Well over six feet tall with short sandy hair and rawboned face, he looked like a giant golden eagle. Pity the vermin who caught his eye.

It was Tom who had intervened when Maeve's drinking had gotten her into rehab. It was Tom who quit his job in solidarity when she came back and was shuttled to desk-duty. He'd been with her ever since.

Like the big brother she had never had, Tom knew all there was to know about her. Almost. You don't tell your big brother everything.

He flipped a rubber knife in the air. The knife slapped solidly as it fell into his hand. Ropey muscles in his arm bunched as he maneuvered the toy. The starched sleeve of his pale blue shirt rode up revealing the gold Rolex watch he said he won in a poker game.

"Man, it's good to see you," Maeve said.

"You okay?"

"Not even close."

On the two-block slog from Arthur's office, Maeve had brooded as she forged through unshoveled snow. It was just light enough that the stars had disappeared, and the silhouetted downtown office buildings were gray against violet blue skies. As she plowed along, Maeve's thoughts plummeted to that dark place where she hid things she couldn't face.

She had screwed up.

By getting Filippo Mataafa acquitted, she had been responsible for the death of an innocent man, Manuel Reyes, a husband and father who worked two jobs to support his family. A warehouse day job and a second job delivering newspapers after midnight. He had just made a drop along his route at a liquor store, a place of known drug dealing and shoot-outs. In the wrong place at the wrong time. Manny was hit by a stray bullet when Mataafa shot at a rival drug dealer. The drug dealer lived. Manny Reyes died.

If only she'd found Tom's note, Mataafa would have been convicted. And Manuel Reyes would be working his day job at this very moment. He would have just spent Christmas with his family.

Since his death, a day had not gone by when she didn't think about Manny Reyes. When she got up in the morning, she imagined how he would just be getting home from his paper delivery job, tip-toeing into the house so as not to wake the family. When she poured another cup of coffee in the afternoon, he would have been pulling himself out of bed to make his four p.m. shift at the warehouse. Every night, she looked at her bedside clock glowing midnight, just when he would clock out at the warehouse and drive to the newspaper office to pick up the first run, hot off the presses.

Maeve had screwed up. Royce knew it. The D.A. knew it. Everyone was going to know. Everyone in the Bar Association and everyone at court were going to talk about how a man had died because of Maeve Malloy. She didn't know what would be worse, losing her law license, public shaming, or her own guilt, but nothing she would suffer compared to the fact that a man's life had been erased and a great hole had been torn in his family.

Maeve peeled her coat off and threw it on the receptionist's desk. She fell behind her own desk. "Arthur called me in. A new bar complaint was filed."

Tom froze. "For what?"

"The Mataafa thing."

Maeve lifted a hurricane glass-cum-pen caddy, a drinking souvenir from a defender's convention in New Orleans. A vague image flashed across her memory of holding the sweating cold glass to her cheek as she sat in a bar next to Addison Royce while beneath the table their fingers lightly played with each other's hands, linking, unlinking, stroking, squeezing.

Maeve spun the glass gently in the air. A bouquet of pens swiveled around, tinkling like ice cubes.

"Who filed it?" Tom caught the knife. "No. Wait. Let me guess. That miserable bastard Royce?"

She spun the pens again before putting the glass down. "How'd you know?"

"I told you he'd screw you if he got the chance."

Tom had said that more than once. Every time he said it, he looked at her expectantly. He must have known about the affair. Not that it was any of his business.

Maeve lifted the hurricane glass again and poured the pens slowly across her desktop.

"It's a man thing." Tom crossed the room, planting himself squarely in front of her desk. He looked down at her. "Men need to dominate women. If they can't, they feel threatened. He couldn't dominate you at the P.D.'s so he ran you off. Now he's still trying to get rid of you."

"I don't understand." What she meant was that she didn't understand why Royce would want to destroy her because of their affair. What Tom meant was Royce was a chauvinist. Maybe they were talking about the same thing.

"You don't think like that. That's why you don't understand." Tom paused. When he spoke again, his voice was softer. "You sure something didn't happen between you and Royce?"

Maeve didn't answer.

A shift in Tom's weight conveyed he already knew. "Like I said, he'd screw you if he got the chance. One way or another."

Time to change the subject.

"I can't take any more cases while the bar complaint is pending," Maeve said.

"We're going to work this bar thing?"

"Arthur said not to. Anything I did would look like I was trying to influence the witnesses." Maeve gathered the pens and dropped them back into the glass.

"Counselor," Tom said sharply. Maeve raised her head to look at him.

"Since when do you do what you were told?"

CHAPTER THREE

F reezing air washed into the room when the hallway door
opened.

"Later," Maeve said quietly.

In the reception office, Maeve found a plump middle-aged
Native lady in a knee-length blue velvet kuspuk trimmed with
white fur. Her skin was the color of chestnuts, her short hair
black and shiny.

A small boy stood next to her in a store-bought parka. He
was lighter skinned than the woman, his eyes the color of green
amber.

"Cora?" Maeve asked. "Cora Fancyboy?"

When Maeve had been an assistant public defender in
Bethel, Cora Fancyboy was an interpreter. At the time, Cora was
raising her baby grandson, Evan, while his mother was in Anchorage finishing college. Cora would bring Evan to the office
and he napped in his carrier at their feet while she and Cora
interviewed clients and witnesses.

Once when Cora had gone to court with another attorney,
she left Evan with Maeve. When Cora placed him in her arms,
Maeve froze, afraid to move lest she drop the tiny body. The
baby with the green amber eyes gazed up at Maeve serenely. And
time seemed to stop.

Now, the boy with green amber eyes was looking at
Maeve, his face tense. Something inside her chest softened.
Could he possibly remember?

"Come in, please," Maeve said as she showed Cora and
Evan into her inner office. Cora sat in the middle of the couch,

her feet barely touching the floor. Evan sat next to her. Maeve took the adjacent chair.

"You remember Tom."

Cora nodded. That was as effusive as Cora got. She had grown up in St. Innocents, a Yup'ik village. Traditional Yup'iks were stoic, especially in the presence of white people.

Tom jammed a toothpick in his mouth and nodded in reply.

"What brings you two into the office on a school day?" Maeve asked Cora.

"We need to find my mom," Evan said.

Maeve looked to Cora for an explanation.

"Esther is missing," Cora said. Her words were formed carefully, spoken slowly and softly, with tiny squeaks added to her consonants.

"Since when?"

"Monday."

"This is only Wednesday," Tom said. Leaning in the doorway, he shuffled his feet, then moved the toothpick to the other side of his mouth. He made these subtle movements when they were interviewing people to convey that he doubted the witness's truthfulness. Tom was suggesting that two days was not a long time to be missing, if she really was.

"Where did you last see her?" Maeve asked.

"Starring," Cora said.

When Maeve had lived in Bethel, Cora took her on a Starring procession, the Russian Orthodox Christmas celebration. In the villages, people went from house to house spinning homemade stars and singing carols. In Anchorage, they celebrated at the Native hospital.

"Who saw her last?" Maeve asked.

Evan grunted, then said, "I did."

Maeve lowered her head closer to the boy's level. "What did you see?"

"She walked outside." Evan glanced at Maeve. In Yup'ik etiquette, one did not lock eyes with another person.

17

"Was she with anyone?" Maeve asked.

"No, but she talked to one of her friends right before she left." Evan's English was faintly accented.

Maeve asked, "Do you know the friend?"

"Someone she works with," Cora said.

"Have you called her?" Maeve asked Cora.

"She don't know nothing." A frown shimmered across Cora's face.

"Did Esther say anything when she left?" Tom asked.

"She was buying new mittens," Evan said. Tears sparkled on the fringes of his clenched eyes. His forefingers on each hand wheedled at his thumbs. The cuticles were frayed and raw. "I lost mine."

"Has anyone reported this to the police?" Maeve asked.

"She's not that kind of girl," Cora said.

"Sorry?" Maeve asked.

"The police said she was drinking with some man she met. She'd come home when she got tired," Cora said.

Tom shifted his weight again, confirming the police had voiced his suspicions.

"Esther is not that kind of girl." Cora spiked a look at Tom. She had known Tom in Bethel too and must have picked up on the meaning of his signals.

Evan reached into the pocket of his parka and dug out a folded paper. "On TV, they draw pictures to help find someone. I drew this picture for you."

Evan slid off the couch and carried the drawing to Maeve. There were three people. To one side was short, round Cora in a brightly flowered summer kuspuk. On the other side stood Evan. In the middle, taller than either of them, was a thin woman with long, black hair falling behind her shoulders. Behind them, a little house. At the bottom of the page was a blue river filled with red fish.

"This is St. Innocent's." Evan pointed to the figures as he spoke. "This is our house where we live. This is the river in front of our house. This is Esther."

"Do you miss St. Innocent's?"

Evan shrugged. "I like living with Esther."

Evan held the picture out, offering it to Maeve. He looked straight into Maeve's eyes with the gravity of an adult and asked, "Can you help me find my mom?"

She stood. "I'm really sorry, Evan, Cora, but I don't do missing persons. I wouldn't even know where to start. That's a job for the police."

"A word, Counselor?" Tom asked.

Tom ushered Maeve into the reception office and closed the door behind her.

"You got anything else better to do?" Tom asked.

"Arthur said I shouldn't take cases."

"This isn't a case. Not a real case. Tracking down missing persons doesn't take a law license so you can't get into trouble. Besides, I'll help."

"Cora doesn't have any money, Tom. And they're my friends. I won't even ask."

"Sometimes it's not about the money," he said. "Sometimes it's about doing the right thing."

Maeve ran her fingers through her hair. Chances were good that Esther had taken off. She'd gone to Fairbanks right after high school, ostensibly to go to college but ended up coming home after her freshman year pregnant and with bad grades. She'd been partying, just like most kids across America when they first escape their parents.

After Evan was born, Esther had left him with Cora while she went to Anchorage to finish her degree. It had been hard for Maeve to imagine how a mother could abandon her beautiful little boy, but Cora said that it was Yup'ik custom for grandmothers to raise the babies while the parents worked. Cora had expected to raise Evan. It was the privilege of being a grandmother.

Still, Esther had a track record of taking off.

Maeve walked back into her office with Tom close behind.

"We'll see what we can do," Maeve said to Cora.

Turning to Evan, she said, "Can I keep this drawing?"

Evan nodded. "I want Esther." He wiped his eyes with a fist. "I want my mother."

¥¥¥

Old Seward Highway
Midtown Anchorage

Maeve pointed down a side street where she'd spotted a car-shaped lump of snow. "Wait! Go back!"

"What?" Coffee choked Tom's voice. He took another sip and slid his travel mug back into the holder.

Tom's truck had been rattling across ridges and gullies, the road a morass of slick ice, soft ice and rock ice. Tom watched the traffic as he drove, alert for vehicles that might suddenly be thrown in front of him by the washboard surface while Maeve searched for snowed-in vehicles. When they'd reached midtown, Maeve felt as if the jostling had rearranged her internal organs. Her arms ached from gripping the dashboard.

"Abandoned car," Maeve said. "Let's check the plates."

Tom eased into the neighborhood. The roads were barely wide enough for one car to pass between snow banks, so Tom drove around the block to bring them behind the abandoned car. He sat behind the wheel, ready to move in case a snow grader came along, while Maeve pushed the door against the berm.

She squeezed out the narrow opening and stepped into thigh-deep snow. Frozen crystals trickled down her boot as it caved in around her leg, locking it into place. Bracing herself against the truck, she edged around it mindfully, careful not to fracture an ankle or knee as she fought to go forward.

Tom lowered his window and offered her an ice scraper. "You might want to check inside."

What he didn't say, but she knew he meant, was maybe someone had passed out in the car and had frozen to death while asleep.

Maeve scraped at the frost until a window was clear. Holding her breath, she peered in. No frozen people. She stood upright and flashed the zero sign at Tom. Then she brushed off the license plate and checked it for the number Cora had given her. Not a match.

Where could Esther possibly have gone? True, a number of missing persons turned up after several days of partying, unaware anyone was looking for them. Equally true, a number were found dead, by accident or otherwise.

Maeve planted her feet in the trail she had made as she waded back to the truck, thinking about Evan. Seven years old. Newly reconciled with his mother, new to Anchorage, apparently fatherless, the next generation of a culture fighting for its survival. He needed his mother.

Maeve couldn't remember her mother.

All Maeve could remember was pulling herself to stand, coming eye level with her mother's crossed legs, the stubby skin, the warm dry, white flesh, some freckles.

It must have been summer. Her mother was wearing shorts. Maeve was aware of bright sunlight. Her mother exhaled a plume of smoke, turned away from toddler Maeve, and flicked her cigarette over an ashtray on a coffee table.

That was all. Maeve couldn't reconstruct the face, the voice, the hair. She couldn't remember her mother speaking to her or caressing her or cuddling her like she had seen women do.

Her father had said her mother left because he knew that Maeve was better off with him. Maeve secretly believed that it was her fault. That her mother had left because there was something deeply wrong with Maeve.

Maeve's current problems, by comparison, were trivial. The bar complaint could wait. Arthur Nelson could wait. Addison Royce could wait.

Evan Fancyboy needed his mother.

⚡⚡⚡

Offices of Neqa Inc.
Anchorage, Alaska

Tom coasted his truck up to a golden glass office building several stories tall. In the south-facing bowed front, Maeve saw a reflection of the sun cresting the snow-covered Chugach mountains. To the west, a purple ribbon crept along the horizon of the blue-black late-morning sky.

In the fifth-story office sat a young Yup'ik woman with long silver dream catcher earrings inside a curtain of black hair, her face a composition of delicate features: epicanthic eyefold obscuring her eyelids, small nose, apple-shaped cheeks, rosebud lips. "May I help you?"

"We're friends of Cora Fancyboy," Maeve said. "She's asked us to look for Esther. We're hoping someone here could help us."

The receptionist appraised Tom and Maeve slowly.

"Just a minute." She rose from her post and disappeared down a hallway. A few minutes later, a short Yup'ik man in an expensive gray suit, gray shirt, and silk tie walked in.

"You want to know about Esther?" he asked Tom. He had the same soft, squeaky accent as Cora, only a little faster and louder.

"I'm Maeve Malloy." Maeve extended her hand, startling the little man. "We're hoping you could give us some information."

Without speaking, he turned and walked to a glass-enclosed conference room behind the reception area. After a moment of hesitation, Maeve, and then Tom, followed.

He stood at the head of the table and motioned for them to take a seat facing the Alaska Range, color blooming across it. Vague lavender shapes formed pink mountain tops and then sharpened into blue-white jagged peaks. Moments like these were the reason Maeve Malloy lived in Alaska even though she hated the cold and dark. But today, she wasn't feeling her usual awe. Today, the landscape looked flat, like a little kid's construction paper art project.

Tom maneuvered around the table, ostensibly to take a couple of photos of the landscape, but Maeve knew Tom was collecting photos of the little man as he snapped away. Tom's surreptitious photographs had come in handy before.

Maeve dug a pen and paper out of her briefcase. "Cora is worried something happened to Esther. Did you see her leave Starring?"

"I was with my family."

"Your wife?"

"My wife, my mother, my children. We went home early. It was a school night."

Tom ceremoniously took the chair beside Maeve's, plucked at the knees of his pressed jeans, then folded his hands on the table, distracting the little man. Tom had spent even more time in western Alaska than Maeve had, and he felt no compunction about appearing rude, knowing that the Yup'iks would both be disturbed by his behavior and write him off as an ignorant white person. He liked to stare at the witness with his raptor-yellow eyes as Maeve interviewed, see if he could knock him off balance, having a theory that an anxious witness gave more away, maybe not in words, but certainly in signs. And so, he stared at the man across the table.

The man held Tom's stare long enough with his own black eyes to establish a cross-cultural pissing contest. Turned away from Tom, Maeve couldn't see him, but she sensed he softened when the man's stare broke away.

Maeve said, "We were told Esther works here. We need information about what she does and who her friends are, so we can track her down." Then she added, "Sorry, I didn't catch your name."

The man's eyes flared, apparently surprised she needed to ask. "Xander George. I am the CEO of Neqa."

"What exactly is Neqa?"

"A cooperative of villages in western Alaska formed for

the purpose of developing and strengthening our economic interests." The response sounded as if it had been written by a marketing agency.

"What exactly do you do?"

"Investments and other economic opportunities."

Still vague.

"What does Esther do?" Maeve twirled the pen between her fingers.

"She doesn't work here. Cora is confused. She works at Turner International."

Maeve stabbed the pad with her pen. "So, what does she do there?" Maeve asked pointedly.

"Analyzes."

Xander must be a politician, Maeve thought. He formed words into sentences yet spoke utterly without substance.

"Why does Cora think she works here?"

"Neqa has a joint venture with Turner International. Esther is our representative in their office. We are working on a water system project for our villages. There is no running water. The people collect drinking water from the river where they dump their honey buckets."

Honey buckets, the wry euphemism for indoor outhouses. A closet in the house would be designated as the bathroom. A wooden bench was mounted against one wall with a toilet seat framing a hole cut in it. Beneath the bench was a five-gallon bucket that was periodically carried to the river and dumped. The first time Maeve had opened a door to the honey bucket room, the stench surprised her and fumes stung her eyes.

Disgusted with the memory, Maeve held her breath. She tried to suppress a reaction but too late. A flicker of movement came from Xander. Maeve forced her features to relax, but she could tell by the look on his face, the damage had already been done.

A Yup'ik's stare was a confrontation. Xander's stare was relentless.

"We'd really like to talk to Esther's friends," Maeve said.

Xander George stood. "Talk to the Turner people."

Maeve felt her eyebrows rise. One would think the CEO of such a small company, a regional Native corporation where everybody was related to everyone else, would know which of his employees were friendly. And, one would think he'd want to help find a missing village girl.

A vein in Tom's neck throbbed. He was thinking the same thing she was. They'd been working together for so long she didn't need him to say it. The little man was hiding something.

"I work mostly with the agencies," he said, as if the excuse explained his apparent lack of concern.

Maeve and Tom followed Xander out of the conference room. He walked back down the hall without a word.

Maeve stopped in front of the receptionist's desk while Tom rang for the elevator. "Do you know anything about Esther Fancyboy, where she might have gone, who she might be with?"

The receptionist opened her mouth, looked over her shoulder in the direction of Xander's departure, closed her mouth in a weak smile and shook her head.

She could be the girl Evan saw with his mother at Starring. Maeve wrote her cell number on the back of a business card and slid it across the desk. "Call me. Anytime."

The receptionist slipped the card under a message pad and said brightly, "Have a nice day."

CHAPTER FOUR

Turner International
Historic Alaska Railroad Depot
Anchorage Alaska

A tall man strode from a back office, paused, made eye contact and held up a finger in the just-a-minute sign.

Tom's cell phone camera clicked.

The man murmured a thanks-for-calling into the slim phone at his ear and then slipped it into his slacks pocket.

"Andrew Turner, pleased to meet you," he said as he stepped into the lobby with arm extended. "I understand you fine people are helping us find Esther. We're lost without her, really lost. I'm afraid we don't have anyone who can pick up the slack. Do you have any news?"

Maeve was so entranced by Turner's clear blue eyes and thick cap of golden hair, she barely noticed the receptionist's eye roll. To punctuate her commentary, the receptionist then tossed her long blonde hair, throwing a cloud of cloying perfume into the air. It was a pretty scent which would have been pleasant if there were less of it.

Tom stood off to the side in his we're-wasting-time pose, weight on his heels, hands jammed in his pockets, tongue exploring his teeth.

"Actually, we came here for information."

"Happy to help. I'm terribly busy, of course. Some crazy I.T. issue. Depends on what information you need. We're not free to disclose client information. Many of our projects are in delicate stages. Don't want the information getting out, you understand. Competitive edge and all that. Coffee?"

"Coffee?" Maeve was sorting out the blur of information when she realized he was offering. "Sure, love some."

"Jerri, bring us some coffee, would you, dear?" He gestured down a hallway. "Let's adjourn to my office, shall we? Last door on your right."

As he led the way, Turner stopped at an opened door. Inside the room was a scrawny young man in a faded t-shirt and jeans hunched in front of a large computer server. "Everything okay, Josh?" Turner asked. The I.T. guy nodded absentmindedly.

"Well, then, I'll leave you to it," Turner said with excessive cheeriness for having just been ignored.

The three proceeded down the hall with Turner bringing up the rear. He spoke into Maeve's ear. "Not very P.C. of me, calling her 'dear.'"

Maeve flinched, startled by his close proximity. She picked up her pace, passing Tom. When they rounded into the office, she turned and saw Andrew Turner smiling wolfishly at her. "Some days Jerri needs a little special treatment, know what I mean?"

Beyond a behemoth desk was a view of the Anchorage port: ships and cranes, boxcars and railroad tracks. Gray ice flowed out to sea while black clouds rolled in from the north. Ravens wheeled and swooped in the churning air.

Tom shot his cuffs, crossed his legs, ankle on knee, and brushed his shiny cowboy boots.

Turner caught a glimpse of Tom's Rolex, as he had intended. "Nice watch. Vintage?" he said, then inched up his sleeve revealing a black-faced watch with silver band. "Wife bought it for our anniversary."

Tom grunted.

"Nice office," Maeve said.

"The clients like posh, makes them feel secure. Especially the Natives. They love expensive things." Turner slid gracefully behind the desk.

"Me, I like urban chic," Turner said. "Simple, clean. In fact, I'm eyeing a piece of property right now. Let me show you the design."

He leapt from his chair, crossed the room, slid out a long thin drawer from an antique cabinet and selected a large sheet of paper. Squeezing in between Tom and Maeve, he spread a drawing across his desk.

Maeve dug her pen and pad out of her briefcase. "Actually, Mr. Turner, we're in a bit of a hur—"

"Won't take but a moment." He flashed a well-rehearsed smile at Maeve and pointed to different parts of the drawing. "The first floor will be rented space, a restaurant or café. Maybe even a bar, something classy, not a dive. The second floor will be completely open, the bullpen where the minions grind away. The third floor will be executive offices and a conference room overlooking the city. Brick exterior. Custom concrete floors. Lots of glass brick, I love that stuff. What do you think?" He smiled at Maeve again.

"Very nice." She nodded, peeked around Turner and caught Tom's eye. "Seriously, we're deeply con—"

Jerri appeared with a tray carrying a carafe, three cups, and little packets of creamer and sugar. She placed the tray on Turner's desk, spun on her heel and left without a word.

Turner cheerfully poured the coffee, offered condiments which were declined, and put a cup each in front of Maeve and Tom.

"Not a problem, anything to help." He returned the plans to the drawer and took his seat. "How's the coffee?"

"Great," Tom said. He hadn't tasted it. He pushed back into his chair, pointedly resigned to what he believed was a waste of time.

Maeve shot Tom a reproachful look, which was ignored, and took a sip. The coffee was thick as tar.

"Fly it in from Hawaii. Kona, the best in the world."

"We're here for information about Esther Fancyboy,"

Maeve interjected. "She's missing, and her family is deeply concerned something has happened to her. Is there anything you could tell us?"

"Barely know the girl." Turner tilted back in his chair. "Nice, nice girl. Will do anything asked of her, great worker. Can't imagine she'd get into any trouble. Don't suppose she wandered off with the wrong sort, do you?"

"Is it possible she's on a business trip?"

"Oh, no." Turner leaned forward and polished a smudge on the desk's glass top with his elbow. "No, no, no. Travel wasn't part of her job."

"What about boyfriends, girlfriends?"

Turner raised his head and frowned thoughtfully. "Not aware of any but you can ask Jerri, she might know."

"What does Esther do?"

"She's actually employed by Neqa. Have you talked to Xander?"

"He sent us here. What's her job?"

"She's the C.F.O. That's Chief Financial Officer, but really she's a liaison between Turner International and Neqa. She does whatever needs to be done, keeps the ball rolling." Turner brushed his bangs out of his eyes and leaned back in his chair again, aiming that smile at Maeve again. "What kind of law do you do? I might be in the need of a corporate lawyer."

"Right now we're looking for Esther. I'm not sure I understand what a C.F.O. does."

"She fills out government forms, reporting stuff. She makes sure men are on site with equipment and supplies. Kind of a bean counter."

"Like a project manager?" Tom asked.

"I'm the project manager, she works for me. More like a secretary, really, but Xander likes impressive titles."

"Xander talked about a water system," Maeve said.

"Oh, good, I'm glad he told you. Don't want to be coy, but it's not my place to discuss the project with outsiders. Since you're in the know, so to speak, we just completed phase one last summer in a village called St. Innocent's. Next summer, we'll iron out any bugs and build in several more villages."

Leaning on his elbows, Turner drew imaginary figures on the desktop. "I've designed a system for small villages where it's impractical to install buried water and sewer lines. In western Alaska, the water tables are so high that when the water freezes and thaws, the ground movement would break apart a buried system. Some villages have pipes above ground, obviously a safety hazard. People are forever crashing into them with snow machines." Turner gave a small, sardonic smile.

Maeve and Tom did not smile. They had been to the villages. They knew what life was like there.

"So where did you get the money?" Tom asked.

"The Native corporations receive federal loans and no-bid contracts to do all kinds of stuff. One group of villages got a contract to replace bridges in Napa, California. Someone else replaced all the windows in the JFK Federal Building in Boston." Turner barked a laugh. "Imagine that, Eskimos in Boston." He shot a conspiratorial look at Maeve.

Maeve didn't react. It wasn't so long ago Eskimos were shocked by the first white people who arrived in Alaska, Russian explorers, disembarking from ships. Absolutely everything, social, political, anything, in Alaska since then had undercurrents of conflict between the Natives and newcomers.

The Natives were forced off their lands. Their children were taken from them and sent to boarding schools. Entire villages were wiped out by European diseases. Unemployment in the villages was in the high ninety percentiles. With no money to buy food and with fishing and hunting heavily regulated, just staying alive was a day-to-day crisis. But the Natives didn't want to abandon their villages. Those villages were their heritage from their ancestors, their legacy to their children.

Maybe Eskimos earning money in Boston wasn't such a bad idea. They could bring that money home.

"Where do they get the know-how for these projects?" Maeve asked.

"That's just the thing, see? They don't have the expertise. They get these contracts because they're Native, but they need professionals to do the work. That's where I come in."

"What's the point of giving them a contract when they have to sub out the work?" Tom asked.

"Our government feels really bad for how they treated the noble red man and now we're making up for it." Turner flipped a hand in the air. "So, the feds came up with this scheme where the Eskimos skim off the top of my contracts. Just hope they use the money for something besides booze."

Maeve's back stiffened. Booze? They're starving.

"Don't get me wrong, I'm totally sympathetic. But I've been in these villages. Have you? They're practically pre-historic. Dirt roads. Crumbling houses. No plumbing. Heated with oil. I don't see the money trickling down to them. It all seems to stop at management." Turner slammed the desk with both hands. "Well, that's my soapbox."

Turner looked at Maeve meaningfully, inviting agreement. His implication was clear. Xander was taking money from the government and fleecing his own people. Maeve had to admit that the optics would look bad to the most naïve villager. Xander wore expensive suits and Neqa's office was opulent, a virtual palace by village standards.

Reading her expression, he picked up again. "But you know of course, what I mean is—"

"Could we see Esther's office?" Tom asked. He looked at his Rolex.

"No problem. Wait here a minute, would you?" Turner strode out of the room.

Tom leaned towards her, speaking in a low tone. "Counselor, this project could make Neqa rich. If it works, they could sell the system all over the world."

Tom slid back into his chair as footfalls in the hallway signaled Turner's return.

"Just down the hall." Turner reappeared and motioned them to follow.

Walking back toward the reception area, Maeve realized they must have passed Esther's office earlier. The door had been closed when they first came down the hall.

"Take your time. I need to get back to work." Turner said. He pushed the door open, flat against the wall. From the threshold, Maeve could see Jerri, the receptionist, head bent over a keyboard with one eye trained on Maeve.

The room had the view of the port but was not furnished in antiques. The desk was walnut veneer, as were the cabinets, all looked to be newly purchased from a big box store. On the credenza behind the desk was a framed school photo of Evan. Beside it was another photo, an outdoor shot of Esther with her arms around her son, both looking shyly at the camera. A third photo was a river with flat, scrubby landscape beyond, the view from St. Innocent's.

Otherwise, the room was bare.

Maeve pointed at Tom and pantomimed opening drawers, then said, "I'll go talk to Jerri."

Tom nodded.

Maeve slipped the photos into her briefcase and walked out of the office, catching the door so it swayed closed behind her. She took a position in front of Jerri's desk on the perimeter of the perfume cloud. "By the way, do you know any of Esther's friends?"

The blonde huffed. "We don't travel in the same circles."

"Then you didn't go to Starring?"

"What's that?"

"It's the Russian Orthodox Christmas celebration," Maeve answered. "Did Esther get personal calls at work?"

"It's against company policy." Jerri's eyes slid toward the closed door of Esther's office.

Maeve raised her voice just a little bit to bring back Jerri's attention. "Not even a quick call here and there?"

"She had a cell. If she got personal calls, they didn't come through me." Jerri ran a finger along the corner of her lower lip, checking to make sure her red lipstick hadn't migrated.

"Esther's family is really worried about her. Anything you think of or run across, no matter how unimportant it seems, might be a clue to finding her. Please feel free to call me." Maeve laid her business card on Jerri's desk.

Jerri rattled her nails on the desktop. "I really don't know her that well."

Esther's office door opened. Jerri spun in that direction, her perfectly cut hair drifting like a wind-blown waterfall.

Tom stood close to Jerri's desk and extended his big, bony hand. "Thanks for the coffee."

Jerri's head dipped as she gave Tom her hand and her eyelashes fluttered. "Happy to help. For sure."

He held Jerri's hand for a moment, eyes locked with hers and a slow smile crept across his face.

Something squirmed deep inside Maeve's chest. "Sorry to cut this short," she said. "We need to get going."

Tom held the door for Maeve. She had just walked into the lobby when Jerri called, "Oh, I just remembered."

They stopped and turned.

"I don't know if it's important, but I just thought of something," Jerri said as she swept the curtain of hair from her face, then brushed her hand across her swelling chest, eyes locked on Tom. "She did get some flowers."

"Really!" Maeve said, a little edgier than she'd meant to sound. "Do you know where they came from?"

"Sorry," Jerri sang. "Tossed the card when I cleaned her office."

Maeve stepped back into the reception area. "When exactly did you clean the office?"

"Yesterday."

"Is cleaning part of your job?" Maeve suspected it wasn't, she just had an urge to needle the woman.

"Oh, hell no." Jerri shot Maeve a filthy look. "Andy, I mean Mr. Turner, told me to."

"Why did he want her office cleaned? Isn't she coming back?"

"He didn't say."

When they exited the building, Tom pointed a remote starter at his truck. Just as Maeve opened the passenger door, the engine sputtered to life. The frozen upholstery felt like a giant ice cube. Cold quickly penetrated Maeve's down coat and jeans. She bounced her feet and legs to keep her blood moving.

With one hand on the steering wheel, Tom pulled into the driver's seat, momentarily hanging out the door as he took one last drag off a cigarette. He blew the smoke at the sky, stubbed the cigarette out in the ashtray, and then slammed the door shut. A cloud of Jerri's perfume filled the passenger compartment. Maeve lowered the window.

"It's freezing out there," Tom said. He cranked up the heat.

"Allergic to perfume," Maeve said. Just that perfume. She fastened her seat belt, stuffed her hands into her pockets, and tucked her head down into her coat like a turtle into its shell. "People don't clean out a co-employee's office unless that person is gone. Gone for good."

"Maybe the flowers were old and needed tossing?" Tom asked.

"I don't see Jerri as someone who naturally tidies up after other people, do you?"

Tom gestured aimlessly with one hand, then turned to watch for traffic as he backed out of the parking space. Apparently, some woman in his past had taught him that sometimes any response was a bad response. He'd learned his lesson well and wouldn't be baited into talking about Jerri. Because he found her attractive. There was no other reason.

"Did you find anything while I was talking to her?" Maeve asked.

"Not a damned thing." Tom shifted the truck into drive. "The pencil drawer was clean, not even little bits of paper or lint. Other than the photographs, there was no evidence of Esther Fancyboy in that office."

Tom paused at the parking lot exit, allowing cross traffic on the road to clear before he pulled out.

"Did you notice the computer?" Maeve asked.

Tom faced Maeve. "What computer?"

"The one that wasn't there," Maeve said. "Everyone has a computer. Why doesn't Esther?"

CHAPTER FIVE

Esther Fancyboy's Condominium
Anchorage, Alaska

A half hour later, Maeve and Tom were sitting on a brown sofa in the Fancyboys' living room with Cora in an adjacent matching recliner. The plain white room boasted a large wall-mounted flat screen television. Disks of woven grass edged with long tufts of fur hung on a wall, a pair of Yup'ik dance fans. Cora, noticing Maeve examine the fans, said, "Esther is a dancer. But now too busy working."

Evan sat cross-legged on the floor. Pages and pages of crayon drawings surrounded him. He was drawing on a sketch pad in front of him when they came into the room, the same drawing that was on all the discarded pages, the same drawing that he had given Maeve earlier that day: Esther, Cora and Evan, their home, and the Kuskokwim river.

"Did you find Esther?" Evan asked.

Maeve hesitated. These were questions she felt better discussed amongst the adults, but since Cora hadn't intervened, it seemed she was expected to talk with Evan. "She's not at work. No one at Neqa or Turner International knows where she could be."

A frown rippled across Evan's smooth brow. Then he tore the drawing from the pad, placed it on the floor beside him, and started another.

Cora reached for a basket at her feet. She plucked out a small piece of hide and began sewing it to a length of fur. Maeve and Tom sat on the couch and watched. Tom rested his elbows on his knees and watched Cora closely if only to prove that he was paying attention. That was how he showed compassion. Over the years, Maeve came to realize the clients felt reassured when a large man like him paid close attention to them.

"We haven't been able to find the girlfriend Esther talked to," Maeve said to Cora. "We were hoping you might have more ideas."

Cora took another stitch as if she hadn't heard Maeve speak, then said, "I don't know her friends."

"Evan, do you know Esther's friends?" Maeve asked.

He shook his head, still concentrating on his artwork.

"What about family?" Maeve asked Cora. "Is there anyone else who might know where Esther went after she left the Star-ring?"

"Her cousin Margaret Alexi, maybe," Cora said. "She's in dental school today."

Tom rocked forward onto his feet and slowly pulled himself to his full height. He slipped a hand into the jeans pocket where he kept his keys.

Maeve stood. "I'll run by Margaret's school in a bit. Meanwhile, can we look at Esther's room?"

Cora put her work aside and stepped around Evan, who had stopped coloring and was bent over his drawing, frozen, apparently too absorbed in the conversation to move.

Cora led them to an upstairs bedroom. A double bed and a dresser, newly purchased but inexpensive, took up most of the space. On top of the dresser, next to a framed school photo of Evan identical to the one in Esther's office, was an earring rack with several pairs of long beaded earrings. The shifts in color and pattern reminded Maeve of tall grass rippling in a breeze.

"Gorgeous," Maeve said.

"I make them. Sell them at the fairs." Cora said with an understated pride. As a Native artist whose work is often shopped by tourists, she would be accustomed to gushing admiration. For all Maeve knew, Cora was beaming in Yup'ik body language. It was well deserved.

Spotting a pile of fur and felt on the nightstand, Maeve asked. "Is this your project too?"

"Esther makes those mittens to give her grandmother back in the village," Cora said.

There were two different pelts of fur. One was a short-haired fur, dark cream with brown spotting, and the other was long chocolate-brown fur.

"What kind?" Maeve asked.

"Seal skin with beaver trim."

On closer examination, Maeve saw one mitten was nearly completed and the other had just been cut. Maeve stroked the silky fur. "Very pretty."

Meanwhile Tom was on his hands and knees looking under the bed. He slid out a black bag and placed it on top of the covers. A laptop bag.

"I didn't know that was there." Cora watched him closely.

"Okay if I look?" Tom asked.

She nodded.

He opened the bag and slipped out a laptop.

"What is it?" Cora asked.

"A personal computer," Tom said, pushing the power button.

The computer didn't respond.

"Dead," Tom said. "Okay if I take it? We'll bring it back as soon as we're done."

"I don't know," Cora said. "It's Esther's."

"There might be something on here that will tell us where she might have gone," Tom said. "Email, or photographs, search histories. Maybe something that tells us who her friends are."

Cora eyed Tom.

"We'll bring it right back. Promise." He slipped the laptop back into the bag and zipped it up.

"What's in the closet?" Maeve asked.

"Just her clothes," Cora said.

Tom opened the closet door.

Maeve's hand flew to her mouth.

The closet was filled with designer dresses, pants and tops, some of which Maeve had seen at Nordstrom's. Across the floor of the closet were neatly stacked shoeboxes, two rows tall with a third row begun.

"Esther likes clothes," Cora said. "I said, 'I don't know why you need so many clothes. You can wear only one thing at a time.'"

"Anything missing?" Maeve asked.

"Just that little coat she likes to wear. Don't know how she stays warm."

Maeve agreed. None of the clothes provided a modicum of protection against the elements. Some were glamorous, some flirtatious, some more reserved, probably her work clothes, but warm they were not. And certainly not cheap.

¥¥¥

Ten-Eighty Pizzeria
Anchorage, Alaska

The sign said *closed* but when Maeve pulled the heavy glass door, it opened. Trailing behind her, Tom had plugged the meter with a few coins and rushed to hold the door. Normally she would have waited for him, but chivalry was optional at five above zero. She swung the door open and stepped inside.

They had stopped in at the Ten-Eighty Pizzeria, the soon-to-be-opened restaurant in a long unused space on the first floor of Maeve's office building. Tom had spent the holidays helping his friend, Sal O'Brien, remodel the space for its opening. The restaurant was empty.

After they dumped their outerwear and Maeve's briefcase in a neighboring booth, Maeve slid in opposite Tom. The room was warm, moist, and rich with the aroma of baking bread. Maeve's stomach growled.

"Hungry?" Tom asked.

"Starved. Where's your friend?"

"He's in the back somewhere," Tom hauled himself out of the booth. "I'll go see if there's any coffee."

Just then, a tall corpulent man in a crisp apron with a slight limp threaded his way through the tables toward them. He waved a carafe in Maeve's direction. "Scoot over, pretty lady. Let the man sit."

Maeve slid over and Tom sat next to her. The man sat on the edge of the bench next to Tom.

Tom made quick introductions. "Sal, Maeve."

Sal extended his hand to Maeve, palm-up. She placed her hand in his and he brought it to his lips.

"*Buon giorno, bella ragazza,*" the man spoke in a fluid baritone. "Salvatore O'Brien, at your service."

For the second time that day, Maeve was caught in the spell of a very charming man. She felt herself glowing.

"Enough of that, Romeo," Tom said. "Mind if we get something to eat? I heard this was a restaurant."

Sal held Maeve's gaze as her hand drifted to the table.

Tom rolled his eyes, plucked two packets of sugar from a bowl and shook them.

"You could learn some patience, Tom," Sal said. "I'm opening tomorrow, but I just passed the health inspection, so you will be my first customers." Sal produced a pad and pencil from his apron pocket, a tiny stenopad just like the one Tom carried. "What'll you have?"

"Pepperoni," Tom said.

"One slice or two?"

"The whole damned thing," Tom said. "Ragdoll here and I got big appetites."

"It's *ragazza*," Sal said, giving the *r* an extra-long roll.

"That's what I said."

"Could I get a small salad on the side? House dressing's fine," Maeve asked. Tom gave her a look. He'd split plenty of large pizzas with her in the past.

"Shut up," Maeve said to Tom.

"*Molto buono,*" Sal said. He filled their coffee cups then limped back to the kitchen.

After the swinging doors closed behind him, Maeve asked, "What's with the limp?"

"Sal's a retired cop. Got shot in the line of duty. Ten-eighty is cop code for a meal break. That's how he got the name for this place. Get it? He's on a break from police work."

Maeve took a sip of her coffee. It wasn't that nasty stuff most restaurants and hotels serve. This coffee was full and rich like good chocolate. She took another sip and held the cup between both hands. From now on, she was drinking only Sal's coffee.

"Unless you got something else for me to do, I'm going out again looking for that missing car. I need a copy of that picture of Esther from your fancy machine upstairs first. Maybe someone's seen her. And someone needs to talk to the cousin."

Tom wouldn't presume to assign Maeve a task, but she knew that someone to whom he referred was her. "After we eat," Maeve said.

Sal stuck his head out the kitchen door and called out, "More coffee?"

"I can barely drink this rotgut," Tom called back, pouring the entire mug down his throat and reaching for the carafe. He shook it. "Yeah, maybe one more pot before we go."

"Gotcha," Sal said. "Pizza coming up."

Another wave of heavy, warm air, pungent with bread, cheese, and meats washed over the table before Maeve heard the kitchen doors swing open. Sal set the pizza, dinner plates, and another carafe of coffee on the table, picked up the empty carafe and stood back.

Maeve could have easily devoured half of Tom's pizza. But she slid a slice onto her plate and promised herself she'd only have two at the most. Tom cocked his head at her.

"Shut up," she said again.

Sal waved a hand in the air. "Eat, eat." He disappeared into the kitchen and returned a few moments later with a tray. He produced a plate and placed it in front of Maeve with a flourish.

"And for Bella," he said, "a salad."

On the plate was a large mound of lettuce with all the pizza fixings arranged on top, enough to feed two people. Sal then laid a bowl of basil vinaigrette on one side of the plate and a second plate of breadsticks in front of her. She quickly added up the calories in her head and figured there were less in Tom's pizza. On the positive side, she wouldn't need to eat again until noon tomorrow. She slid the plate of pizza slices back across at Tom. She pulled it back, took one bite off the tip of one piece, and then pushed the plate away as far as she could reach.

"So, what's this about a missing girl?" Sal said as he flipped a chair around and took a seat at the next table.

"Ragdoll's friend," Tom said. "Native Alaskan, late twenties. Single mother. Seven-year-old son. Last seen leaving the Native hospital during the Christmas party."

"Party girl?" Sal asked. Taking in Maeve's frown, he added. "It's not a prejudice thing you know. When you've been on the force for a while, you figure out that when a Native girl turns up missing, she's probably gone off partying or hooked up with the wrong guy."

"Chief financial officer," Maeve said.

Sal lifted his eyebrows. "Well, then, that's different. So, did you take a look at the boyfriend?"

"What boyfriend?"

"Unbelievable!" Sal said. "Pretty girl like that? There's always a boyfriend. That boy of hers must have come from somewhere. First rule is, you look at the boyfriend."

CHAPTER SIX

Buddy Halcro's trailer
Anchorage, Alaska

By mid-afternoon, when Maeve cruised through the trailer park, the sky and snow were cobalt blue. The sun had barely skimmed across the southern horizon before dropping below it, leaving a greenish-blue ribbon in the southwest sky.

Maeve drove slowly in the lanes of the trailer park, narrowed by snow berms on either side. At any moment, hitting a speed bump camouflaged by packed snow, gravel and sand could toss her car into the path of another car or into a bank. Flurries made the street signs and trailer numbers hazy.

After their late lunch, Maeve and Tom went up to her office. She stashed half the leftover salad in her office mini-fridge and plugged the laptop into a charger while Tom copied the photo of Esther. Maeve called Cora, who found the address for Evan's father in the kitchen junk drawer. Cora remembered that Esther had taken Evan to visit his father for Christmas, but she was unaware of any other boyfriends. Maeve left her office to visit Buddy Halcro, Esther's ex, while Tom kept looking for the car. Tomorrow she'd find Margaret Alexi, the cousin.

"There," Maeve said aloud when she saw a dingy white single-wide at the end of an icy driveway. An old battered Chevy Blazer with a primed fender and duct tape holding on a side mirror was parked in front of the trailer. She parked behind the Blazer and held on to her Subaru as she skated up the driveway.

When she reached the door, Maeve suspected that she had

strained a groin muscle on the ice. Something didn't feel quite right. There might have been a popping sound when her legs had splayed on the ice.

Maeve pushed the doorbell button. An artificial bell tone sounded. There was no response. She rang it again, then knocked. From within the trailer, there was the muffled sound of a man yelling.

Someone was up. Maeve checked her watch. It was just after three o'clock.

Maeve wrapped her arms around herself and stomped her feet to keep her blood circulating. A pain shot from inside her upper thigh deep into her pelvis.

The sound of footsteps grew louder before the door was thrown open.

"Yeah, what d'ya want?" said a young man, jeans unzipped, shirtless. He was so thin, Maeve could see ripples in his sternum. The second thing she noticed was his movie-star blue eyes, the kind of eyes that would stop any woman in her tracks. "Whatever you're selling, I don't want none."

"I'm not selling anything," Maeve said. "I'm—"

"Not interested in religion either." The man yawned and scratched the sparse hair on his chest. Across his knuckles were blue jailhouse tattoos spelling *Free*.

"I'm looking for Esther Fancyboy," Maeve said.

"Ain't here." He studied Maeve's face. "Who are you?"

"My name is Maeve Malloy," Maeve said as she stuck a business card between the glass storm door and the jamb. "I'm a friend of Cora Fancyboy. Esther's missing. Cora asked me to look for her. Are you Buddy Halcro?"

Buddy looked at the business card. "None of your effin business who I am, lady. She ain't here and I ain't seen her."

"You do know her then?"

"You sure you ain't a cop?" He shifted his weight. "If you're a cop, you can't lie to me. That's entrapment."

Criminals love the entrapment defense. Maeve lost count of the times she sat in the jail visiting room with her new client crying that he'd been entrapped. They didn't know that the law had been so shot full of holes, the police would have found a way around it.

So why would this guy be worried about the police when Maeve was just looking for the missing mother of his child?

"I'm not selling anything and I'm not a cop. When's the last time you saw her?"

"Haven't seen her. She won't have nothing to do with me. Won't let me see my kid."

Maeve tilted her head. In videos of her clients' interrogations, she had witnessed the police technique of silent pressure. When the cops asked a question the accused didn't want to answer, the cops turned into mannequins, like they went into suspended animation until they got the answer they wanted. Detectives could wait for a long, long time.

"Well maybe that one time at Christmas. Merry effin Christmas." Buddy said as he looked down and noticed his jeans weren't snapped. The zipper had slid down revealing, to Maeve's relief, dingy briefs. He bent to zip his pants. "If you don't mind, it's freezing out there."

"Did you send her flowers?"

"Who the hell has money for flowers?"

As Maeve leaned closer, she could smell that burnt-metal smell of the screen door. She looked past Buddy, her eyes adjusting to the gloom inside the trailer. Crushed beer cans littered the floor around a worn lounge chair. Buddy Halcro didn't look like a flower-sending kind of guy.

"If you hear from her, please give me a call," Maeve said.

"Darned tootin', I will. Adios, amigo."

With that, Buddy Halcro slammed the door.

≇≇≇

Maeve Malloy's Condominium
Anchorage, Alaska

It was past dinnertime when Maeve unlocked the front door to her condo. Just inside the door, she kicked her boots off and felt a twang deep in her pelvis. She ground her thumb into the spot. The twang ripened into a stab then softened as she massaged. She knew the rules for treating a sprain, having done it enough, but a lapful of ice didn't sound like fun. She'd put her feet up instead.

Maeve hung her parka on the hook in the foyer of her split-level condo. Half a flight up led to her bedroom and bath. Half a flight down led to the kitchen, dining area and living room. She went downstairs.

Maeve dumped her briefcase on the kitchen table, her make-shift home office, next to her laptop, then examined the contents of her freezer. After a lunch salad made mostly from pizza toppings, something calorie-conscious, like a chicken and vegetable TV dinner, would be a good idea. Then she saw the box of frozen macaroni and cheese. It was only a salad, after all.

As the mac and cheese spun in her microwave, Maeve dug her cell out of her briefcase. A call had come in a little after five o'clock, about the time she was standing on Buddy's doorstep. Her phone displayed the number of Addison Royce's cell phone.

Maeve stared at the number. A cold fog wrapped around her.

What could Addison Royce possibly have to say to her?

Weeks had passed since she last saw him. He'd shown up, drunk, for a booty call. She threw him out. Back when she was an ascending star in the P.D.'s felony defense unit, they had been lovers. Lovers, boyfriend-girlfriend, fiancés, whatever you call it. She thought they had a future together. She thought it was real.

She thought they were going to start a high-powered firm together. She thought that right up until the day she came into his office and saw a shiny gold band on his ring finger. That's when everything changed.

Sure, he'd been moody, remote even, in the months before he married someone else but she thought it was because he was worried about the budget. The legislature always seemed to be cutting back on the P.D.'s budget, shifting the money over to the D.A.'s, which meant fewer defenders but more cases.

She hadn't read the social page. She didn't have time for office gossip. She'd noticed that when she walked into the bullpen, the secretaries and paralegals clustered in little flocks stopped talking and averted their eyes. They all knew. Everyone knew except her.

When you're working eighty hours a week, you don't have time to supervise your boyfriend. You pass out in the clothes you wore to court, you get up the next morning, shower, change into another suit, and put in another fifteen-hour day. After a while, texts and calls from the boyfriend become fewer and fewer. And you don't notice.

In retrospect, Royce had kept her that busy because he didn't have the balls to break up with her.

How stupid could she be?

And now he had filed a bar complaint against her, accusing her of negligence because she hadn't seen Tom's note on the Mataafa case in time. She had believed her client. She had defended him and gotten him acquitted. She had done her job.

She had nothing to say to Royce and nothing she wanted to hear from him. She deleted his message before she heard his voice.

Crap! There must be some way to access even deleted messages. Weren't the I.T. guys always saying that nothing goes away? It's all in there somewhere. But where? She went into her phone app and scrolled around, looking for an "undo" delete button.

The cell chirped. Tom's number showed on the caller I.D. Maeve took a deep breath, shook her hair out of her face, and thumbed the accept button. "Hey, Tom. What's up?"

Behind the roar of the truck's heater, Maeve heard a squawk-box and the ding-ding of a fast food drive-through.

"That car isn't at the hospital. No one saw it get moved. Some of the folks there recognize Esther and they know Cora, but they didn't see her leave. The car isn't at the mall either.

I'm getting something to eat, then I'll cruise the bars and drug houses. You get anything?"

"I checked out Buddy Halcro. He lives in a trailer court on the east side of town, not far from Esther's condo. Knows nothing, saw nothing. At first, he claimed he hadn't seen her or Evan, but Cora told me Evan had been over there at Christmas. So, I used that cop trick, stare at him until he talks. He folded pretty quick, admitted the Christmas visit. I caught him just after three o'clock. It looked like he was just getting up. He wouldn't let me in. There were beer cans all over the floor."

"Probably some small-time dope dealer," Tom said. "It'd make sense if the girl met him in Fairbanks when she was partying."

"Right," Maeve said, feeling like her soul was smeared across two lifetimes. That lifetime from before when she and Royce were an "us." Her lifetime now when she was just her waiting for a microwave dinner to finish cooking while Royce was curled up with his glamorous wife in the luxurious home Maeve imagined for them.

"You okay?" Tom asked.

"Yeah, sure," Maeve said. "I just slipped on some ice, wrenched something. I'll be fine in the morning."

"What you got on for tomorrow?"

"Take a look at Esther's laptop then go by the dental school, talk to her cousin."

"When are you going to do something about that bar complaint?" Tom asked.

"Cut me some slack. I haven't even looked at it. Hadn't had time because of Esther."

"Yeah, you might want to read it."

Not reading a file had been the problem in the first place. "Right, I know my job. I have to call Cora first."

"I wasn't saying..."

"Forget about it."

After Tom disconnected, Maeve realized the microwave was beeping and had been for quite some time. She pulled the box out, pried the lid open, and stuck her finger in the macaroni and cheese. Lukewarm, garish orange curds had separated from the soupy whatever.

Maeve tossed the box into the garbage can under the sink. She grabbed a towel, filled it with ice, sat down behind her kitchen table, jammed the towel into her lap. Within a few minutes, the pulsing pain relaxed. She dug into her briefcase, found the bar complaint and put it on the table.

Maeve picked up her cell and dialed Cora's number. Cora answered with a meek "hello."

"Tom's out looking for the car. I saw Buddy Halcro. He hasn't seen her in a couple of weeks. Tomorrow I'll go over to the dental school and talk to Margaret."

Silence.

"Tom's going to keep looking for her car through the night. If I hear anything, you'll be the first one to know."

More silence.

"I'm sorry, Cora. We're doing our best."

No response.

"I'll touch base with you tomorrow, okay?"

A pause, then Cora said, "Okay." The line went dead.

Maeve felt small. The hum of electric lights and appliances seemed to roar. The night's heavy darkness smothered her little home. Looking through her sliding glass doors, she couldn't see the lake beyond her deck or the snow-covered mountains she knew were just a few miles away. What dim glow her overhead fixture cast broke up into tiny shards of light radiating in all directions before they disappeared into the gloom.

On the table in front of her was the envelope. The Alaska Bar Association's address was set in a heavy bold traditional font that said "We're important and we know it." Her name had been typed in an everyday font that said "And you are just another person under our command."

She ripped envelope open.

On the first page was the case caption: *In the Matter of the Discipline of Maeve Artemis Malloy*. On page two, she saw the name that had been printed over every letter and every pleading she had signed when she was as an assistant public defender: Addison Royce.

Bastard.

※※※

Arctic Roadrunner Parking Lot
Anchorage, Alaska

Tom pulled his rig into a parking space, stubbed out his cigarette, unwrapped the cheeseburger, and bit off half. While he chewed, he dug out his tiny stenopad and reviewed all the dives he'd cruised. Then he made a list of the establishments to visit next: that bar in a falling down cabin on the east side of town, that "pool" room, really a strip joint, and all the other sleazy hideaways in town. Then he listed the two slums where crack houses and meth labs had been found. He'd cruise those last after the bars closed.

That'd be plenty for tonight. As the night wore on, he wouldn't find anyone sober enough to talk to. Tonight, he was looking for the car. If he found it, he'd go inside. Otherwise, he'd save the talking for tomorrow night when he would do a bar-by-bar search, starting with the strip joint where he'd found the redhead. Not that she had anything to do with this case, but she'd been good luck before.

During the Mataafa trial, that bastard Royce had authorized Tom only one night to check out Mataafa's alibi witness and then shipped him out to Bethel the next morning on the first flight. Tom spent that night hanging around Belle's Olde Time Saloon looking for Enrique Jones, Mataafa's alibi witness.

Belle's had old-timey trappings, frayed and faded red velvet curtains behind a stage, old-fashioned snowshoes, head mounts of snarling wolverines, and dangling fur pelts hanging on the walls. But the bouncers' handle bar mustaches and the girls' can-can dancer outfits were long gone. No one cared. The men came to Belle's for over-priced booze and cheap skin.

That night, Tom had watched sad men and women, coming and going, looking for excitement, looking for drugs, looking for someone to fleece, looking for something to fill the holes inside them. Skeletal girls with caked-on make-up covering their acne and crack sores swayed as seductively as they could while peeling off chintzy costumes, stoned out of their minds. But he never saw Enrique Jones.

One of the girls, a redhead almost six feet tall, had sashayed by his table, stopped and offered a lap dance, which was technically illegal. He followed her to a small room behind a frayed red velvet curtain. It smelled of sweat, smoke, booze, and sex.

Tom let his sleeve ride up as he shed his coat so she'd be sure to see the Rolex. Girls liked flashy, expensive looking things. Girls like her wouldn't know if it was real or a knock-off but they both knew he was telegraphing that he had enough money to pay for whatever he wanted.

Tom told her about the robbery and Mataafa's alibi, that he'd spent the entire night of the robbery in this very strip joint with Enrique Jones, and that Enrique was backing him up. Tom tossed a twenty-dollar bill on the table. She glanced at the money before drawing the curtain closed and sidling up next to him in the booth.

"Didn't happen," Big Red said. "They were in the next night, both of them."

"How can you be so sure?"

"Because after closing I went to a motel with Ricky, Enrique, everyone calls him Ricky, and he told me all about the robbery. That's where Filippo got all the money. Ricky wasn't in on the job, but he always managed to be around when there was money to be spent. I know he didn't do the robbery 'cause he was across town doing a deal. That's where the coke came from. Mountains of it. Filippo had the money and Ricky had the coke. When I woke up next morning the sonofabitch was gone. Didn't even give me a ride back to my place. I had to call a cab."

When Tom went back to the office, he found the file on

top of Maeve's desk, flipped it open to the comments page, and wrote *Alibi NG*. He wasn't willing to put the full interview in the file, because he had promised Big Red. Girls like that turn up dead for a lot less than blowing someone's alibi.

Tom couldn't hang around for Maeve to come in. He had that plane to catch. Maybe he should have written it all out, leaving out the redhead's name. He should have blown off the Bethel trip. He should have slept in his truck in front of Maeve's house and blocked in her car so she couldn't go to court without going past him.

Tom looked in the greasy bag. The cheeseburger was gone. Most of the fries were gone, the rest had gone cold. He wadded the leftovers into the bag, opened the truck door and took the garbage to a bin. The freezing wind blew open his Carhartt jacket, waking him up.

As soon as he got the okay from Maeve, he'd find that redhead again. This time he'd find out who was in on this drug deal Enrique Jones was doing when he was supposed to be hanging at a strip joint. Because Tom would be damned if Maeve was going down for this cluster fuck. It was just as much his and Royce's fault.

And now, Royce was using it to run her out of town. Because that's how men treat women who refuse to disappear.

CHAPTER SEVEN

Thursday, January 10
Old Seward Highway
Anchorage, Alaska

B y morning, the snow had stopped and a low gray ceiling of clouds hovered over the city. When Maeve's car was perched on a hill waiting for a red light, Anchorage spread out before her. It looked like a fairy village with sparkling hoarfrost blanketing the ground, trees and tree branches, diffracting into tiny specks of lavender, green and blue.

A few cars ahead of her, a John Deere grader, taller than any truck and twice the length of a car, crawled like a giant insect. Traffic inched around the yellow monster. Stuck in the procession, Maeve punched through the search menu on her C.D. player. Classical music. No. Pop music. No. Celtic music. No. She turned the player off.

She hadn't called Royce after she read the bar complaint. She couldn't piece together a rational question for him. "Why are you screwing me?" didn't seem designed to elicit an honest, thoughtful response as if she expected the truth from him now.

When traffic stopped again, Maeve tore into the cold bagel sitting on her passenger seat and chased it with black coffee she'd bought at a parking lot kiosk, wondering what she'd do about Esther's laptop. Earlier that morning, she had gone into the office and fired it up only to find the dreaded blue screen of death. After she turned it off and on again, there was nothing but blue. A virus must have crashed the hard-drive.

After a long slog of stop and go driving in morning traffic, Maeve found the dental school tucked away in an abandoned shopping center. It had been one of Anchorage's oldest malls until an outside chain erected a modern five-story structure downtown and put it out of business. After it was sold to the state university, classrooms replaced shops. Typically Alaskan. If something could be reused, it was.

Inside the school, Maeve followed a track of gray slush and lumps of snow to an open room lined on both sides with dental chairs. Young Natives, men and women, in green scrubs, masks, and paper hats probed patients' mouths with dental picks. An older woman, also in scrubs, strolled from chair to chair. She spotted Maeve.

"Can I help you?" she asked.

Other than the instructor, Maeve was the only white person in the room and felt as conspicuous as a brown bear at a picnic. "I'm looking for Margaret Alexi. I'm a friend of her aunt, Cora."

Better to be a friend of the family than a lawyer investigating a case. People don't want to get caught up in a legal dispute, but Alaskans would give the shirt off their back to a friend, or even a stranger, if she wasn't a lawyer asking questions.

The instructor stopped at one of the chairs and spoke quietly into the ear of the student. The student cut her eyes to Maeve, nodded, and returned to her work.

The class broke up a few minutes later. The student pulled off her hat and mask. She was a short, stocky young woman with a pretty, round face and silky, black hair knotted on top of her head, a younger version of Cora. Margaret Alexi rooted under a counter, grabbed a large designer purse and crossed the room to Maeve. "You're a friend of my auntie?"

"I knew her in Bethel," Maeve said. "She asked me to help find Esther."

"It's our break," Margaret said. "I only have a few minutes."

"It'll only take a few minutes."

Maeve followed Margaret to another former shop where

groups of students settled around cafeteria tables drinking pop and coffee from vending machines.

Margaret looked at Maeve expectantly.

"I need to know more about Esther, her friends, boy-friends, anything you can tell me. We checked with Neqa, Turner International, and Buddy Halcro but we've come up with nothing so far. We checked the hospital for her car. It's gone. It isn't at the mall either." Maeve didn't add that Tom had cruised the bars, hotels, and motels, and he had planned to cruise the drug houses last night. Esther was the family golden girl. Maeve didn't want to offend her relatives with the same assumptions the cops had made.

"Cora called the cops, you know, the morning after Starring," Margaret said with the composed affect that seemed inscrutable to white people. "They aren't doing anything. You know the old saying 'A good Indian is a dead Indian.' Nothing changes."

Margaret eyed Maeve defiantly. She was daring Maeve to prove she was different.

Since Maeve had first come to Alaska, she had felt pressure to compensate for those who had pushed Native Alaskans to the brink of extinction. This conversation felt like another test of her sincerity.

"Got any idea where Esther could have gone?" Maeve asked. "Maybe she had another errand. Maybe she wasn't going to the mall."

"I didn't talk to her."

"You were at Starring?"

"I was coming in one door when she was going out of the other door."

"What did you see?"

"There was a big black SUV parked in front. Esther leaned in, looked like she was talking to someone."

"Did she get into the car?"

"No. She walked off into the blizzard. Disappeared. Cora's afraid she turned into a ghost."

Maeve shook her head. The way Margaret had said it, there must have been some cultural significance Maeve didn't understand.

Margaret continued. "In the village, when someone gets lost, their soul wanders the tundra. They look different from real people, all white. If you see them, they run away. They're afraid of living people."

Esther had been missing three days. No call, no text, no message from her at all. No effort to assure her seven-year old son that she was alright, that he was loved, and that he didn't need to be afraid. By now, there was a pretty good chance she was a ghost.

But until there was proof, Maeve would assume she was still alive and needed help. "Got any idea who was in the SUV?"

Margaret shook her head.

"What can you tell me about Esther?"

"We used to be friends in the village but not so much anymore."

"What was Esther like in the village?"

"Traditional girl. We were raised by our Grandma Agatha. Back home, grandmas raise the children while parents hunt and fish. Grandma Agatha took us berry-picking. Esther liked to dance. She was a good dancer back in the village. She was close to our grandma."

"Then what happened?"

"She went to the university in Fairbanks. Her first year there she met a white boy and got pregnant. She came back home and had the baby. Then she came to Anchorage, finished her degree, business something, and got a job with the corporation. Cora and Evan came to live with her last summer. When I came here for therapist school, she had friends of her own. I only see her at family things now."

"I thought you're learning to be a dental assistant."

Margaret shook her head, just barely. "We don't have dentists in the villages. They don't want to go there, no money to be made. Dental health is very bad." She dug an apple out of her bag. "Villagers like lots of sugar, lots of soda, and don't know to brush their teeth. Dental therapists teach basic hygiene and perform many of the services dentists do."

"When you finish school, where will you go?"

"Back to western Alaska. I'll have my own territory, a group of villages."

"Getting back to Esther, do you know who her friends are?"

"Someone from work, she said. Maybe you should talk to Ana Olrun, her friend in Anchorage. She works at the corporation, she should know."

⚶⚶⚶

On the way back to the office, Maeve pulled into line at another drive-through coffee kiosk, a bright blue wooden shack in the middle of a parking lot. While she waited, she dialed the number for Neqa. When the receptionist answered, Maeve asked to speak with Ana Olrun.

"I am Ana Olrun," the voice said, shrinking away.

Ana had to be the receptionist who looked like she wanted to talk. Maeve reminded Ana who she was and explained Margaret's suggestion that Ana might know Esther's friends.

"Why would I know?" Ana's voice was flat.

"Margaret said you're Esther's friend."

Ana answered with silence.

"Margaret seemed to think you might be helpful." Maeve added as she inched her Subaru forward in line. "If you think of something, would you give me a call?"

"If I think of something," Ana said and hung up.

The car behind Maeve honked. An untenable gap had grown in front of Maeve's car as the line had moved up while she was distracted by her phone call.

Never had Maeve run into so many saw-nothing, know-nothings: Xander George, Andrew Turner, the ex, Buddy Halcro,

Cousin Margaret Alexi, even Esther's mother, Cora, and now Esther's alleged friend, Ana Olrun.

"Unbelievable," Maeve said to no one.

꽃꽃꽃

Maeve Malloy's Office

Maeve looked out the window, checking dawn's progress. The sun would just crest the Chugach mountain range around ten a.m., a long time off yet. The sky was gray. Fat snowflakes passing through the halo of streetlights.

The door opened. Without greeting, the mailman dropped a package of mail on Maeve's reception desk then left as quietly as he came. On top of the bundle was a small envelope, the kind law firms use to send out announcements or invitations, stamped for bulk-rate postage. Inside, an inexpensive photocopied, not printed, single card announced the opening of the Law Office of Ryan Shaw.

Ryan Shaw came to the P.D.'s office a couple of years after Maeve. A short man, he was clean-shaven and always wore a suit even when jeans would do. His analytical skills were just good enough to pass the bar. Unaware of his limited abilities, he sometimes mounted nonsensical arguments any other lawyer would have choked on. After a few embarrassments to the public defender's office, Addison took Ryan under his wing. Ryan interpreted Addison's attention as a recognition of his extraordinary gifts. In a way, it was. But Maeve had to admire his tenacity and ambition. Ryan never stopped talking, never seemed aware of people moving away from him, and never stopped seeking the limelight.

She was surprised that he had left the P.D.'s office. With her gone, he was lined up for the chief of the felony unit, a job which had more administrative duties than litigation, a nice place for a lawyer who doesn't belong in a courtroom.

Back at the P.D.'s, Maeve had seen Ryan Shaw in Addison

Royce's office. It was during the Mataafa trial, when she and Royce were having a short hiatus from their relationship because of work demands, he'd said. She'd gone into Royce's office to ask for investigation time on her case. Shaw walked in, congratulated Royce on his wedding the weekend before with a you-devil-you punch in the arm.

That's how she'd found out.

When she saw the gold ring on Royce's finger, it took all the strength she could muster to keep from fainting.

That night she got drunk. Stinking, crying, vomiting drunk. She spent most of the night sleeping on the cold bathroom linoleum with her arm wrapped around the toilet. That was the night Tom couldn't roust her with the news of the perjured alibi.

Maeve could just imagine Ryan Shaw puffing his sunken chest out, bragging to all his friends about all the money he was going to make in private practice. The twerp. She'd seen him strut before, managing to recast every situation into a win for himself. If his client got a few less months than the co-defendant, it was because of his brilliant advocacy. If a witness turned up who changed the entire case, it wasn't because Tom had scrounged through pool halls and drug houses night and day, it was because Shaw was the captain of the ship. And if the prosecutor dismissed a case against his client, it wasn't because they had bigger fish to fry, it was because they were frightened of Ryan Shaw's golden oratory.

The phone rang. It was Tom. Maeve punched the speaker button.

"How's it going?" Maeve asked.

"Up 'til four this morning. The car isn't downtown parked in front of, near, or behind any bars. It isn't at any of the hotels or motels. It isn't parked in front of, near, or behind any of the drug houses. If the girl was holed up in some crack house or some hotel partying, I'd have found that car by now. You got anything on the computer?"

"I looked at it this morning," Maeve said. "I can't get it

open. Looks like a virus."

"Swell," Tom said. "Tell me again how you got onto the ex, Buddy whathisname?"

"Cora had the address in the kitchen junk drawer."

"Yeah?" Tom said. "What else you think might be in that junk drawer?

⚹⚹⚹

Esther Fancyboy's Condominium

Cora opened the door with a hopeful look.

Maeve pressed her lips. Stating the obvious, that they had no news about Esther, seemed too vulgar to say aloud.

Cora's expression darkened.

"Tom looked all night. He's catching some sleep now while I keep looking."

Cora nodded her head once.

Evan came down the stairs, pausing on the third step up. He searched the space around Maeve and peered down the hall into the living room. When he saw Maeve had come alone, he seemed to deflate.

"Sorry, bud," Maeve said. "No news yet."

Evan nodded once just as his grandmother had, then slowly climbed back upstairs.

After his bedroom door closed, Maeve turned to Cora. "Shouldn't he be in school?"

"He wants to be here when Esther comes home."

"Sure, of course," Maeve said. She wanted to say something kind, something soothing, but realized she didn't have the language for it. She only knew how to battle in court.

Cora waited for an explanation of Maeve's visit.

"About that junk drawer," Maeve said. "You know, the one where you found Buddy Halcro's address. Do you suppose I could have a look at it?"

Cora nodded. She hadn't spoken since Maeve arrived. She walked into the kitchen. Maeve followed.

Cora stopped in front of a drawer and opened it. Maeve began taking the contents out carefully, sorting them on the counter. She found Margaret Alexi's cell phone number, a permission slip for Evan's school, pens, pencils, crayons, bits of lint, paperclips, flyers for Chinese food take-out, and keys. There was an extra set of keys to Esther's car with a remote door lock. There was a house key attached to a key ring with a paper disc on it. On the disc was written *#1401*. The house number of the condo was 26, not 1401.

"Is this key for the condo?"

Cora shrugged. She still had not spoken.

Maeve took the key to the back door with Cora in tow. She tried the #1401 key in the back door. It jammed.

Maeve went to the front door. Again, the key got jammed.

"Can I take this with me?" Maeve asked.

Cora nodded again.

≇≇≇

Turner International

Ana slipped into Andrew Turner's private office.

Turner hadn't heard her. His head was stuck in the grant papers, re-reading them, trying to find a loophole for filing the damned report, any excuse to buy time. He saw something flitter at the corner of his eye and looked up to see her standing there, watching him.

"What are you doing here?" Turner asked.

"I needed to see you," Ana said. "Don't worry. Jerri's on her lunch break. No one saw me."

"Does anyone know you're here?"

"No one. Xander's gone for the day. He doesn't pay attention to what I do anyway."

Andrew rose from his desk and met Ana at the door. He peered down the hallway. Jerri's desk was empty. Then he remembered Jerri sticking her head in and telling him that she'd be late coming back. She had an appointment, hair or nails, something.

Turner let his hand drift down Ana's back, pausing for a slow squeeze. He looked down the hall again, closed his door, pushed in the lock and grabbed Ana's ass, jerking her close.

He ground into her.

She giggled.

He checked his watch. They might have just enough time.

"I need to know something," Ana breathed into his ear.

Crap. His interest softened.

"Esther," Ana said. "She's a pretty girl."

Crap. One of those talks. He let Ana go.

"She is," Turner said adjusting his slacks as he crab-walked across the room. He turned and leaned against the desk top. "Why bring her up?"

"I was wondering..." Ana said.

Turner cocked his head, staring thoughtfully at Ana. He knew exactly what she meant but he wanted to look innocent, that her suggestion was so unimaginable that it would take him a few moments to decipher it.

He put on a sympathetic face. "Oh, no, no, no, baby, not in a million years." He reached a hand toward her, beckoning. "She wasn't my type."

Ana drifted across the room to him. She ran a finger under the length of his tie.

She'd never done that before. Turner wondered what old TV show she had watched the night before.

"But I am?"

He wrapped his hand around the back of her warm, soft neck, thin as a sapling, and rubbed his thumb up and down along her windpipe, pausing on the spot just under her chin where he could feel her heart beat speeding up. He didn't dare do more than that now. Jerri would be back too soon. "You know you are, baby."

He knew what she was waiting for. She was waiting for a list of reasons why she was different, better, and preferable to Esther. He also knew that giving her those answers was the wrong move. What he needed to do was let her mind grope for what she wanted to believe, that she was special to him, that they could have a future together, and let her wrap herself up in that illusion. That promise of a dream come true, rags-to-riches, pauper to princess. Wedding bells. That is what they all wanted. If he waited long enough, caressing her tenderly, not sexually, she'd retreat to her dream again.

"I'm sorry," she said. "I just didn't know with all the drama. Esther missing. Everyone looking for her. Xander's being weird. He liked her a lot, you know. That's how she got this job, because Xander liked her so much and after she got this job, she didn't want to go partying with me so much anymore, so I was thinking, you know, maybe you and her."

Turner smiled with what he hoped looked like deep compassion. He shook his head as his mind whirled. If Esther had cut ties with Ana, her bestie in all the world, there must have been a reason. "She must have hooked up with some new guy."

"You think she's coming back?"

Turner lifted his eyes and looked around the room for an answer, one that wouldn't come back to haunt him. Finally, she was getting to the real reason for her impromptu visit.

Ana loved palace intrigue. There were things she had told him that she shouldn't have known, things she must have learned from Esther, who shouldn't have been telling them, things Ana should not have repeated. Knowing her love of the shadowy and forbidden could work for him.

Ana got to the point. "If Esther doesn't come back, can I have her job?"

"Too soon to tell, baby," Turner murmured softly, not in a forbidding way, but in a do-keep-your-hopes up way. "Hey, I got an idea. That Maeve Malloy. After she came to your office, you called me and told me she asked you some questions."

"She called me again. Margaret Alexi told her to."

Turner's neck stiffened. "Did you tell her anything?"

Ana shook her head.

"Well, this is what I want you to do. Why don't you call her tonight? Don't tell her anything Esther told you about, the business stuff. Just tell her what you know about Esther's love life, girl talk. See if you can find out what she knows."

Ana pouted.

"I'll stop by later tonight."

"Promise?"

"Promise."

Then he kissed her long and deep until her body softened against his. If he had just a few more minutes, she would be his. But he didn't. Jerri would be back anytime. He slowly untangled from Ana, turned her toward the door and steered her out of his office, down the hall and out of his reception area toward the elevator. Ana never knew when to leave. He literally had to shove her out the door.

Turner stood beside her, primly waiting for the elevator door to open as they shared the naughtiness of their secret affair. He could feel her eyes flitting up towards him, a smile breaking on her face. He gave her his pretend frown. She tried to look serious and faced the elevator. When the door opened, Jerri stepped out. She shot Turner a filthy look as she passed them.

"Have a good afternoon, Ms. Olrun," Turner said as Ana stepped onto the elevator. "Thank you for stopping by."

When Turner opened the reception-area door, Jerri was at her desk with her back so straight, she appeared to be tied to a broomstick. She wouldn't look at him, pretending to work on the computer.

He glanced at his watch again. The afternoon was still young. He didn't have anything on his calendar. It would be a long, quiet and boring afternoon unless...

He stopped a yard from Jerri's desk. "Miss Ebersole," he said. She turned her head in his direction, deliberately, stony faced, eyes hard and watery.

"I need you to take some dictation." He turned without waiting for her response. Before he was halfway to his office, he heard her heels clacking behind him in a deliberate step, a step he knew so well. He imagined how her hips rolled as she sashayed behind him.

Turner looked at the lush carpet in his office space, smiling. He'd get some relief this afternoon, after all.

CHAPTER EIGHT

Maeve Malloy's Condominium
Anchorage, Alaska

Maeve dropped her briefcase, picked up the remote and turned on the television for the background noise. The meteorologist, a peppy middle-aged man recently hired from the Lower 48, was predicting freezing temperatures and snow.

Hardly news in the middle of an Alaskan winter.

Beyond her sliding glass doors, the frozen lake glowed with a pale grey light. A pitiless north wind had been replaced by equally pitiless falling snow. Large fluffy flakes descended. In the morning, driving on a couple of feet of the new accumulation on top of ice would be a horror.

Suspended from practice.

Arthur's words sounded as clearly as if he were in the room with her. It didn't matter that she had won the Mataafa trial. The bar association would think she knew Mataafa was lying before she put him on the stand, that she had knowingly suborned perjury.

The growl of a snowplow thrust into her consciousness as it raked back and forth on a nearby street. Engines ground as it geared up to push the snow, a bell rang as it backed up.

A black wall formed in Maeve's mind. She pictured herself sitting in the bar association conference room with a tableful of people staring at her. Again. What kind of work could she do if they suspended her? How long would it last? Did she even want to be a lawyer anymore?

Maeve flopped down on her couch and surveyed the room. The ugly brick on the fireplace she had planned to cover with a nice stone. Maybe a coat of paint instead. The frost building on the inside of the sliding glass door she'd planned to replace. Heavier curtains instead. Thin beige carpet that smelled of the previous owner's animals and made her sneeze every time she walked into the room. She had wanted to tear it out and install hardwood floors. Maybe she'd live on the bare concrete slab for a while. Urban chic.

Suspended from practice. If she had enough money set aside, she could travel. But there were no savings. She was barely getting by from month to month as it was.

Addison Royce was trying to annihilate her. She punched his number on her cell phone. When she put the phone to her ear, her hand was shaking. She hadn't spoken to Royce since she threw him out of her condo.

A woman answered.

Maeve thumbed the disconnect button and threw the phone across the room. She wondered if Royce's caller ID had displayed her name. Would the wife know Maeve had called? Maeve wasn't sure why she should feel guilty. She hadn't had an affair with that woman's husband. That woman had married Maeve's boyfriend. It's Mrs. Royce who should feel guilty. Guilty and insecure. Just a few months ago, when they were still newlyweds, her husband had been at Maeve' apartment, drunk and horny.

Maeve wandered into the kitchen, opened the refrigerator and found a Styrofoam box of pad Thai, the noodles dry and brittle. She put it back. In the freezer was an unopened pint of Ben and Jerry's Super Fudge Chunk ice cream. She grabbed the container, pitched the lid into the garbage and sleep-walked back to the couch.

Halfway through the pint, her cell phone rang. She jumped up and reached for it.

"Tom?" Maeve asked.

"Sorry?" A feminine voice replied.

"I thought you were somebody else." Maeve tried to iden-tify the voice. "Sorry. I meant 'hello'"

"Hello," the young woman said.

Maeve waited for the caller to identify herself. Clearly the caller was waiting for Maeve to initiate the conversation.

"This is Maeve Malloy. Is there something I can help you with?"

"This is Ana Olrun."

Ana, the skittish girl at Neqa. Esther's friend.

"Ana! I'm so sorry, I didn't recognize your voice," Maeve said. "How are you doing tonight?"

"Okay," Ana said and went silent. The snowplow's bell chimed in the distance while Maeve waited for Ana to explain the call. Another snowplow rumbled past the condo. Maeve no-ticed a spiderweb, no spider, for the first time in the corner of her ceiling. Did spiders live through the winter? She didn't know, but she'd leave it in place until the spring just in case it came back.

Ana still hadn't spoken.

"How was your day at work?" Maeve asked.

"Xander hung around the office all day. That's why I said what I did when you called."

"That's okay, I should have known. Sorry to put you on the spot like that."

"I wanted to tell you about Esther. It's better if Xander doesn't know we talked."

"Why's that?"

"He hangs around a lot, listening in. He always wants to know what's going on. I figure it's none of his business."

"I promise not to tell." Changing the subject, Maeve said, "Evan said he saw Esther talking to someone at Starring. Was that you?"

"She said hello, then she went outside and talked to some guy in an SUV."

"Do you know who the guy was?"

"Maybe her new boyfriend or something. I seen her with

him once before in the alley behind the bars on Fourth Avenue. I asked but she wouldn't say. I figured he was married or something.

"She used to tell me things a long time ago, but not anymore. We went out a couple of times after she came back from fish camp but then she was always, like, too busy or something. Even when she came to the office to see Xander, she didn't hang around me. It was like we weren't even friends. She talked to the I.T. guy more than she talked to me. I don't know why she changed. Does Cora know anything?"

"She has no idea, that's why she asked me to help. Did Esther say where she was going when she left Starring?"

"She just said she had to take care of something. Like it wasn't anything important. She was coming back. She had to take Cora and Evan home."

"Do you think she went partying?"

"Esther doesn't do drugs."

"Would you know if she did?"

"Back before she went to fish camp, we went out almost every Friday night, sometimes Saturdays too. Dress up and go downtown. She likes to dance. All the men ask her to dance, she's so pretty. I don't mind. There's plenty of guys to go around."

Wingman to a prettier girl. It's no fun when all the men want to get next to your best friend. You're either invisible to them or they see you as a stepping stone. Unless Ana was the most spiritual woman on the planet, she minded very much indeed.

"Did you know any of Esther's boyfriends?"

"Just that loser she met in Fairbanks. Evan's father. He came into the bars looking for her."

"Recently?"

"New Year's Eve. Esther called me and said she wanted to go dancing. We went down to Fourth Avenue. He showed up just before midnight. Tried to drag her out of there."

"She didn't want to go?"

"No way! She was done with that dude. Buddy something. She called him Buddy Poor Boy. Not to his face. She said that when she was talking about him." Ana's use of modern lingo in her soft western Alaskan accent sounded strange, almost comical. "No child support, crummy little job working nights, just out of prison. She's moved on. She had the rich guy in the fancy SUV."

"Have you seen Buddy Poor Boy since Esther disappeared?"

Ana was quiet for a few moments.

"No." Her voice was soft, thoughtful. "No, he hasn't been around."

"One last thing," Maeve said. "We found this key at Esther's house. It looks like a house or an apartment key and it has a tag on it with the number 1401. Does that sound familiar to you?"

"Nuh-uh," Ana said.

≱≱≱

Last Frontier Bar
Fourth Avenue

"Willie, you old badger, can I buy a drink for you and your lady friend?" Tom patted the neighboring bar stool. Willie Pike was Tom's source for all things Yup'ik. Tom had done him a favor once a long time ago and now Willie provided him information otherwise withheld from nosey white people.

Willie smiled. He was skinnier than Tom remembered and had fewer teeth, but his hair was still black and he still had that mischievous look in his eye. The woman with him was stocky with thin hair cut at her shoulders. Out in the village, she would have been a hardworking mama, hunting moose, butchering, wrangling a snow machine. In town, she spent most of her time drinking beer by the look of her bloated face.

Willie hauled himself up onto the stool. The woman tried to climb onto a stool next to him and slipped off on her first attempt. She hit Willie's arm. "Help me."

Willie grunted, got down, pushed her up on the stool and then hauled himself back up.

"Brewskies?" Tom asked.

"Brewskies!" The little lady said.

Tom laid down a large bill and the bartender pried the caps off two bottles, setting one each before Willie and his girlfriend. They took long pulls on the beer. Willie put his bottle down and faced Tom with his usual curious look. The girlfriend tossed hers back as expertly as a college frat boy.

"Impressive," Tom said, nodding at the woman.

She burped, then said, "Don't you flirt with me. My man's here. He sees you."

Willie assumed a patient expression.

"I'm looking for a girl," Tom said.

Willie smiled broadly. He had way fewer teeth than last time Tom'd seen him. The girlfriend hit Willie's arm again.

"Yeah, not like that," Tom said. "It's business, a missing person." He placed the picture Maeve had taken from Esther's office in front of Willie. "Esther Fancyboy."

"Where's she from?" Willie asked.

"St. Innocent's," Tom said.

"Who's her family?" Willie asked.

From Tom's time in Bethel, he'd learned that family connections were the passports of western Alaska. Nothing transpired until it was established how you were related and whether you're happy about it. If Willie's great grandfather had a run-in with a Fancyboy way back when, Tom was out of luck.

"Cora Fancyboy is her mother," Tom said. "Agatha Alexi is her grandmother."

"I seen her but I don't know her."

Tom pushed the photo towards the girlfriend. "Know her?"

She hit Willie again. "Alexis are my cousins. You know that."

Willie shrugged.

She studied Tom. "Why do you want to know?"

"I'm working with Maeve Malloy. She's a friend of Cora's and Cora asked us to help find Esther. That's why I want to know."

"What about that little boy of hers?" the woman asked. "The half-white one?"

"Cora is taking care of him."

"That's the way we do things, we Eskimos," she said. "My grandmother raised me, but I got no one to raise. I ain't got no grandkids." She wiped her eyes with a dirty sleeve.

Willie held his empty beer bottle eye-level and shook it, looking for dregs. He looked over at the woman's bottle. It was empty too.

Tom needed to get back on topic before Willie and the girlfriend both drifted into oblivion.

"Esther ever come down here?" Tom asked.

"I seen her a few times. She's young, all the boys like her." She tilted the bottle into her mouth again.

"Anyone special?"

"Just that no-count white boy. Buddy Poor Boy. Comes in sometimes looking for her. She won't talk to him. Must be the baby's father. Or maybe some other no-count white boy. Who knows when a good Eskimo girl starts hanging out with white boys."

"You remember when you seen him last?"

"Christmas, maybe. Yeah, around Christmas time." She looked in the distance, like she was trying to focus on something. "Or maybe it was New Years. They had all that tinsel stuff hanging all over."

"When's the last time you seen Esther?"

"A while ago," she said. "She came in here dancing with that friend of hers, that Ana Olrun. I went outside to get a smoke and saw Esther out back behind the bar, getting into a shiny black SUV." She upended the bottle over her mouth, frowned when she remembered it was empty and smacked it down on the bar.

"When was that?"

"Same time. Christmas, New Year's." She shrugged. "Maybe same night even."

"Know who was driving the SUV?"

"Nope," she said staring into the bottle. "But I seen him."

The girlfriend slid off the stool. She stumbled to the back of the bar, aimed for the hallway where the restrooms were and barely missed hitting the wall.

"You seen him?" Tom asked Willie.

"Nope." Willie spoke and belched simultaneously.

Tom held up two fingers to the bartender. When Willie's girlfriend returned, a fresh uncapped bottle was waiting for her. Willie's new bottle was already half-gone.

"You still here?" she asked.

"The guy you saw in the black SUV with Esther. What did he look like?" Tom asked.

"Big white guy," she grabbed the bottle. "Like you."

"Anything else?"

"Naw, all white people look alike to me." And she and Willie laughed.

CHAPTER NINE

Ana Olrun's apartment

A na heard the front door open just as she disconnected the call. The visitor stepped inside. The door closed. A coat rustled as it was hung on a hook. Boots dropped onto the floor. A man padded heavily down the hallway.

She shook her shoulders a bit, letting the pink satin bathrobe fall open, her hair spilling across her shoulders. She adjusted her feet so that her newly polished pink toenails peeked out.

Ana held the receiver as if the call was still connected and lifted a wine glass off the coffee table. She didn't understand why people liked wine, it smelled like diesel fuel. But sipping wine looked classier than sucking beer out of a bottle.

When Andrew Turner entered the living room, Ana smiled at him. He liked it when she smiled. That's how they had gotten together. One day, when he was visiting Neqa's office, he stopped at her desk and said, "Put a smile on that face, pretty lady." Later that week, he invited her to lunch at a local hotel.

"Have a nice day," she said into the cell phone and then acted as if she was disconnecting the call again.

Turner went into the kitchen, found himself a wine goblet and dropped on the couch next to her. He poured himself a glass and asked, "Was that her?"

Ana arranged herself around Turner.

"Hmm...mmm."

"She know anything?" he asked.

Ana shook her head, then rested it on his shoulder.

Turner slipped out of Ana's embrace and leaned forward. He turned the goblet in his hands, studying the thin sheet of liquid clinging to the glass as he tipped it one way, then another.

There was something on his mind and it wasn't Ana. She was low on his list, somewhere after his work, his wife, Esther, and that lawyer. Even the glass of wine was more important to him.

"Cora didn't tell that lawyer anything," Ana said. "That's why she's asking questions. She didn't know about Buddy. She didn't know about Esther's secret boyfriend. Oh, but she did find the key to the Neqa suite."

He looked over his shoulder at her. "How does she know it's the Neqa suite?"

"All she knows is that the key is to a room 1401. I didn't tell her about the suite."

"Good girl," Turner said, patting Ana on the thigh. "What's this about a secret boyfriend?"

"The one I was telling you about. The guy she talked to at Starring. You know, Christmas? The guy she met in the alley."

Turner put his glass down and leaned away from her. He looked at her with an expression she'd never seen before, crazy like a beaten dog, always scared for its life, every hair on its face vibrating, nostrils wide. Any moment it could strike, tear your face off.

"What guy?" There was a hardness in his voice.

Ana froze. "I told you. In the black SUV."

"You've seen her talking to him more than once?"

Ana nodded.

"You get a look at him?"

Ana shook her head.

Turner stared straight ahead, hands clamped together, his knuckles white, his fingers flushed and fat with blood. "This Malloy woman say anything about finding a thumb drive?"

❦❦❦

When Turner first scanned the room, Ana looked to him like a teenager imitating an old-time screen siren. Her small skinny body was wrapped in a cheap polyester robe and when she took a sip of the wine, she grimaced.

Now she looked like a teenager in a horror flick, just realizing that she was alone in a house with a madman. He knew that it was the expression on his face, the tone in his voice. He was never good at hiding rage. The Malloy woman had the key to the Neqa suite. She didn't know what she had yet, but she was bound to figure it out.

And what's this about Esther and a secret boyfriend? God knows what she was saying to him, maybe as much, or even more, than she told Ana. She was probably screwing that guy in the Neqa suite.

If that weren't enough, Esther's thumb drive was missing. On the last afternoon he'd seen Esther leave for the day, weeks before she disappeared, he'd seen her pull a thumb drive out of her computer and drop it in her purse. When she looked up, she saw him standing in the hall. "Back up," she'd said. Josh, the I.T. guy, confirmed to him that Esther was in the habit of backing up the day's work and taking it home with her, just in case a virus took out the computers.

That meant that somewhere there was a thumb drive with all the information anyone could want about Andrew Turner, his business and his money.

And now because of Turner's stupid, stupid mouth, Ana knew that he wanted it. She's uncontrollable. She'd leak it to the wrong person at the wrong time. He just knew it.

He needed Ana to forget what he said.

He took the wine glass from her hand, put it on the coffee table. She was pushed back into the couch as far as she could go. With one finger, he slowly unworked the knot of the robe's tie. He put on his naughty smile, slithered the belt out from under her, held it up for her to see, and let it drop into a lazy pool of pink ribbon on the floor.

Ana relaxed. He took her hand and coaxed her to stand. He swung down and lifted her off her feet, carrying her into the bedroom Clark Gable style. Soon she'd float back into that magic dreamland of hers, where lovers live happily ever after, and forget everything he had said about the thumb drive.

CHAPTER TEN

Friday, January 11
Suite 1401, Inlet Towers

T urner's hands were so sweaty when he tried to turn the key that it slipped from his fingerss.

Last night when Ana was drifting off to sleep, he realized that if Esther had a key to Neqa's corporate suite, she might have stashed the thumb drive there. He didn't have time to check the suite after leaving Ana's. He needed to go home. There was only so far "sorry, honey, working late, meetings, couldn't answer the phone" would go. As he was zipping up his pants with his cell phone wedged between his neck and shoulder, he had listened to four voicemails. When he sat down to pull on his socks, he thumbed through the texts, each shorter than the one before. The last text had only two letters: *F.U.*

When he got home, the bedroom door was locked, and a pillow and blanket had been dumped on the living room couch.

Still in the doghouse this morning, he slipped out with the promise of bringing back a *New York Times*, a *Boston Globe* and freshly baked croissants. He only had a few extra moments he could blame on standing in line, there being no traffic in Anchorage on Sundays to slow him down.

He wiped his hands on his slacks. He could feel his face and ears warming as he tried the key again. This time it worked.

When the door opened, there was a fat, hairy man standing in the middle of the living room wearing only a towel, hair damp from a recent shower.

"Who the hell…" the fat man started.

Turner held up a hand. "So sorry, I didn't realize Xander had someone here. I had an out-of-towner visiting last week and he called this morning, frantic. He just realized he lost his thumb drive with some very important documents on it and asked that I check the suite."

Dammit, that was stupid cover. Xander would know there weren't any out-of-towners last week. He'd fix it later.

"Where would it be?" the fat man asked.

"Could be anywhere," Turner said. The air sang with tension for Turner, but the fat man looked slightly bored.

"Knock yourself out," the fat man said, picking up his highball glass and rolling into the bathroom. The door closed.

Turner opened the desk drawers, looked under the desk around the edges of the carpet. He rummaged through the kitchen drawers. He tossed couch cushions on the floor and ran his hands through its crevices. He went into the bedroom, looked through the drawers, looked behind and under the dresser and nightstands. He was on his hands and knees scooting around the bed, alternately peeking under the bed and running a hand under the mattress when the bathroom door opened.

"Your visitor keeps his thumb drives under the mattress?" the fat man, now shaved and robed, asked.

"Hope against hope," Turner laughed. "He's desperate and he's already back in Florida so figured I'd help him out, see if I could find it."

"Did you?"

Turner peeked one more time under the bed for effect. That's when he saw the tiny bit of light flicker, a reflection. He reached under the bed and pinched the shiny thing.

"Just this," Turner said, holding a long beaded earring in the air.

"Your buddy wears some pretty fancy jewelry," the fat man said.

⚡⚡⚡

Medical Examiner's Office

The wind couldn't be heard inside the building. Maeve ran her hands through her hair, pulling it out of her face while Tom gave the heavy door an extra tug to make sure it locked into place.

On the drive over, Tom's truck had splashed through ankle-deep water as it fish-tailed through intersections. The Chinook wind, like a blasting furnace, had melted too much snow too fast. Typical January. When the temperature dropped at night, Anchorage froze. Then the hot winds melted the top layer of ice leaving water standing on a base layer of ice. Cars crashed into each other. People slipped and fell. It was a personal injury attorney's dream come true.

Maeve found Evan sitting alone in the row of plastic chairs against a wall. He looked small and fragile. She sat down next to him while Tom walked down the wide hall looking for the medical examiner's office, his footsteps ringing on the linoleum floor.

Street crews sanding the roads had found the body. After any big snow melt, a body or two turned up, usually homeless people. Fatigue, a symptom of hypothermia, compounded by intoxication, overwhelmed them. They'd lie down, fall asleep, and die.

This body had not been a homeless person.

Maeve slowed as she approached Evan. He gripped his chair so hard, his knuckles were white. The effort he took to control his emotions contorted his small face. He stared straight ahead.

Maeve leaned towards him. "Is Cora here?" she asked in a hushed voice.

Evan nodded and clenched his eyes.

A window overlooked a landscaped knoll. The sun hadn't crested the mountains yet and the dawn sky was streaked with pale green and pink. Wind had swept away the snow, revealing grass as green as when it had frozen. One young, leafless birch tree stood atop the knoll, its black and bony branches reaching upward.

Shuffling feet approached. Cora and Margaret Alexi came into view around the corner. A middle-aged, sturdy woman wearing surgical scrubs and a lab coat accompanied them. Tom walked a couple of paces behind.

The procession halted.

"The death certificate will be available in a few days," the doctor said. "Meanwhile, Mrs. Fancyboy, if there is anything you need, anything at all, please don't hesitate to call." She smiled politely, pivoted, and strode away.

"I'll meet you in the car, Auntie," said Margaret, handing Cora car keys.

Evan looked even paler than before. He stood and took Cora's hand. Then, he and Cora shuffled toward the exit.

When the door closed soundly behind them, Maeve turned to Margaret, her eyebrows raised in inquiry. Tom stood off at a distance.

"Beaten to death. Not raped. But the doctor said something like," Margaret paused to recall the words, "there was evidence of sexual encounter not long before she expired. 'Expired.' That's the word she used."

"I am so sorry," Maeve said.

Margaret nodded, then walked out the door.

Tom moved closer to Maeve.

"Sexual encounter," Maeve said.

"The night she died," Tom added.

❦❦❦

Saturday, January 12
Ten-Eighty Pizzeria

The Ten-Eighty wasn't open yet, so Tom had led Maeve in

through the back door that faced the parking lot behind the building. When they walked in, Sal was punching a giant lump of pizza dough, and the smell of yeast filled the room. It struck Maeve how much raw bread and beer smelled alike.

"Just put the coffee on," Sal said. "You two grab yourselves a seat and I'll be out in a minute."

Tom flipped on the restaurant lights as they stepped through the swinging doors. The dining room looked like any other diner: a long counter immediately in front of them with stools still up-ended on top following mopping the night before. Beyond that were metal tables with fifties style red upholstered chairs. Red booths lined the floor-to-ceiling glass exterior walls.

"It's cold in here," Maeve said.

"Hold on." Tom reached back to the thermostat on the wall just behind them and turned the dial. "Where do you want to sit?"

"Where it's warmest," Maeve said.

"The heat from the baseboard comes up over there." Tom pointed to one of the booths against the window.

By the time Maeve and Tom had settled into the booth, the heating system was creaking. She kept her puffy coat on, shoved her hands into her pockets and pulled her head down into the coat as far as she could. Tom kept his working man's heavy brown canvas jacket on.

The kitchen doors swung open and Sal came out with pot of coffee and two tall plastic glasses of ice water.

"Looks like you need some of this," he said as he poured coffee for Maeve and then Tom.

She would have been offended if it wasn't true. "Worked all night." She rubbed her face with her hands, trying to wake herself up. "Margaret called just as I was going to sleep. Buddy found out about Esther and showed up at the condo, pounding the door, demanding his son."

"That was fast," Tom said, lighting a cigarette.

"He'd heard it from Ana in the Neqa office. Margaret had

called Esther's job to let them know..." Maeve didn't finish the sentence. Let them know that Esther wouldn't be coming back.

Maeve swirled her ice water. The cold of the glass seeped into her palm but didn't make her feel any more alert.

Sal stood next to the booth, the coffee pot held aloft. "So why's that mean you have to work all night?"

"Typing up emergency custody petition." Maeve looked at her watch. "I'm meeting Margaret in my office upstairs in fifteen minutes, then we're going to the courthouse to file. Hopefully the magistrate will give us an emergency order. That should get us protection for the weekend at least, when Buddy's likely to show up drunk again. Monday, when court opens, I'll file a formal custody action."

She took a sip of her coffee. It had no flavor. It might as well be hot water.

"You could do all that typing when you're awake. You got the whole weekend," Sal said.

"Didn't Arthur Nelson tell you not to take any cases?" Tom asked.

Maeve shot him a frown.

"When did Nelson say that?" Sal asked.

"I was up anyway," Maeve said.

Sal put the coffee pot down on the table, pulled a chair up, and sat down. "Why did Nelson tell you not to take cases?"

"I could have waited until today but then I have to type up a bunch more paperwork for the custody case. Besides, I wanted to make sure we got an order as soon as possible, best while Buddy was still sleeping off last night's drunk."

"Why no cases?" Sal asked.

"It's no big deal," Maeve said.

Tom put his mug down a little too hard. "No big deal?"

Maeve threw herself back in the booth and stared at Tom. "Do you mind?"

Tom flicked his cigarette over the ashtray. "As a matter of fact, I do mind. We need to deal with this and we need to deal with it now. If the bar takes your license, you can't run around saving anyone."

"Take her license!" Sal said. "What in the hell is going on?"

"You mind if I tell him?" Tom asked.

Maeve threw a hand gesture in the air which could have been interpreted as resignation. Or an insult.

While Tom droned on about the Mataafa trial and the bar complaint, taking more responsibility for not telling Maeve about the perjury than was his, Maeve's mind drifted back to Evan drawing picture after picture of his mother as if he could have conjured her from crayon.

Sal's voice penetrated her thoughts. "Well, that don't sound right to me. Have you talked to Bennett?"

Tom scoffed.

"I worked with him before, back in the day. He's not a bad guy. Seriously. He tries to do the right thing."

Maeve could feel her brow furrow. She didn't need someone to tell her she looked pissed. "Jefferson Bennett is not a bad guy? The last case we had, he tried to railroad my client. He lost the evidence. Hid more evidence. The judge sanctioned him and ended up dismissing the case."

Sal pulled himself to a crooked stand and picked up the coffee pot. "He's got a job to do like anyone else, Ms. Criminal Defense Attorney. You never thought about what you guys look like to the cops and prosecutors? The ridiculous stuff you guys come up with? The crap you feed to juries?"

Maeve shoved her coffee mug aside and took a deep breath as she dredged out her "ethical obligation of the prosecutor versus the defendant's right to day in court" argument from the recess of her mind. She was about to launch into it when Tom put his big hand on her forearm. His grasp was warm and firm.

"Maeve, hear anything from the cops yet about Esther?" Tom had dropped his voice, a trick she had taught him for drawing in someone's attention.

She'd let him get away with it, this time. "They'd just left Cora's condo, giving the family an update on the investigation when Buddy showed up. He must have been watching the house."

"It's too soon to have anything for the family," Sal said. He had stepped back a pace from the table and watched Maeve with a mask of police professional poker face.

"They asked a bunch of questions and said they had no suspect. They're not sure when she was killed or dumped."

"Forensics, DNA?" Sal asked.

"Some semen. It appeared she had consensual sex in the hours before she died. They might get DNA off that. But that won't necessarily tell us who killed her, only the man she had sex with."

"And if it doesn't match someone in the database, it won't tell us anything," Sal said.

Us? Maeve let that go, too. She was too tired and needed to stay focused.

Tom leaned back and put a toothpick in his mouth. "The cops could get search warrants."

"And search who?" Sal asked. "There aren't any suspects."

"What about the guy in the black SUV?" Tom asked. "The guy she was talking to outside at Starring. My sources saw her getting into a black SUV with some white guy behind the Last Frontier bar."

"Your *sources* get a name?" Sal asked.

Tom shook his head.

"Pretty sure you'll need more than her voluntarily getting into a car with some guy on some day seen by some barfly to get the D.A. excited," Sal said. "I'm no lawyer, but..." His voice had lost its battle-hardness. He looked at Maeve with big, sad brown eyes.

She took his hand and squeezed it. He squeezed back.

"I heard the same thing from Ana Olrun when she called Friday night," Maeve said. "Some guy in a black SUV was waiting for Esther at Starring, and a few days before that in some alley."

Maeve looked at her watch again and scanned the road outside the window for signs of Margaret.

"Don't the courts usually give the kids to the parents?" Tom asked. "Is there any chance Buddy will win?"

"Not if I got something to say about it. Cora's raised Evan since he was born. That makes her *in loco parentis* and puts her on even footing with Buddy. And if you're comparing Buddy to Cora, he hasn't got a chance. But until I get a court order, he can take Evan any time and the cops won't do anything about it."

Sal nodded. "The lady lawyer is right."

Spotting Margaret walking toward the building, Maeve said, "There's my client. Catch you guys later."

❦❦❦

Nesbitt Courthouse

Maeve and Cora sat in cold plastic chairs in a waiting room that looked like a bus station for over an hour before they got their chance to talk to the magistrate. Two petitioners were ahead of them. A young woman with a black eye and split lip sat in the first row with an infant car seat at her feet. Every few minutes she bent over to peek inside, sometimes putting her hand in to stroke the baby or rearrange a blanket, then sat up again. A court clerk, a young man in slacks, a pullover and tie, came out of a side door and called her name. She picked up the infant carrier, winced a bit as she did, then followed him through the door.

Almost half an hour went by before the mother and baby came out. She looked frightened, all alone, with paperwork in one hand and the baby carrier in the other. She spotted the green neon exit sign and headed toward it, hesitating a long moment before she pulled the big door open with the hand that clutched her paperwork and stepped out into the world.

The court clerk came back fifteen minutes later and called a man's name. Across the room, an older couple had been sitting. The man had been a ball of fury, crossing and uncrossing his arms, rolling his neck. The woman looked exhausted and on the verge of tears. They followed the clerk into the side room and were gone for twenty minutes.

Maeve could hear the man's deep voice rise and drop while he must have been telling his story. When they came out of the room, the man was calmer, the woman no happier than before. She slipped their paperwork into her purse. He held the door for her. Just as she passed him on her way out, he patted her shoulder and murmured, "It will all work out, Mother, you'll see." She paused to listen, nodded, and stepped out of the room.

All the while, Cora hadn't said anything. It was always awkward keeping clients distracted and calm while waiting for something to happen. Maeve was grateful that Cora could occupy herself while Maeve leaned her head against the wall and closed her eyes.

The court clerk called Cora's name. Maeve jerked awake. She hadn't meant to fall asleep and was aware of a purring sound she'd heard just before she woke up. She hoped it hadn't been her.

When they stepped into the side room, they found a sad looking woman in a judge's robe behind a desk in a small office. She had long, dark curly hair, smoky eye makeup, puffy eyes, and a hang-dog expression. She turned an audio recorder on, introduced the case and said to Maeve, "You may proceed."

Maeve explained that Esther's body had recently been found. It was too soon to provide a death certificate to the court. The magistrate would just have to accept her representation that Esther was in fact dead. Margaret testified that Buddy showed up, drunk, beating on the door the night before, and threatening to call the cops to get his kid.

And Cora had called the cops while Buddy was yelling. As they had just left the condo after interviewing the family, they came back minutes later. Evan wouldn't leave the kitchen window overlooking the street as Buddy stumbled through a field sobriety test and was loaded into the back of a patrol car. One of the officers came back to the house and explained to Margaret and Cora that had he been sober, there was nothing they could have done to prevent him from removing Evan.

Cora told the magistrate that she had raised Evan his

entire life, as was the Yup'ik custom, and that the police had said Esther had died under suspicious circumstances, but they didn't who had done it. Maeve handed the magistrate a copies of Buddy's criminal convictions.

"Very well," said the magistrate as she signed the order. "A copy of this will be sent over to the state troopers to serve on Mr. Halcro. Meanwhile, keep a copy with you at all times. If he shows up again, you call the police and show the order to them. They will enforce it." She stood and handed the papers to Maeve.

Maeve led Cora back to her office, made a copy of the order for her file, and then gave the original to Cora.

"What happens next?" Cora asked.

"We'll file a custody action first thing Monday. As soon as I get everything typed up, I'll need some signatures and I'll give you a call."

"This paper means we get to keep Evan?" Cora asked again.

"Absolutely. If Buddy shows up, don't answer the door. Just call the cops and they'll send him away. Give a copy to the school too, so they know not to let him on the grounds."

Maeve walked Cora to her car, then went back into the Ten-Eighty using the front door. A few tables had filled with diners. The room was warm and now smelled of freshly baked bread, cheese and pepperoni.

Maeve took off her coat and slipped into the booth opposite Tom. It seemed he hadn't moved since she left. The ashtray was full. Sal came out of the kitchen with a platter for one of the tables, served the pizza and then came over to the booth.

"So where were we?" Sal asked.

"Large, half pepperoni, half sausage," Tom said.

"Statements, alibis," Sal said. "Who saw what when."

"Buddy Halcro said he hadn't seen Esther in a long time," Maeve said. "Except for when she dropped off Evan at Christmas. Who knows what a long time is to him, but according to Ana, he showed up at the bars looking for her at New Years."

"My sources confirm that," Tom said. "When can we order?"

"Is he lying or just living in an alternate reality?" Sal asked. "This guy's a drunk? Probably takes drugs too."

"We talked to the C.E.O. at Neqa, knows nothing. Andrew Turner, he's the head of Turner International where Esther's office was, knows nothing. The receptionists at both offices weren't cooperating. Nothing, nothing, nothing. But I found a key at Esther's condo."

Tom took the napkin he'd had wadded up in his hand and threw it on the table. He lurched his body out of the booth. "I'm getting us some bread sticks."

Sal ignored him. "What key?"

"I found a house key in Esther's junk drawer at her condo," Maeve said. "There's a tag on it with the number 1401."

Sal took Tom's seat and filled a mug of coffee for Maeve. "Does it open her condo?"

"Nope, tried that."

"Definitely a house key?"

"Yup."

Tom came back with a basket of warm bread sticks and a couple of bowls of tomato sauce and put them down the table. "Could be a hotel room key."

"Nah, not anymore, they all use those electronic card things," Sal said. "It's got to be a house key, or an apartment key."

Sal and Maeve sat in silence, thinking. Tom pulled up a chair, sat down, and chewed on a breadstick.

"Let's assume for the moment it's an apartment key," Sal said. "How many apartment buildings have fourteen floors in Anchorage?"

Tom slapped the table. "Inlet Towers."

"Good boy," Sal said, patting Tom on the back. "I knew you'd get there."

Tom shot Sal a dirty look. "So why would Esther Fancy-boy have a key to apartment 1401 in the Inlet Towers?"

"Here's the thing," Sal said. "You don't have a search warrant. You should turn it over to the police and let them look into it."

"If you're not a cop, you don't need a search warrant, buddy," Tom said.

"That's burglary! You can't admit illegally obtained evidence, can you? That's what the D.A. always told us."

"Who cares?" Maeve asked. She just needed to know why Esther had died. Besides, for all they knew, apartment 1401 belonged to Esther, so using her key wouldn't be illegal. It could have. Maybe.

Tom saw the look in Maeve's eye. He opened his wallet and dropped a twenty on the table. "Thanks, Sal, we're out of here."

"This is a police matter," Sal warned. "You don't want to go stinking up the trail before they get there."

Maeve fluttered her fingers in a good-bye. "Or it could be a wild goose chase. Besides, the police don't seem to be doing anything."

"That's not fair," Sal said, "It takes time for them to pull the team together, make a plan. There's a right way to do things. They got to check all the boxes or some smartass defense attorney will say they screwed something up. Besides, police don't publicize their theories and lines of investigation. They don't want the bad guys knowing and they don't want the crazies out there trying to help them."

Maeve grabbed a breadstick and took a bite, then a second bite. She realized how hungry she was. "Box up that pizza for us, we'll be back."

"What pizza? Oh yeah, that. I lied." Sal edged out of the booth.

"Figures," Tom said. He wrapped the breadsticks in a napkin and shoved them into his pocket.

"Look you two, don't say I didn't warn you. It could be dangerous."

"I hope so," Maeve said. "Then we're on the right track."

≠≠≠

Suite 1401 Inlet Towers

Maeve paused before the door, looked down the hallway, saw that it was empty, then checked the other direction. Empty too. Behind her, Tom kept lookout while she slid the key into the lock.

The key turned smoothly. Maeve pushed open the door to suite 1401, then stepped inside, and listened. Dead quiet. Tom followed her into the suite.

Inlet Towers was one of two matching towers that had been erected in Anchorage in the late 1950's. Standing fourteen stories tall, the towers—one on each side of town—were the two tallest buildings in Anchorage at the time. Both were badly damaged in the 1964 earthquake.

There was only enough money to save one of them.

The Inlet Towers had been renovated into a high-end hotel and apartment complex. The eastern tower, the Pepto-pink McKay building, was abandoned and left to rot, its derelict frame now providing shelter to the homeless.

Maeve and Tom stepped past a galley kitchen separated from the living room by a granite-topped island. The apartment was decorated in creams and grays, the focus of which was one large picture executed by an art-institute educated Native artist Maeve had seen in the local galleries. The painting was a bear in bright colors, mostly blue. It was the only color in the room.

The couches and chairs looked like typical hotel room furniture, clean lines, hard-wearing. The tables and a desk in the corner were dark wood. An open laptop was on the desk. When Maeve ran her finger across the mouse pad, it came to life. The screen said *Attorney Client Work Product* in bold letters across the top of the page. Before Maeve thought to turn away, she noticed the client's name: Xander George.

"Shit," Maeve said. "There's a lawyer staying here."

"Yeah, so what?" Tom asked.

"So if the bar association gets wind of me burglarizing a lawyer's suite and accessing his client files, I'm dead. Skip the hearing. Tender my bar card."

"It's not burglary if you got the key." Tom said, but he was halfway to the front door when it opened.

"Who the hell are you people?" said a corpulent, robust man, face flushed from the cold. He was wearing a long cashmere coat, elegant but not nearly warm enough for an Alaskan winter, over slacks, and a dress shirt open at the throat. A paper cup was in hand and a newspaper was tucked under an arm.

The truth was Maeve's sword and her shield. If the bar found out she lied on top of everything, it could only get worse.

Maeve strode to him with her arm extended. "I am so sorry," Maeve said. "I had no idea anyone was staying here. I'm Maeve Malloy and this is my investigator, Tom Sinclair, Mister..."

"Edelson," the man said, giving Maeve and then Tom a once-over look. "Robert Edelson."

Edelson was a big, beefy man. When he spoke, his jowly cheeks shook. Furry eyebrows would have dominated his face were it not for the bulbous nose with red spidery veins. He'd be a back-slapping bon vivant if he didn't have you in his crosshairs.

"I have a key to this suite, Mr. Edelson. It's a long story."

"Tell me or tell the cops," Edelson said.

Maeve took out her business card and handed it to him. "I'm following up on the death of Esther Fancyboy and I found this key in her condominium. I was hoping I might run across something here that could steer us in the right direction."

Edelson peered at her from under a frown. He examined Maeve's card, flipped it over, scowled, and flipped it right again. "Like maybe you're looking for a thumb drive?"

"Why do you ask?"

"Some blond guy was here first thing this morning, looking for a thumb drive. He said a business associate lost it. I figured he worked for Xander George over at Neqa, since this is their corporate condo for out of town visitors."

Tom produced his cell phone. He accessed the photo he'd taken of Turner surreptitiously on their first visit to his office. "You mean this guy?" Tom showed the photo to Edelson.

Edelson set his coffee and newspaper on the granite counter, rummaged in his breast pocket for glasses and slipped them on. He looked at the photo for only a moment. "Yeah, that's him."

CHAPTER ELEVEN

Maeve Malloy's condominium

M aeve unlocked her condo front door while Tom stamped snow off his boots.

"You think Esther's office was searched? Turner looking for that thumb drive?" Tom asked.

"It was only a couple of days after Esther disappeared and no one knew she was dead yet," Maeve said. "For all Turner knew, she'd come back any minute ready to go to work. Unless, of course, he already knew she wasn't coming back."

"Seems he's pretty twisted up about that thumb drive. You think it was important enough to kill her?"

Maeve had just pulled off her boots when someone rang the doorbell. She and Tom exchanged looks.

Maeve opened the door. A young man in a parka and boots stood in front of her. He was a little over six feet tall, probably in his thirties although his strawberry blond hair, fair complexion, and round baby face made him look younger. Maeve felt the heat of Tom's body as he loomed behind her.

"Peters, what are you doing here?" Tom demanded.

Peters froze to his spot, his eyes locked on Tom. Then he seemed to remember the large manila envelope in his hand. His look darted back and forth between Tom and Maeve.

"Maeve Malloy?" he asked in a quiet voice.

When Maeve said "yes?" Peters shivered.

He handed her an envelope. "You have been served." Then, he turned and trotted down the driveway.

Tom pushed past Maeve to follow him.

Maeve grabbed his arm. "It's legal, Tom. You know that."

"Crappy way to do business. Someone should teach that kid some manners."

"Not you, not today, okay?"

"What d'ya got there anyway, more bar crap?"

"The bar association would have mailed it," Maeve said. She tore open the envelope and tossed it to the floor. Inside was a complaint that read *The Estate of Manual Reyes versus State of Alaska Office of the Public Defender and Maeve Malloy*. It was printed on Ryan Shaw's pleading paper.

"I need to sit down." Maeve whisked past Tom, handing him the papers on the way.

Downstairs, she dropped onto the couch, shoeless but still wearing her coat. She looked around the condominium, feeling like a visitor. She remembered pushing the chairs and tables into place when she first moved in, but her memories were distant, like a story that had been told to her. Like she didn't belong here. Like any minute now, it would be time to go home. To her real home.

Tom came down the stairs. He tossed the documents on her kitchen table and loomed in front of her. "The bastard! We already knew this. Never liked that Shaw guy. What an effin' ambulance chaser he turned out to be. Someone should have strangled him in the crib."

"I already knew Royce filed a bar complaint against me. I didn't know Shaw was trying to take everything I own."

"You think maybe Arthur Nelson should know?"

She looked at Tom curiously. Arthur who? She was sure she should know who Tom was talking about. Then Arthur Nelson, her mentor, snapped into mind.

"You want me to call him?" Tom asked. He stood in front of her like he could stand there for hours, his body perfectly balanced for the act of waiting. The furnace rumbled into life, its fan whirling. Maeve envisioned arm air streaming through the conduits. She wondered how she'd pay the gas bill next month.

"Counselor?"

"What?"

"We should call Nelson. You got his number?"

Maeve rummaged through her coat pocket for her cell phone and dialed. Arthur picked up on the second ring.

"What's happened?" Arthur asked.

Maeve had never called him during the weekend before. It was understood that she would only use his private cell line in an emergency. Otherwise she called the office.

"I just got sued," Maeve said. She filled him on the details.

"Bring the papers by the office first thing Monday," Arthur said. "I'll file an entry of appearance. Meanwhile, don't do anything. Just put your feet up."

"Arthur, your office's parking bill is more than my entire gross earnings. I can't afford you."

"You were a state employee and you're being sued in your official capacity. The state has an obligation to defend you. I'll get them to pick up the tab. Don't worry about it."

"I'm so sorry, Arthur. I've caused you nothing but trouble."

"We do for one another, Maeve. That's why we were put here on this earth."

After Arthur disconnected, Maeve flipped the phone shut and dropped it on the coffee table. She fell back into the couch. Maybe she should just sell the condo before she defaulted on the mortgage payments. At least she could live off the money rather than let Ryan Shaw get his hands on it. She could buy a motor home, an old used one, and drive around Alaska all summer. Incognito, important to no one.

Tom looked at her expectantly.

"Arthur told me not to do anything," Maeve said. "Again."

"Did you do anything after you got the bar complaint?"

"I called Royce but didn't get through."

"I'll go make coffee." Tom picked up her cell and tossed it at her. "Try again."

She caught the phone. What was the point? Royce was an

experienced lawyer. Even if he hadn't been in a courtroom in a decade, he'd choose his words carefully. Nothing factual. Nothing true. Nothing that could be used against him. And definitely nothing that would make her feel better.

Royce's personal cell phone number was still on her autodial. She punched in the call. Royce answered the phone on the second ring. "What?" he whispered loudly.

"What? I'll tell you what. I just got sued. And you filed a bar complaint against me. What the hell is going on?"

"Look, I got sued, too. That's why I filed the bar complaint. Risk management made me do it. It wasn't my choice. You know how those pencil-pushing bureaucrats are. They want to minimize the exposure to the P.D.'s office."

"If Shaw wins, I pay the judgment?"

Royce scoffed. "That's a long way off."

"So how the hell did Ryan Shaw find out what happened?"

"I can't talk to you about this. You know that. And do me a favor," Royce hissed, "don't call this number anymore."

The line went dead. Maeve had been right. She didn't feel better. She felt worse. The man who she had made look good by winning case after case when she worked for him was now minimizing the impact on his budget by blaming her for the one thing that went wrong.

The same man who she had planned a future with.

The same man who didn't even break up with her before he married someone else.

There had been signs but she ignored them. The romantic Christmas retreat at the Girdwood ski resort, champagne, a room with a hot tub, maybe even some skiing, that he canceled at the last minute. He said he had to spend the holidays with the governor, his best friend from high school and the man who had appointed him to the P.D.'s job. He couldn't turn down the offer after everything the governor had done for him. The governor's sister would have been there.

On Valentine's Day, he canceled the romantic dinner in favor of an early night at her condo. He was flying to Juneau later that night to lobby for more money for the department. And then as the summer wore on, he called less and less, came over less and less.

By the time she saw the gold ring on his finger, she hadn't seen him for a month.

She had been such an idiot.

Tom had been right. Royce got his chance and he screwed her.

Maeve scrolled through her cell phone directory, found Royce's entry and deleted him.

She picked up the lawsuit again and thumbed through it. Her mind raced too much to read it thoroughly, but she recognized names: Ryan Shaw, Addison Royce, Filippo Mataafa, Maeve Malloy, and, almost as an afterthought, Manual Reyes, the man who was killed.

Tom came out of the kitchen carrying two mugs of coffee and handed her one. She held the mug beneath her face, the steam penetrating her skin.

Screw Royce. Screw Shaw. When someone backs you into a corner, you have a choice. Take a beating or fight. If you sit back and let them do this, everything is lost. You have nothing to lose by fighting hard and dirty.

"Tom, you know we never really talked about the Mataafa thing after it was over. No point since there was an acquittal," Maeve said.

"Yeah?"

"So how did you find out that the alibi was perjured?"

"Now, you're talking, Counselor."

༈༈༈

2:30 AM, Sunday, January 13
Parking Lot of Belle's Olde Time Saloon

Tom looked at his watch again and re-started his engine. The temperature had dropped to ten below and the truck cab was frigid. His jeans, stiff from the cold, scratched his thighs. Inside his boots, his feet went from too hot when the heater blew freezing air a few minutes after he shut it off. If Big Red didn't come out of that strip joint's side door soon, he was going to burn up an entire tank of gas on nothing but staying alive.

He lit another cigarette. The smoke warmed his lungs.

A side door opened and a group of girls wandered out in stiletto boots, tight pants, and waist length fake fur jackets. One of them was a head taller than the rest. Under the yellow security light, her hair was a river of copper.

Tom crushed out the cigarette, opened the door, and strode across the parking lot. Girls should look scared when a strange man comes at them in at 2:30 in the morning but all these girls did was stand around watching him as he headed for Big Red. When she noticed him, she dropped back and put one hand in a pocket, like she was going to pull a knife.

A few seconds later, she relaxed but her hand stayed in the pocket. "You again?"

"Got time for breakfast?"

Big Red gave him the once over slowly, toe to the wrist where she had seen his Rolex before, now hidden under his parka sleeve, and back to his eyes. "You driving?"

"Got the limo over there." He nodded at his truck.

"You girls run along," Big Red said to the audience. "I'll catch up with you later."

Big Red was quiet on the ride to Soapy Smith's. She must have been tired after a night of dancing, loud music, and putting up with bull, too tired to fight the truck engine's roar.

Soapy's was a dive. A soupy trail of melting gray snow led from the front door to booths. Tom escorted Big Red to the back wall, their shoes crunching on the fine layer of gravel tracked in by boots. Along the way, they passed red-faced drunks, rogue young men who didn't have a woman to go home to, guys who'd been tossed out of the bars at closing time but weren't broke yet.

Tom steered Big Red to a far booth near the kitchen, usually the least desirable location in a restaurant, but in this restaurant, the warmest spot. The drunks sitting by the entrance were still wearing their coats.

Tom threw his Carhartt jacket in one side of the booth. Big Red tossed her fur jacket into the other side. When the drunks caught the spillage of Big Red's breasts from her sequined red halter top, their drunken mutterings halted for a moment, then one of them snickered. She took no notice.

She slid into the booth. Tom sat down. A more than middle-aged woman in a waitress uniform, her unnaturally brown hair stuffed under a white cap appeared at the table with a carafe stained by years of rancid coffee.

"Morning, Tom. Red," she said as she flipped over two cups and poured. "Welcome to Soapy's."

The coffee tasted as bad as it smelled.

Their waitress, Iris, made no comment about them coming in together, although Tom had never brought Big Red to Soapy's before. He wasn't surprised Iris knew her. Soapy's was the favorite place of bar workers and the only all-night diner in Anchorage.

"You know who Soapy Smith was, don't you?" Big Red asked.

Tom shook his head. He thought Soapy Smith was make-believe, like Paul Bunyan.

"He was a rip-off artist down in Skagway, during the gold rush. He got shot to death over a rigged card game."

Figures. A dead criminal is what passes for mythical hero in Alaska.

Iris cocked a hip and tapped her pencil on her order pad.

"Whatever you want," Tom said.

"Denver omelet, hash browns," she said.

"Ditto," Tom said. For once, he'd met a woman who wasn't on a diet.

Under the yellow florescent lights, Red's face looked ravaged. Dull brown roots showed beneath the brassy hair. Make-up filled the crevices like a bad grout job. Eye shadow caked in her creased eyelids. Flakes of mascara dotted her cheeks. Harsh red lipstick made her thin lips look like a knife wound.

When she spoke, one eyetooth jutted out. Her eyes were an unreal shade of green. As she doctored her coffee with powder creamer and sugar, Tom saw the edge of a contact slither across her eyeball.

Red polish was chipping off her fake fingernails. The nail of her left little finger was painted silver and was long, all the better to shovel cocaine with. No wonder she was so thin.

Still, she was a woman who had a hard life or she wouldn't be stripping for drunken jerkoffs like the fools huddled at the far table. He'd heard the story a million times before. It started with a creepy father or an uncle, the girl running away as soon as she was old enough. It ended with the one of the only two jobs an underage girl could get: stripping or hooking.

After that, what future was there for a stripper? College, ha! Most of them didn't have high school diplomas. Working in an office, ha! Who's going to hire a girl with no office experience, one with "exotic dancer" on her resume.

Most girls hoped some nice doctor or lawyer would wander into the saloon one night and rescue them just like Cinderella. If that didn't happen before they were too old to bring in the jerkoffs, they'd end up on the streets.

Big Red was a woman who worked for a living just like Maeve worked for hers, just like Tom worked for his. She deserved respect.

She sipped her coffee, leaving a bloody red lip print on the cup. When she put the cup down, she looked at Tom and waited.

"You don't mind this place?" Tom asked, remembering that the last time they'd talked, she did not want to be seen with him, an investigator. She didn't want people thinking she was a snitch.

She shrugged. The sequins twinkled. He couldn't help but notice how light rippled across the halter top when she moved. The room went quiet again.

"About Enrique Jones," Tom said.

"What about him?"

"Seen him lately?"

She didn't answer. Big Red stretched her body across the booth like a panther. The sequins glittered. The drunks tittered. Man, she was good at controlling men.

Of course she was. The one and only thing she'd learned was to manage men, how to get what she wanted, how to keep them at a distance. It wasn't mercenary on her part. It was the lessons life had taught her.

"You remember me and you talked about Enrique Jones a couple of years ago? You called him Ricky. You and him, motel room, Filippo Mataafa, gas station robbery, coke deal."

Big Red rocked a leg and her body followed it like a wave. The sequins were probably still doing their work, judging by the quiet from the other booth, but Tom was getting bored with the show. His eyes burned. He rubbed them. His low back ached from sitting all day. He twisted and stretched.

"I didn't rat you out, or someone else would have been here by now," Tom said. "And I'll do what I can to keep your name out of it. But I need some answers."

If Big Red were younger, she would have rolled her eyes at him. Instead her stare drove straight into his.

"We broke up," Red said.

Tom frowned.

"Last time I talked to you, he'd just dumped me," Red said. "I was pissed, so that's why I said what I said."

Tom made his living from pissed-off ex-girlfriends. When they wanted to hurt Mr. Wrong, they didn't make stuff up. They dug up the darkest, most vulnerable secret the guy had, the best way to hurt him, and they gave it away to anyone who wanted to know. For free. They just didn't want to get caught in the backlash. Just in case he might come back.

"You might have talked to me because you were pissed," Tom said flatly, "but you and I both know what you said was true."

Big Red tilted her head in a way that said she was a wiser woman now. Tom noticed then the bump in her nose, beneath which it took a slightly different direction. And the healed cut on her left cheekbone.

"Enrique Jones gave Mataafa up a couple of months ago," Tom said. "He won't come back on you. He told the cops he lied about being with Mataafa in the club the night of the robbery. He's already admitted Mataafa robbed the gas station. If Mataafa comes back on anyone, it'll be Ricky. He sold Mataafa out because of the drive-by, to save his own ass. You heard?"

"Everyone has."

"What do you know?"

As she looked up at the ceiling, editing her thoughts, Iris appeared with the two plates of food. Before she could serve them, Tom waved her away. With slit eyes, Big Red followed her breakfast going back to the kitchen.

"Ricky done a bunch of deals with some guy named Sonny. And then everyone around Mataafa started going to jail. Everyone but Sonny. Filippo figured Sonny was a snitch, or maybe an undercover cop, so Ricky set up a meet on Gambell Street. It was late at night when no one was supposed to be around so Filippo could do a hit...you know, kill him. Sonny drove off while Filippo was shooting at him and the paper boy got killed instead."

"The paper boy that got killed was a father working a second job to support his wife and kids."

"Oh, that's too bad," Red said rotely. Home, marriage, kids, all that stuff was like a fairy tale to a girl like Red.

"You know this Sonny?" Tom asked.

"Only seen him a few times. Biker looking dude. Tall, skinny, lots of leather, long hair, big beard."

"You seen him lately?"

Big Red shook her head.

Tom turned around, caught Iris's eye, and motioned for their meals. Red had told him everything he needed to know. Mataafa was right. Sonny was an undercover cop. All that hair and beard, now long gone, was there to hide his face. He was probably working in some new disguise in Fairbanks. Or he went back to his suit and tie job as a detective at Anchorage Police Department, or he might even be a fed and had since moved out of state. Tom might never know who Sonny really was.

But he did know Enrique Jones had set up the coke deal with Sonny on the same night Mataafa robbed the gas station. And a year later, Enrique Jones had set up the meet that had ended up in Manny Reyes's death. No other way around it. Enrique Jones was the cop's contact. Enrique Jones was Sonny's snitch.

Big Red tucked into her omelet like a truck driver. Tom was beginning to like this woman.

"So you girls having a party or something?" Tom asked.

"Or something," Big Red said. "We're watching *Casablanca*, making s'mores and doing our nails. Girls' night. No men. We get enough of them at work." She cut her eyes toward the now hungover young men. Their sallow faces stared into their coffee, now realizing that the most excitement they'd get that night had come and gone.

"I'll drop you off," Tom said.

CHAPTER TWELVE

Home of Cora and Evan Fancyboy

M aeve followed Margaret to the dining area and placed her briefcase on the table. Cora sat on the couch in the adjacent living room, her hands busy sewing fur trim onto a spotted seal skin.

"These are the mittens Esther started for her grandmother, Agatha." Cora said without lifting her eyes. "We'll give them to her when we take Esther home."

"When will that be?" Maeve asked.

"In the summer, when the ground thaws." Cora stabbed her needle into hide.

Rustling sounds from upstairs drifted down to them. In the stillness, traffic noises seemed distant, hushed by the falling snow.

"Neqa is paying for the plane," Margaret said.

"Is that something they do for all the shareholders?" Maeve asked.

"Xander said he'd make sure it got paid because Esther was his employee."

Funny, Maeve thought, Xander was so magnanimous now. Before he'd acted as if he barely knew Esther.

"I found out where that key went to, the one we found in your kitchen drawer," Maeve said to Cora. "Neqa keeps a condominium in Inlet Towers for out-of-towners. There's an attorney staying there. Andrew Turner went there yesterday looking for a thumb drive. Has Turner called you?"

"We don't know anything about a thumb drive," Margaret said. "But Xander asked about Esther's computer."

"Wasn't it her personal property?" Maeve asked.

"It was, but he was hoping it would have something on it he needs."

"The hard drive is ruined," Maeve said. "A virus probably. Nothing can be reconstructed from it."

"Can you tell that to Xander?" Margaret asked.

"Happy to," Maeve said as she opened the briefcase. "I need Cora's signature on the custody papers. I'll leave them with you. Just give me a call when they're signed."

Quiet as a ghost, Evan entered the room and tucked himself tightly beside his grandmother.

"Was Esther dating anybody?" Maeve asked Margaret quietly.

"You asked that before," Cora said, her eyes trained on her work.

"Yes, we did."

"Why do you ask again?" Margaret frowned. "The police asked us that, too. Is there something you're not telling us?"

Maeve deliberately eyed Evan for Margaret's benefit. His little ears didn't need to hear his mother had sex before she died. Margaret followed Maeve's look and nodded. "No, no one's called or come by."

A long uncomfortable moment stretched out when no one spoke. Margaret's stare bored a hole into Maeve, like she was trying to read Maeve's mind. Cora sewed. Evan watched Cora.

"Is there anything we can do for you?" Maeve asked Margaret.

"No, thanks. We have friends from the village who come by. We're fine."

Maeve stood.

"She had a boyfriend." Evan said, his eyes still on Cora's sewing.

Cora laid her project in her lap.

"How do you know that, Evan?" Margaret asked.

"I heard them talking on the phone."

⁂

Monday, January 14
4539 Nunaka Drive

Irma Reyes sat on her couch passing a fat, energetic toddler back and forth to the white-haired woman sitting next to her. Irma was a plump woman in her middle forties, but looked older, with a kind face, and thin, dark hair drawn into a loose braid. The other woman, the very image of Irma only a few more lines in her face, was her mother, Isabel Martinez. The wall behind them was covered in school photos of many children, too many to count because of the family resemblance. Maeve knew from her prior visits that there were seven children in all, ranging in ages from fifteen months to seventeen years.

The Reyes family lived in a modest three-bedroom, one-bath home that had been built by the army to house military dependents. Each small square home looked much like the small square home on either side of it. The families who bought into the neighborhood cared about their homes. They mowed their lawns in the summer and shoveled their driveways in the winter.

When Maeve and Tom had stepped inside, they passed the little font nailed to the right side of the door beneath a portrait of the Blessed Virgin. Maeve dipped her hand and crossed herself without thinking. Tom stopped abruptly behind her.

Irma Reyes had always been kind to Maeve even on her first visit. During the Olafson trial, Maeve had learned that Filippo Mataafa shot and killed Manual Reyes. After the trial was over, she visited Irma Reyes and her family to extend her condolences, to apologize for her role in allowing Filippo Mataafa wander the streets, and to offer whatever help she could give them.

Irma didn't blame Maeve then and she didn't look resentful now. She wasn't the kind of woman who stewed in revenge. She took care of her family, went to Spanish-language Mass and volunteered with the Legion of Mary, the ladies' auxiliary. After her husband's death, she took a night job cleaning one of the downtown hotels so she could be home when her children came back from school.

Maeve sat on the edge of a chair, in the lady-like pose she'd been taught by the nuns, straight back, knees together, ankles crossed. "How are you, Mrs. Reyes?"

Tom was in another chair striking his sympathetic pose, elbows on knees, hands clasped, peering from beneath his brow. No toothpick.

"Little Manny is starting college in the fall," Irma Reyes said in a quiet voice with a soft Mexican accent. "He's going to be a doctor. Maria Teresa made honor roll again. Angelo and Miguel get into trouble but just little stuff. They're really good boys. Gabriella wants us to call her Gaby. Iliana just started kindergarten. And little Diego," she kissed the baby's curly black hair, "is the image of his father."

That is how Irma answered every time Maeve asked her how she was. She answered by telling Maeve how the children were.

Diego curled up in his grandmother's lap while Irma wiped an eye.

"Are you getting by okay?" Maeve asked.

Irma nodded. "We're getting a little bit from the workers' comp and the Social Security. The money I make helps. Little Manny wants to get a job this summer. I won't let him work during the school year. His education is too important. And Maria Teresa does some babysitting."

"The reason I ask," Maeve said, "is because I got this lawsuit." She pulled a copy of the complaint from her briefcase and handed it to Irma.

Irma took the document and read each page closely. "I don't understand," she said as she handed it back. "Can you explain it to me?"

"What this says is that you're suing me for your husband's death, that you want me to pay you money."

Irma covered mouth. "But why? I didn't do this thing. How did this happen?"

"The name of your attorney listed on the complaint is Ryan Shaw. Do you know him?"

Both Irma and Isabel nodded at the mention of Shaw's name. "That's the man who came to the house, said he'd help us."

Tom lifted an elbow, adjusted his feet.

"When was that, do you remember?" Maeve asked.

Irma consulted her mother in Spanish.

"Before Christmas, after Thanksgiving," Irma said.

Ryan Shaw was still working at the public defender's office during the Olafson trial in November. Maeve was certain. Shaw had represented one of the kids who had assaulted her client, who had cut a deal snitching out his codefendant to get a lighter sentence. Shaw must have quit his job soon after that, opened his little office and driven straight over to the Reyes' house to sign up his first big case.

Before visiting Irma, Maeve had gone by court to file the custody action against Buddy Halcro and then visited the court's record room where she picked up several files, including the probate one Shaw had opened giving him the legal authority to file suit against the state and Maeve. She also copied Enrique Jones' criminal cases. Six in all. Two misdemeanors as a young man for fighting and reckless driving, and four felony cases as he matured, all drug related except the last one. That was the murder case in which he was indicted along with Filippo Mataafa for the killing of Manual Reyes. And Ryan Shaw was his attorney.

So when Shaw suggested to Enrique Jones he could get him a deal if Jones cooperated, Jones told Shaw about Mataafa's gas station robbery, the bogus alibi, and how he and Mataafa had lied to Maeve to get Mataafa off. Shaw wasn't stupid. He saw an opportunity to make money. He quit his job, drove to the Reyes' home and signed her up.

"What was he going to help you with?" Maeve asked.

"The life insurance from Manny's work. We didn't know how to fill out the forms. And he said that there was a victim's fund, money the state gives people to help them with their bills. But no lawsuit. He didn't say anything about a lawsuit. He wants money from you?" Irma's hands twisted in her lap. "No, he never said anything about that."

Maeve took the probate file from her briefcase and handed it to Irma. "Do you know Jennifer Dominski, the woman who was appointed personal representative of Mr. Reyes' estate?"

"Si," Irma said. "His secretary. She came with Mr. Shaw. She said she'd help him with the paperwork."

"How are you paying them?" Maeve asked.

"I have some papers," Irma said. She left the room, came back a few minutes later and handed documents to Maeve. One was a contingency fee agreement by which Irma agreed to pay Ryan Shaw thirty-three and one-third per cent of anything he obtained against "any liable party." The second fee agreement was with Jennifer Dominski for seven per cent for any funds she administered through the estate.

In sum, Ryan Shaw and his secretary were getting more than forty percent of the money they recovered, including the Violent Crimes Victim Fund, which only required one form filled out. There was nothing in the fee agreement that explicitly authorized Ryan Shaw to sue the state or Maeve.

Tom grunted, his code for he had something to say. Maeve had something to say, too, but it wasn't to Irma Reyes. Irma had been duped by the ambulance-chasing Ryan Shaw.

"I am so sorry, Mrs. Malloy," Irma said. She always called Maeve Misses, no matter how many times Maeve asked her to use her first name. "Did I get you into trouble?"

"It wasn't you, Mrs. Reyes. I'm sure it's just a big misunderstanding. Do you mind if we go over what we said one more time? I'd like to get it recorded. It'll help us clear this all up."

ƒƒƒ

Law Office of Maeve Malloy

The pizza ovens had started up and Maeve's office was humid with the smell of baking bread. Sooner or later, she would need to develop immunity.

She was studying half of the files she'd copied that morning. Tom was on the couch reading the other half. He stood, crossed the room and dropped one of the files on her desk. "You'll never guess who Enrique Jones's lawyer was back when you were trying the Mataafa case. Back before Shaw represented him."

"Someone at the P.D.'s?"

"The P.D."

Maeve sat up and dragged the photocopies closer. On top was an old indictment in *State vs. Enrique Jones*. He had been charged with conspiracy to distribute a controlled substance, to wit: cocaine. His attorney in that case was none other than Addison Royce.

The public defender rarely handled cases personally. His real job was administrating the agency, but occasionally he would pluck a file from the office caseload. Usually it was because the case was receiving a lot of media coverage, television cameras in the court room, reporters asking for a statement. But this wasn't one of those cases.

It was just a routine drug bust. Or should have been.

Enrique "Ricky" Jones had been caught in a motel room with mountains of cocaine during an undercover sting. He was the only defendant. There wasn't anyone else to snitch out so he could leverage a good deal. Yet when that case wrapped up, Jones had a conviction in name only. No jail time. No fines. Just probation. That meant one thing: He had done someone a favor to get that deal.

Maeve dug a legal pad out from the bottom of the pile on

her desk, dropped the other files on the floor, and wrote out a timeline.

In 2011, Jones got busted in the motel room. Addison Royce was his attorney. Royce and Jones cut an unbelievably good deal and according to what Big Red told Tom, Jones was setting up buys and feeding dealers to the cops.

In 2012, the gas station was robbed. On the same night, Enrique Jones was doing a coke deal with an undercover cop. The other people at the scene were busted, but Jones wasn't. Because he was the snitch.

In August 2013, Jones testified for Mataafa. Royce had to have known Enrique Jones's alibi testimony was a lie because Royce negotiated the deal by which Enrique Jones turned snitch and set up buys between drug dealers and the undercover cop, Sonny.

And look who the prosecutor was in all these cases: Addison Royce's friend at the district attorney's office, Jefferson Bennett. Bennett had to be in on the deal when Jones agreed to start working as a confidential informant for the police. Bennett was the same attorney who prosecuted Mataafa. When Jones took the stand in the Mataafa case, Bennett had to have known he was lying.

Maeve looked harder at the dates. Bennett was the D.A. assigned to the case before his good friend, Royce, entered appearance for the public defender's office. It looked like Bennett had called Royce and told him to pull the case for himself, there was a sensitive deal to be done.

Had Royce kept Tom on a short leash during the Mataafa trial, hoping that he wouldn't find out about Jones's activities and blow the whistle? And had Royce handed the file off to Maeve, who he was then distancing himself from because of his impending marriage? If so, Bennett and Royce knew the alibi was perjured. Yet they watched silently as Maeve put Jones on the stand. They used her.

"Bastards," Maeve said.

Tom was silent, his jaw working.

"But why?" Maeve asked.

"Counselor..." Tom's voice was soothing, almost motherly. "They hung you out to dry because you were expendable. What are you asking? What, did they sneak around like they're James Bond or something? Secrets are seductive. Knowledge is power. Both of those clowns are power hungry, especially Royce. If he wants to be judge, he needs the police vote and the D.A.'s support. There's only one way to do get the cops and prosecutors on a defender's side and that's by playing ball. He's a snake in the grass. Always has been."

Maeve's stomach lurched. Bile burned her throat. It took all the focus she had to force her breakfast down.

She had been so naïve. Criminal defense is supposed to be about the constitution, about fairness for everyone, for the public, for the accused. It isn't supposed to be a platform for a political career.

"You drop off the recording?" Tom asked.

"Hmm," Maeve said. "The court reporter said she'd have the transcript by tomorrow."

On the street below, traffic crunched by on the snow. A fighter jet zoomed low, engines screaming as it approached the nearby military base. Then another fighter. And another. Maeve could no longer smell the baking bread.

"You were right," Maeve said. "About him, about them."

CHAPTER THIRTEEN

Neqa, Inc.

A s Maeve and Tom watched from the conference room window, heavy gray clouds blanketed the landscape and a
gauzy curtain of ice fog obscured the divide between sky and
earth. The mountains she had seen on her first visit were gone,
as if they had never existed. Color, too, was gone, as if it had
never existed.

"Roads'll be slick tonight," Tom said as he checked his
Rolex. "How long we got to wait? It's been forty-five minutes
already."

"He needs to learn we're not going away," Maeve said.

In the parking lot below, light fixtures on tall poles
winked on, faintly glowing at first, then brighter and whiter.
Gloom above. Gloom straight ahead. Ice particles danced in the
cones of light shining from the poles looking like fairy dust.

Xander George entered without greeting. On his heels was
Robert Edelson, the attorney who had busted Maeve in suite
1401. Xander sat at the head of the table. Edelson now dressed
in an expensive suit, sat to his right, facing Maeve.

"We meet again, Ms. Malloy." Edelson tossed a card across
the table at Maeve, ignoring Tom as the hired-help. She picked
up the card and examined it. Heavy linen paper, raised lettering.
A Seattle firm. The card snapped as she placed it on the table.

"Sorry again about yesterday," Maeve said.

Edelson held up a hand. "Think nothing of it. Seems there
are a lot of keys floating around to that condo." His tone was

overly gracious in a now-you-owe me way.

"I'm surprised to see you here today, Mr. Edelson," Maeve said. "Does Mr. George require an attorney to speak with us?"

Maeve eased back in her seat and waited. She didn't expect Xander or Edelson to answer that question, but she wanted them to know that she had thought of it and let them mull over the inferences she no doubt had drawn. Edelson must have evaluated the situation and spotted a vulnerability. Edelson was there to protect his client. Protecting his client meant keeping him from talking to another lawyer.

Lots of people think they're smarter than lawyers. They want to match wits, mince words, turn tables, and dumbfound their suit-wearing adversary. They don't realize the only reason a lawyer talks to them is to collect damaging evidence. Every statement, prevarication and lie hurts them. Prisons are full of people who thought they were smarter than lawyers.

Xander stared at Maeve like a bear stares at an unexpected intruder, figuring out whether they're a danger to them or good to eat. Edelson kept a poker face.

"I happened to be in town and Xander asked me to sit in," Edelson said.

"Does Neqa have a problem?" Maeve asked.

"Esther Fancyboy's files are missing. Ms. Fancyboy was responsible for preparing financial documents. Without her data, Neqa is unable to file mandated reports needed to obtain future funding."

"I'm listening."

"In phase two of the project," Edelson said, "Neqa was to install water purification systems in another five villages. Neqa needs to dig when the ground thaws so it can finish the systems by next winter. Without government funds, there will never be water systems in these villages."

"Ever?"

"The project will be shelved."

"What does that have to do with Esther's laptop? Cora said you wanted it."

"We hope she made a back-up," Edelson said.

"The hard drive was destroyed by a virus. If the files were on there, they're gone now."

Xander blinked.

"We'd like an expert to look at it," Edelson said.

"It was Esther's private property. I don't have the authority to give it to you."

Edelson's face darkened. "Perhaps you could approach her heirs, whoever that would be, and explain how important the success of this project is to the corporation and to the communities it represents."

Perhaps she could. But not until Maeve knew what was on that computer and why it was so important to Neqa. If Xander was only interested in reports, you'd think he could recreate them from the data that was available to him. Surely, Esther was not the only person with access to that information. It would be on Turner's computers. It would be on Neqa's computers. It would be on paper somewhere in someone's files. If Xander was only interested in the reports, that is.

"And the thumb drive Turner was trying to find for a client who had supposedly lost it in the suite?" Maeve asked.

Edelson laughed. "Turner obviously didn't know who I was or he'd have been more forthright. And I didn't know who you were. By the way, Mr. George would like to have that key back." Edelson extended his beefy hand, opened, to receive it.

Whatever had been in the condo was gone now. If not before Turner searched, certainly afterwards. Edelson would make sure of it.

Maeve dug the key out of her briefcase and handed it over. She felt Tom shifting in the chair beside her. He wouldn't have handed over the key. But his law license wasn't on the line.

"We're trying to find out who killed Esther," Maeve said. "She was dating someone but no one seems to know who he was. We were wondering if Mr. George might be able to help us."

A light flashed in Xander's eyes.

Edelson threw a protective arm across him. "I'm afraid

Mr. George can't help you. Ms. Fancyboy's personal life was just that. Personal."

Xander recomposed his inscrutable expression.

"We're asking everyone," Maeve said. "She was seen talking to a man at Starring. We suspect he was the boyfriend. Maybe she had a date with him later that night."

They didn't need to know Esther had sex before she died. Xander was with his family at Starring and went home with them, so he couldn't have been the mystery man. Besides, Tom's sources had said the man in the SUV was white.

Still, Xander George shouldn't need a mouthpiece just to talk about grants and thumb drives, unless there was something else he was hiding.

"Did you see Esther at Starring?" Maeve asked Xander.

"That's all the time we have today." Edelson stood. Xander pulled himself to a stand slowly. With an arm extended like a maitre d', Edelson escorted Xander out of the room.

Maeve turned to Tom. "That's okay. We'll show ourselves out."

ψψψ

Edelson followed Xander down the hall to the presidential suite. Five hundred square feet of space showcased a mahogany desk and leather upholstery. Ultra-modern bone carvings, weighing at least a hundred pounds each, were displayed on custom built shelving with hidden spotlights. A bit much.

It's all about the money, Edelson thought. It's always all about the money.

He loosened his tie and released the top button of his shirt before dropping onto the buttoned leather sofa. "There's a dead girl, I take it. What exactly is going on here, Xander?"

Xander George stared out the window, hands clasped behind his back.

Beyond the darkened glass, grayness swallowed the city. Anchorage wasn't much to look at anyway, as far as Edelson was concerned. Nothing but a miniscule downtown surrounded by arctic ghetto. Like a rundown Russian outpost.

Several months ago, the Neqa directors had asked Robert Edelson to fly up to Anchorage immediately. They had a problem. He wasn't surprised. How much business acumen could primitive hunters have? Sixty years ago, Alaska was just a territory, not even a state. The American equivalent of Siberia rumored to be floating on oil. Even now, the biggest city in the whole state was smaller than a suburb anywhere else. Edelson couldn't wait to get back to home and get a decent meal.

What could Xander possibly be looking at?

"Is this the girl we had problems with a few months ago?" Edelson asked.

Xander flinched.

Not talking. Again.

During the last visit, Xander George hadn't talked when Edelson explained the Board's findings. Someone had caught him with this girl in the act, or close to it anyway, in the copy room one night after hours. Some receptionist had forgotten her cell phone, came back to retrieve it, heard noises, and investigated only to find her co-worker and their boss *in flagrante.*

Where would we be these days without our cell phones? Stuck in traffic and not billing, that's where Edelson would be.

Confronted, the girl admitted the affair. She was young and frightened. She didn't know when to keep her mouth shut, and she didn't know who her friends were. In corporate politics, no one has friends, only allies and adversaries and they switch on you when you're the most vulnerable. The girl didn't know that. But she wasn't Edelson's problem. Xander was. He was one of the directors of Neqa and Neqa was Edelson's client.

Xander was a respected member of his tribe, if "tribe" was the politically correct term these days. Either way, he had figured out how to squeeze money out of the feds and the tribe needed him to keep squeezing. The federal money paid for the swanky offices and the directors' generous salaries.

So naturally, the directors were averse to a scandal. More

like scared shitless. Edelson suppressed a laugh. Xander didn't notice. They were afraid if the feds got wind of Xander dipping his quill in the company ink, that river of money would dry up. The directors might be stuck with Xander. But they weren't stuck with the girl.

Xander hadn't said a damned word when Edelson explained the terms. The girl needed to go. Whether the sex was consensual didn't matter. Whether it was true love didn't matter. Edelson never knew. Xander had never said. But, honestly, true love isn't consummated on top of a photocopier.

What mattered was simple. Xander was the girl's immediate supervisor. He had the authority to hire, fire, promote, and demote her. Any sexual relationship was considered coercion legally and therefore exposed the Board to significant, and worse, uninsurable liability.

Which meant if something went wrong with Xander's little dalliance and the girl filed suit, the scandal would go public embarrassing the corporation. The Board would pay a ton of money in its own attorneys' fees and then a big, fat settlement to the girl. And that federal funding that the directors so enjoyed would vanish.

Edelson had laid the cards on the table. He appealed to Xander's civic duty, explaining it was better for everyone to end it as cleanly as possible. The girl was given a significant sum, too much to refuse. She received a new title and new job duties elsewhere in satisfaction of any claim she might make.

And Xander kept his job. This time. Conditioned on one non-negotiable concession. Xander couldn't see the girl anymore. Couldn't see her, couldn't touch her, and sure as hell couldn't screw her.

"You know, Xander, I'm in your corner." Bad choice of words. Xander probably didn't understand a boxing metaphor.

"I'm your attorney," Edelson said patiently. "Anything you tell me is absolutely privileged. I'm not allowed to share our talks with anyone."

Xander shot a look at Edelson.

Edelson hauled his bulk off the couch, his knees crunching as he rose. He slowly approached Xander and stopped as close as he dared. "Sure, the Board pays my fees, but you're the client. My duty of loyalty is to you." Not technically true, but Edelson would say whatever he had to say to protect the corporation.

In the reflection of the glass, Edelson saw what Xander was watching his own image.

"Tell me the truth," Edelson said. "Now. Were you still seeing that girl?"

⚜⚜⚜

Tuesday January 15
Law Office of Maeve Malloy

Maeve was sprawled across her desk like a morose teenager in high school English class, playing with a hurricane glass pen caddy, the New Orleans souvenir she'd repurposed when she quit drinking. *Betrayed*, she heard in her mind. With one finger, she twirled the pens and the word faded. Then, she heard *used*. The word scattered when she spun the glass.

The jostling pens sounded like ice cubes swirling in a Long Island Iced Tea, those deadly drinks that quickly led to a blackout, a hangover, and tales from one's buddies that started with "do you know what you did last night?"

Hypnotic. She spun it again.

While she waited for Mrs. Reyes's statement to be transcribed, there was nothing more she could do about the lawsuit. If it was dismissed, the bar complaint should go away too. The state would no longer have a reason to pursue her.

The front door opened. Tom's heavy footsteps strode toward her inner office. "You ever look at the victim?" he asked.

Maeve stopped twirling the hurricane glass. "What about her?"

Tom tossed his jacket in the visitor chair.

"You do know," Tom said, "that in a murder case, you always start with the victim."

"It wasn't a murder case when we started, but I did get some background on her. You know what I know." Maeve spun the pens again.

Tom slipped a small stenopad from his breast pocket. "There's an old domestic violence case up in Fairbanks." He spoke as he read his notes. "She filed against a guy named Buddy Halcro."

"Evan's father. I already talked to him. You know that," Maeve said.

"Could he be the secret boyfriend?"

"I doubt it. Everyone says she hated him. And where would he get a shiny new SUV? He's living in a trailer park."

"Did you know he went to prison for counterfeiting and assault?"

"Counterfeiting what?"

"He photocopied hundred dollar bills and tried to pass them at McDonalds." Tom smirked. "What an idiot."

"That's our Buddy. And the assault?"

"Pounded the crap out of some guy who talked to Esther in a bar. He was drunk at the time, so one of his conditions of probation prohibits drinking or going into bars."

Maeve recalled the beer cans littering Buddy's trailer. "Well, he's still drinking."

"And my sources say he's hanging around Fourth Avenue."

"Ana Olrun said the same thing."

"You suppose he followed Esther to Anchorage? That he's been stalking her?"

Maeve looked at Tom as she thought about it.

"Maybe. And if Buddy had been following Esther, he could well have seen a lot more than he's letting on." Maeve gave the pens a stir.

"Enough of that, little daydreamer," Tom said. "Focus. Did you know Esther Fancyboy owned a condo?"

"I knew she was living in one with her son and mother. I thought they were renting it. Was Esther paying the mortgage?"

"No, she was not paying the mortgage on the condo, Counselor. She owned it outright. Paid off. In full. Free and clear."

CHAPTER FOURTEEN

Buddy Halcro's trailer

A lthough closed, the trailer's front door sagged so much that a stream of warm air seeped out, building a thick layer of frost on the metal frame. Tom knocked on the door again, louder this time.

A skinny man in jeans, t-shirt, and a few days' growth of beard yanked the door open. Had to be Buddy Halcro.

Stiff-arming past Buddy, Tom said, "Mind if I come in?"

"Yeah, as a matter of fact, I do." Buddy, still holding the door, watched Tom circle the small living room.

"Won't take long." Tom shrugged out of his jacket and tossed it on the harvest gold crushed velvet couch. When Tom sat down, the sagging couch collapsed around him. Objections played at Buddy's lips as he shifted from one foot to the other.

"Cold out there," Tom said.

Buddy closed the door and the room darkened. Heavy curtains were drawn across the windows. The only source of light was the flicker of an oversized television. Beer fumes mixed with the stink of old sweat. Possibly other bodily fluids too, Tom suspected when he noticed a small, stiff stain on the upholstery. As the room heated up again the spicy green aroma of growing plants reached him. Buddy grew pot?

Buddy slouched over to a threadbare recliner, positioned directly across from the television. Crushed beer cans littered its perimeter. "Why are you here?"

"I'm following up on the death of Esther Fancyboy."

Buddy reached to the floor and picked up an open can.

"You don't look surprised," Tom said.

"Not really." Buddy shrugged. "It wouldn't be like her to leave Evan."

"Got any idea what might have happened to her?"

Buddy eyed Tom as he guzzled, then said. "Hooked up with the wrong guy?"

"Got any idea who that wrong guy might have been?"

Buddy drained the can, crushed it, and dropped it over the armrest. "Nope, haven't talked to her in a year."

"You were seen hanging around Fourth Avenue, trying to hook up around Christmas and New Years."

Buddy stood and crossed the room to the kitchen area. He opened the fridge and took a can from a shelf lined with beer. The only other contents were ketchup, mustard, and a quart of milk. Only Methuselah would know how old that milk was.

"Who said that? Whoever it is, he's a friggin' liar." Buddy popped the can. "I already told that lady lawyer, I didn't see Esther."

Tom twisted, cracking his back. "I'll just give the names of my witnesses to your probation officer and you two can sort it out." But instead of wrenching himself up, Tom settled back into the smelly couch.

"Want a beer while I'm up?" Buddy asked.

"Don't change the subject."

Buddy crossed the room and sank back into the recliner. "No need to start something, mister. Yeah, I went downtown. Found Esther in the Last Frontier. She came out to my car. She didn't want people seeing us together."

Buddy's eyes darkened. He took another sip of beer. "Besides, I'm not supposed to be in no bar."

Tom listened, not moving. Never interrupt a talking witness is the second rule of interrogation. The first rule, don't let them refuse to answer the question.

"But as soon as she gets into the car with me, she tells me what a loser I am, gets back out again, and takes off." Buddy made a little walking gesture with two fingers. "You know..." He swallowed a belch. "On foot like."

"You go after her?"

"Hell no! I had to get out of there. Didn't want no one ratting me out to my P.O. Chasing a woman down the street attracts attention, you know?"

"When was this?"

"Few weeks ago. Maybe around Christmas."

"What kind of vehicle you drive?"

"That Blazer in the driveway." Buddy gestured toward the front door with his beer can. Tom had noticed the beater when he came in, weather-dulled red, replaced fender still gray with primer, windshield cracked just above the dashboard, side mirror secured by duct tape. No one would mistake that rig for a shiny new SUV.

"Anyone see you with Esther?"

Buddy considered the question for a few moments. "There was a big rig parked in the alley."

"What'd it looked like?"

"New. Figured it was the bar owner's. He's the only person down there with that kind of money."

"Color?"

"Dark, hard to tell. Blue, maybe black. It was late." Buddy up-ended the can over his open mouth.

"The night Esther disappeared, where were you?"

"At the comic book store, playing games."

"Anyone who can vouch for that?"

"My man, Igor."

"Igor," Tom repeated.

"Yeah, Igor Cave Dweller. Short, fat, bald, wears all black."

"Where do I find this Igor?"

"Try the bingo parlor tonight. He's the pull-tab guy."

"Another thing," Tom said.

"Come on, dude, I've told you everything I know."

"You know about Esther's money?"

"She had money?"

"Her condo was paid for."

Buddy barked a laugh. "Knew it."

"Knew what?"

"She must've had a sugar daddy. Why else didn't she want to be seen with me?"

⚹⚹⚹

Turner International
Historic Alaska Railroad Depot

While Tom was visiting Buddy, Maeve went back for a second round of questioning with Andrew Turner.

"Please." Andrew Turner sat down behind his desk and gestured to the guest chairs. "To what do I owe the pleasure?"

"We're following up on Esther's death," Maeve said as she sat.

"Aren't the police doing that?"

"They don't seem to have any leads."

"I don't know how I can help you."

"We've learned that Esther recently came into quite a bit of cash. We wondered if you knew anything about it."

Turner's face slackened. "No, no. I had no idea."

"Could she have received some sort of bonus?"

"We had no reason to do that and frankly I'd be surprised if Xander could afford it." Turner tapped steepled fingers against his mouth. "As far as I know, Neqa barely has enough money to meet administrative expenses."

Maeve waited without speaking. She looked out the window for something to watch. The ice fog was gone. The sky was crystalline, and the ground so white it burned her eyes.

Turner's hands fluttered to the desktop. "What have you found out so far?"

"She seemed to have quite a bit of disposable income. Her condo was paid for. And we have reason to believe that she was seeing someone."

Turner leaned forward. "How do you know that?"

"She was overheard speaking to him on the phone."

Turner spun his chair to view the port behind him as a cargo ship slowly headed towards the Pacific Ocean. Ravens wheeled over the shoreline.

He spun back again. "Tell you what. We seem to have a bit of a problem here."

Maeve lifted an eyebrow, inviting Turner to say more, to tell her about the missing financial records.

"I don't know if Xander told you, but Esther's files have disappeared. She was working on our annual reports. Without the reports, the feds won't give us any more money, and we won't be able to finish the project. The whole thing will collapse. Frankly, I can't survive much longer if the money isn't there. That's why I had the I.T. guy here. He was trying to reconstruct her records."

"Uh-huh." Maeve said. Would he admit to searching Suite 1401?

"So much is electronic these days," Turner continued. "I don't know that we have enough documented on paper to recreate them. Much less the expertise. Esther was the only one who understood what was going on with the accounts. Maybe she had a backup."

"I looked at her laptop. Got the blue screen of death."

"You looked at the data?"

"I tried but can't get anything to open."

Turner slammed a fist on the desktop. "But there's confidential material on there. I told you that. You have no right to pry through my business."

Maeve flinched when Turner struck the desk. She hadn't suspected he was violent. Next time she came, she'd bring Tom.

Turner waved in the air, as if to wipe away his outburst. "No harm, no foul. It's just that Turner International's Alaska operation was dependent on the federal funding of this project. I invested a lot in opening the Anchorage office. We're newcomers to the area and, I'm sure you know, the locals are reluctant to hire someone they don't know."

That was one way to put it. Alaskans don't trust Outsiders, who are seen as carpetbaggers draining money from the Alaskan economy. Turner had little chance of competing with the local engineering firms. His competitors would do all they could to freeze him out and send yet another Cheechako packing.

Turner leaned toward Maeve. "I'd be happy to pay for the investigation. Esther's family couldn't possibly afford you."

Money was always nice. Money would especially be nice for Maeve given that she was facing an involuntary vacation. But, the bar hadn't suspended her yet and she was still free to earn fees. It was Arthur who suggested that she shouldn't take any new cases.

"I'd insist on regular updates," Turner said.

If he was paying the bill, he was the boss. She watched Turner rock back in his chair with the air of the self-satisfied.

Over the port, one raven caught a thermal and rose higher, then higher, wings spread wide, climbing effortlessly, delicately adjusting his feathers. The bird settled onto an invisible wave of air, dropped a few feet and beat his wings lazily as he drifted away.

When this case began, Maeve had promised Evan she'd find his mother. Implicit in that promise was bringing her back alive. She failed. Nothing would repair the trajectory of Evan's life now that he was motherless. At the very least, though, Maeve could find Esther's killer and bring him to justice. Turner's agenda would drain her time and attention.

The door swung open. Turner looked up and put on a wide smile. "Darling!"

In the doorway, striking a pose, was a tall, dyed-blonde thirty-something, her shoulder-length hair expensively cut to maximize volume. False eyelashes, virtually unseen in Alaska, rimmed heavily colored eyelids. She wore so much makeup Maeve could smell her cosmetics from across the room.

Not a local girl.

"Sweetheart!" she responded, sweeping into the room. She slid her fur coat onto the antique map chest, revealing a jewel blue sleeveless sheath so tight she had to be wearing a full-length girdle. She planted a peck on Turner's lifted cheek.

Turner stood. "Darling, this is Maeve Malloy. She's looking into Esther's death for us."

"Oh?" Darling said. She affected a frown. "Poor girl, very sad."

"Ms. Malloy, may I present my wife, Stephie."

Maeve waved from her chair. "Hi, Stephie."

Stephie's gaze slid over to Maeve and hovered. The room cooled around them.

Maeve stood. "I won't take up any more of your time, Mr. Turner."

"Andrew," Turner said.

"Andrew," Maeve repeated. "I'm afraid I'm declining your offer. I already have a client."

Turner's head reared. "Who?"

"Evan Fancyboy."

"Surely the boy can't afford your fees." Turner smiled.

"Sometimes, Mr. Turner, it's not about the money."

¥¥¥

Neqa Inc.

"I don't think you appreciate the seriousness of this situation," Turner said as he slammed the conference table, making the three crystal highballs glasses in front of him clink into each other.

Xander hardly blinked. The doctors must be giving him some really good meds, Turner thought. He looked like a zombie. Edelson, on the other hand, looked bored. He wasn't on meds but he didn't care what was happening, he got paid by the hour.

"The files are gone." Turner felt his entire body tighten.

His neck ached from the tension. "That lawyer woman has the computer. She says it's trashed, but do we really know that? For all we know, she's already downloaded everything and handed it over to the feds."

"The feds? You're paranoid, Turner," Edelson said. "Get a grip."

Turner stood, knocking his chair into the wall. "Paranoid? Me paranoid? You aren't paranoid enough! I'm behind in my rent. I can't pay my secretary. My car payment is late. I have to park it in alleys so the dealer won't find it and tow it away. I need that money."

"Exactly. You're letting your financial situation cloud your judgment. If you don't get a grip on yourself, you're going to do something stupid." Edelson reached for the bourbon decanter between them and topped off Turner's high ball. "Here, have another drink."

Turner looked at the glass as if it was poison. Maybe it was. He watched Edelson take a sip. Well, if it was poisoned, Turner was already screwed. He'd downed two drinks since he got here. If he was lucky, he'd die before shit hit the fan.

Turner reached for the glass, took a generous mouthful, and hissed as the whiskey burned its way down his throat. He strolled around the room, calculating. Even if the computer *was* trashed, all the data had to be on Esther's thumb drive. But where?

"Okay, okay," Turner said as the booze warmed his veins. "But what about the thumb drive? She kept it in her purse."

"You're worried the cops found the purse when they found her body?"

"Yes," Turner hissed. "Don't you see? We don't know what she was backing up. Xander and I could go to jail."

When Xander heard his name, his head pivoted slowly. Turner couldn't tell if anything was registering.

"I'm not so sure about that," Edelson said. "My client has done nothing wrong."

"Really?" Turner said. "Maybe you don't understand federal bribery law."

"And you do?"

"Been there, done that, Bobby my boy," Turner said. In big business, it was customary for a grateful contractor to slip the project owner some cash. Everyone did it. A plain envelope thick with a few hundred dollar bills. "Appreciate the work, pal," was the by-line.

Turner dropped into his chair, suddenly exhausted. Back in Beantown, he found out not everyone saw it his way. The feds especially. They called those kickbacks "bribes." If the money was traced, or if someone talked, you'd be looking at five years in the pen. With real criminals. The noise in his head sounded like a tornado. Once the feds found those little accounting fictions, it wouldn't be long until they found the rest of it.

Even though he had given Xander cash, it could be traced. Any serious examiner would figure out the entries he made in the bookkeeping system were bogus. For all he knew, Xander had deposited the money in his checking account. Idiot.

With Esther's body showing up, it was only a matter of time before the cops would start asking questions. Xander was so stupid, he'd admit to taking the money, not realizing that he had incriminated himself and Turner and nailed their coffins shut. Next thing you know, it would be search warrants, indictments. Game over. Once the feds dug up the Boston thing, they wouldn't let Turner go. Not this time.

Turner inched his chair to the table. He shoved the decanter aside so he could look Edelson straight in the eye. He leaned as far across the table as he could, not wanting his voice to carry outside of the room. Ana Olrun would be lurking just outside the door, eavesdropping.

"You don't suppose Esther Fancyboy was cooperating with the F.B.I.?"

Edelson gave Turner a sharp-eyed appraisal. "Is there something you're not telling us, Turner?"

Turner scoffed and pushed his chair back. Edelson wasn't *his* lawyer. There weren't any confidentiality rules keeping

Edelson from testifying against him. The less he knew the better. Turner had already said too much. He needed a plan. He needed to find out if Esther was talking to the feds, and if she was, he needed to come up with an escape.

⚹⚹⚹

Aurora Bingo Parlor

Tom huffed out a lungful of smoke and opened the glass door patched together with duct tape. Inside, a smattering of players scattered amongst rows of folding tables were entranced by the bingo caller. An oily mist pungent with hot dogs and popcorn hung low in the room.

On the back wall was a retail stand that displayed carnival toys and pull-tabs. If anyone won at bingo, they were welcome to lose their money buying cheap toys for the kiddies they were neglecting. Or they could gamble the winnings away on pull-tabs. Neat arrangement, Tom thought. Fleece the customers coming and going.

Behind the pull-tab counter lounged a short fat kid with a shaved head. Dressed in black, he had beluga whale white skin. Thoroughly engrossed in a comic book, he didn't notice Tom's approach.

Tom rapped on the counter. The kid looked up.

"I'm looking for a guy named Igor Cave Dweller." Tom winced as he said the ridiculous name.

"Who wants to know?" The kid didn't seem embarrassed.

Tom tossed his business card on the counter. "Buddy Halcro sent me, Igor."

"'Bout what?" Igor's face closed into a mask.

"'Bout what the two of you were doing the night Esther Fancyboy disappeared."

"How am I supposed to know when Esther Fancyboy disappeared?" Igor closed his comic book and crossed his arms. "I didn't even know her."

"You're claiming you never heard of her?"

"Sure, I heard of her. She's Buddy's ex-old lady. Won't let him see his kid. That's all he talks about once he gets a few beers in him."

"It was Tuesday, January seventh, six days ago."

"On Tuesdays, we play *Magic of Merlin*. It's my night off."

"Every Tuesday?"

"Every Tuesday."

"You don't want to take a minute to think about that?"

"Every Tuesday," Igor repeated.

CHAPTER FIFTEEN

Wednesday January 16
Nelson and Associates, Attorneys at Law

A rthur frowned as he scanned the pages of transcript that Maeve had given him. Then he turned to the beginning and read it again, slowly.

Maeve stared out the window, waiting for him to finish. In Cook Inlet, slabs of ice jammed into each other and drifted with the outgoing tide. Above, layers of gray clouds hid the setting sun. An occasional pink sliver blazed over the horizon and then faded again.

Arthur gingerly laid the transcript on his desktop, as if it would explode.

Maeve had never seen him look so grave.

"Mrs. Reyes's statement raises some very serious questions."

The metallic taste of adrenalin seeped into Maeve's mouth. "Serious questions" was lawyer-speak for "someone's going to get in a whole lot of trouble." Maeve hoped that someone wasn't her.

Because Irma Reyes was represented by counsel, ethical rules forbade Arthur, who was acting as Maeve's attorney, from contacting her directly. Everything needed to go through the lawyers.

However, nothing prohibited Maeve from contacting Mrs. Reyes directly. Although Maeve was a lawyer herself, in this instance she was a party in the lawsuit, which put her on equal footing with Irma Reyes. At worst, Ryan Shaw might claim that Maeve had used undue influence or tricked her. That would be conduct unbecoming an attorney, what the bar called an "appearance of impropriety." Even if she did nothing wrong, a lawyer could get into trouble for *looking* like she was doing something bad, a giant vortex where anyone could be swallowed whole.

Maeve had nothing to lose. One more infraction didn't worry her.

"And Tom sat through the entire interview?" Arthur asked.

Maeve nodded. Sometimes witnesses waffle, say one thing and then deny the statement, come up with excuses about why they didn't mean what they said, or were tricked into saying it.

It only had to happen once for an attorney to learn. As much as she trusted and believed Irma Reyes, Maeve had recorded the statement and asked Tom to sit through the interview. If Mrs. Reyes waffled, Tom would testify to what she had said.

"I'll prepare a motion to dismiss the claim," Arthur said. "No doubt the state of Alaska will join. The judge will have no choice but to dismiss the case unless Mrs. Reyes recants her statements to you."

Hope fluttered in Maeve's stomach. "And the bar complaint?"

"That's a different matter," Arthur said.

"Royce said the only reason he filed it is because risk management made him do it, in reaction to the lawsuit," Maeve said.

Arthur lifted an eyebrow. "You contacted him too? I told you not to do that. If the bar gets wind of your behind-the-scene machinations, you could lose your license even if we defeat the negligence claim."

"And if I don't do anything, I could lose my license. You said so yourself."

"Here's the thing, Maeve. Even if we defeat the negligence

claim on the letter of the law, the bar takes a dim view of rule breakers. Bar association counsel are people who have lived by the rules all their lives. They join the association because they felt a calling to supervise the profession, like internal affairs of a police department. They will be watching you. Your colleagues will be watching you. The tiniest infraction that would have been ignored before will result in another bar complaint. You will have to keep your head low and tiptoe on a very straight, very narrow line."

For the first time since the bar complaint, someone was imagining a future for Maeve as a practicing attorney. And that someone was Arthur Nelson, a man who'd been around almost since Alaska became a state, who knew every scandal, shouted and whispered.

"Got it."

"I also warned you against taking new cases," Arthur said.

"I haven't. Tom and I were looking for a missing person for a few days. It was a favor. Her body turned up in a snow bank last weekend," Maeve said.

"I read about that in the paper. A young lady?"

"Esther Fancyboy. I worked with her mother in Bethel years ago. Esther was the chief financial officer for a joint venture between Neqa and Turner International. They're designing and building water treatment and delivery systems for the villages."

"Neqa? That would be Xander George. He's a dogged advocate for his people."

"The people at Neqa and Turner are frantic. She was working on a section eight contract," Maeve said. "The project is collapsing because her files were lost."

Arthur took a moment to process, then said, "Does her death have something to do with the missing files?"

"No reason to..." A knock on the door interrupted Maeve.

The door opened a few inches. A young woman peeked through the opening. "Mr. Nelson, these motions need to be filed this afternoon. Do you have a moment?"

Arthur motioned her in.

The secretary slipped through the door without opening it further, glided across the room, and slipped papers before Arthur. He signed his name on several pages and handed them back to her. As she crossed the room again, her footfalls squished on the carpet. She closed the door so softly that Maeve could barely hear it click into place.

"You were explaining about missing documents," Arthur said.

Maeve recollected her thoughts. "Oh, yeah. Tom's been looking into the ex-boyfriend. And Andrew Turner tried to hire us to look for a thumb drive."

"You turned him down?"

"Sure, we're already reporting to Cora and Evan. It's pro bono but if Turner paid us, he'd run the show and could distract us from finding out who killed Esther."

"The last thing you need is an accusation of conflict of interest. But why is it your business to find the killer?"

"The police don't seem to be doing anything. They chalked her up to another villager in the big city, partying with the wrong people. That isn't right. Esther was a hard-working young mother. Her family needs to know what happened to her."

"Poking your nose into a murder investigation could be dangerous to you personally. Is there any way I can talk you out of this?"

"Cora is my friend," Maeve said. "Would you turn your back on your friend in need?"

Arthur smiled. He didn't have a come back. She knew how much pro bono work he did quietly because he believed that the purpose of life was to serve his fellow man.

"I thought not," Maeve said. "So, what do you know about these section eight contracts?"

Arthur looked into space, collecting his thoughts. "Section eight of the Small Business Act has been around a long time, even before Alaska was a state. It was originally passed to give tribes in the Lower Forty-Eight a one-time opportunity to receive a no-bid federal contract to help boost reservation economies. In the 1980s, the legislation was amended to permit Alaska Native corporations to participate. The amended legislation eliminated the one-time only feature."

"Apparently, there are some reporting mandates," Maeve said. "Without Esther's data, Neqa can't receive the additional funds for the next phase of the project. Xander George and Andrew Turner are in a panic. Xander even has some Seattle attorney up here."

"That's not surprising. There have been serious problems with the contractors taking advantage of the Natives. Several Native corporations were stolen blind. They're easily duped because of their lack of business acumen. I'm not surprised Xander keeps his attorney close."

"You think Esther's job was to watch Turner?"

"Perhaps. You might want to ask Xander." Arthur tapped on his desk absentmindedly. "You know he's received quite a bit of criticism from his fellow shareholders about his standard of living. They don't see the tireless work he does for them in the halls of power, they only see him in the context of their own lives. The quality of life in the villages hasn't improved. So when they come to town, visit Neqa corporate headquarters, see how much money is being spent, how well Xander is dressed, the nice car he drives, they're concerned. I've heard talk of the shareholders replacing him at the next annual meeting."

"Is he suspected of stealing money from the corporation?"

"I'm unaware of any proof." Arthur stood, signaling an end to the meeting. "But there's talk."

※※※

Law Office of Maeve Malloy

Tom was sitting at Maeve's desk, hanging up the phone just as she walked in. "That was Cora Fancyboy. She wanted to know what was going on with the case."

"What's that in the fax machine?" Maeve pointed to the page resting in the in-coming tray.

Tom swung around, plucked the paper out of the drawer, glanced at it, and handed it to Maeve.

Maeve read the fax. "We have a hearing Friday morning. And the judge continued the emergency custody order." Maeve pulled off her knit hat and coat, tossed them into the visitor's chair, and reached for the phone.

"Where you been?" Tom asked.

Cora's phone kept ringing. "Arthur's office. Say, you think Xander is embezzling Neqa?" Maeve asked.

Cora picked up. "Who says that?"

"Sorry, Cora, I was talking with Tom. I was just calling to let you know we have a hearing Friday morning first thing. And the judge continued the custody order."

"Should Evan come too? He wants to talk to the judge."

"Judges don't like that. It's traumatic for the kids. He's too young to have a preference, legally. But I'd like to have Margaret there. She's a good witness."

Cora was silent.

"I'll meet you at the office half hour before court and we'll walk over together, okay?"

A moment hung in the air before Cora said "okay" and hung up.

"That's what business is about, right?" Tom asked, stashing a pen behind his ear news reporter-style as he swung his legs up on her desk.

She batted his feet down. "What business?"

"Someone puts themselves higher up in the food chain and the good stuff sticks to their hands." Tom began to push himself up.

"No, you stay there," she said as she flopped into the visitor's chair. She looked around the office, a little disoriented from the different point-of-view. A little intrigued.

"Do you suppose that's why everyone is so interested in the laptop?" Maeve asked.

"Could be. Could also be just what they say, missing reports needed for funding."

Maeve's window faced the D.A.'s office which blotted out most of the view except for the darkening night sky. The temperature would drop below zero tonight with the sun's disappearance. If she was suspended, she'd huddle in her condo with the temperature set as low as she could stand it to save money.

Or maybe get a job washing dishes somewhere. That'd be nice. Pleasant, even. Pick up a dirty dish, wash, rinse. Clean dish. Quick gratification. No one complaining about their rights. It was a variation of the flower shop fantasy spun by young female lawyers frustrated with the business. Wouldn't it be lovely to sit in a shop all day surrounded with flowers, moist warm air heavy with their perfume, color abounding?

But Maeve once had a florist client who told her what the business was really like, grumbling never-satisfied customers, high overhead. They made washing filthy dishes sound good.

"Earth to Maeve," Tom said.

"What? I miss something?"

"You're far away."

"Arthur went over the bar complaint and Shaw's civil case, hashing out what might happen. I gave him the transcript of the Irma Reyes interview. He's going to file a motion to dismiss the lawsuit."

"Then what?"

"The civil case goes away."

"And the bar thing?"

"That's going to hearing." Maeve felt emotion surfacing, something dark and ugly. In the rehab group counseling room, there was a "name your emotion" poster that had perplexed her. As far as she knew, the only emotions she had were happy and mad. This emotion roiling in her chest and into her head was neither. She covered her face with both hands, took a deep breath, and then dropped them in her lap.

Tom changed the subject. "Interviewed Halcro. Says he saw Esther downtown on Fourth Avenue around Christmas, talked to her in his car. She told him to pound sand. Claims he never saw her again after that. And when she disappeared from Starring, he was with some friend all night."

"Did he look credible?"

"Not even. Career criminal. They lie so much they don't know how to tell the truth. But he's got an alibi that checks out. Guy named Igor. Halcro thinks Esther had a sugar daddy. He saw a big black SUV in the alley."

"Which is exactly what the others said. Margaret saw Esther talking to someone in an SUV at Starring. Your sources saw her getting in the SUV behind the bar. Evan said she had a boyfriend. And, there's what the medical examiner said."

"She had sex sometime that afternoon. In her office, on her lunch break maybe, or on her way home. But we can't tie down whether she got into the SUV that night or on some other night. Time has no meaning to my sources."

"You think she may have been meeting a man behind the bar on a regular basis?"

"Sneaking around, meeting her boyfriend for a quickie. It's been known to happen. We need to look for that late model black SUV." Tom stood. "Enough of this chit-chat, Counselor. On your feet."

※※※

The silver blade jabbed at Maeve.

She crashed her arm across the extended forearm so hard that the plastic knife flew across the room. Her heart pounded in her ears. Her breath was shallow and fast. Maeve shoved the mop of sweaty auburn hair out of her face. "Sorry, did I hurt you?"

"Forget about it," Tom said. "Take a deep breath before you pass out."

Maeve was still hyped-up from her talk with Arthur. "I can't seem to control myself today." The knife was just a replica, she told herself, willing her heart to slow down. Just a toy to help practice self-defense moves. And, boy, had she moved.

"It's the adrenalin," Tom said. "From that bar complaint, the lawsuit. That's okay. You need to get used to adrenalin dumping on you when you're in a confrontation. It'll make you faster and more powerful. But, it'll also give you tunnel vision and make time slow down. Messes with your brain. You got to have muscle memory. You got to practice these moves over and over until your body can do them without being told."

"Do we really have to do this today? I'd rather be working on Esther's case."

"I can't be around to protect you twenty-four seven, Counselor. That Coffer thing last year was not a fluke. People like you attract jerks."

Eli Coffer was a vigilante Maeve had run across in the Olafson case. He believed in natural justice, not courtroom justice. And Maeve had gotten in his way. One night while she had been walking from her office to her car after working late, he had tried to kidnap her. As it happened, Tom had given her rudimentary self-defense lessons and she'd gotten away. It could have been worse. Much worse.

In the months since then, Tom had insisted on weekly martial arts lessons. Every lesson felt like an electrocution, Maeve being zapped with a new awareness. As soon as Tom noticed that she was comfortable with the lesson, he added another element of danger.

"People like me?"

"People who speak their minds. It's not a bad thing."

With swan-like grace, Tom plucked the knife from the floor and faced her. "Next time follow up with an elbow to the face. The down block will jerk his head toward you and you'll be lined up for it. After you hit him in the face, he'll stagger back.

Reach down and grab his foot and push it straight into the air."

"Really?" Maeve asked. Tom had six inches and sixty pounds of muscle on her. No way could she take him down.

"It's not about matching your opponent's strength." He balanced his weight evenly over his feet, rooted to the earth. "You'll never win a wrestling match with the bad guy. He's pumped. He's taken you by surprise and he's stronger than you'll ever be. It's about being smarter than him. You study, you learn body mechanics, you practice the technique, you develop muscle memory."

An image popped into Maeve's mind, the disappointment she had seen on Arthur's face earlier.

"Focus!"

"Arm, face, foot, got it."

They squared off again. She wiped moisture from her hands onto her pants. *Arm, face, foot.* He pointed the knife at her and lunged. She stepped in and crashed down. An electric buzz shot through her own arm. *Face.* His head popped forward. She snapped her elbow at his nose. He avoided the strike with a small step backwards. *Foot.* She grabbed his ankle, pushed it up over her head. The floor whomped when he crashed to the ground and a dust cloud floated up from the carpet. He rolled over backwards and sprung to his feet.

He tossed the knife at her. "Your turn."

CHAPTER SIXTEEN

Smith & Jones Restaurant and Bar

"**H**e's here." Tom nodded in the direction of the door, interrupting Maeve's reverie. As they sat at a window-side table overlooking Cook Inlet, she had been watching chunks of ice drift towards the ocean, their jagged surfaces pink and lavender like the low-hanging clouds floating overhead.

Maeve broke away from the scene and searched the room.

Andrew Turner snaked through young adults crowded around tables, perched on bar stools and standing in small groups, his dark blue wool coat glistening with melting snow. He draped the coat across one chair and slid gracefully into the empty seat at their table, then raised a hand to attract a passing waitress's attention. "Gin and tonic?"

The waitress nodded without breaking step.

Turner spun toward Maeve and Tom. "Thanks for meeting me. Helluva day, really. What are you having? Can I buy you a drink?"

"Thanks, but we've ordered already," Maeve said.

The waitress returned with Turner's cocktail, coffee for Tom, and sparkling water with a twist for Maeve.

Maeve rearranged the down parka she'd inverted across the seat back, moving the fiberfill clump that jabbed her in the back.

"Put it on my tab, would you dear?" Turner creased a hundred-dollar bill down the middle and dropped it on the waitress' tray. She examined the bill as it lay there. Her eyes slid up to his. He eased into his flashy smile. She struck a model's pose, hips thrust forward, and smiled warmly at him before she slithered off to the next table.

"Pretty girl." Turner winked at Tom.

Tom grunted. He hadn't flirted with the waitress when they'd placed their orders. In fact, he usually acted as if Maeve was the only woman in the room. Except that time when he met Jerri, the receptionist. Straight-haired blondes, lots of make-up, was that his type? Maeve combed her fingers through her curls and got caught in a tangle.

Or maybe bimbo is his type. Not that it mattered.

"You wanted to meet with us?" Maeve asked.

"Yes, thanks for making the time." Turner sampled his drink and took a moment to savor it.

A phantom gasoline-like flavor hit Maeve's tongue. Even in her drinking days, she hadn't cared for gin. Sure, she'd drink it if it was in front of her, holding her breath and grimacing with every swallow. It was an efficient way to get drunk. What alcoholic drinks for flavor anyway?

Maeve fished the twist of lime out of her glass and crushed it. She took a sip, pausing while her nose filled with citrusy mist. It's all about choices. Maeve set her glass down. "Is there something we need to know?"

"How's the investigation coming?" Turner cocked an elbow on the seatback and nursed his cocktail.

"We don't know much more than we did when we last met." Maeve stirred her glass with a red plastic swizzle stick. She used to save these. Whatever happened to the collection? "But we heard a rumor. Shareholder unrest over Xander's standard of living."

Turner's highball glass froze in mid-air. He looked at Tom and then back at Maeve. Slowly Turner's highball floated down to the table. He placed it precisely in the middle of a soaked cocktail napkin and smoothed the edges with his free hand. "The dirty dog."

"Sorry?"

Turner's face clenched as he kept staring at the table. "I never thought…" His head bobbed in small oscillation. Turner scooted towards them and cleared his throat. "Here's the thing. I don't want this going public, you understand. It's a delicate situation."

Maeve waited and Tom fidgeted. Maeve's to-do list was only getting longer while Turner milked this moment for drama. She needed to interview the witnesses again, look at the evidence more closely for a hint of who was driving that SUV, and, oh yeah, figure out the rest of her life if she got disbarred.

"It seems there's some money missing."

"Missing from where?"

"From the joint venture accounts." Turner pushed the condiments between them aside and scooted even closer. "I was hoping it was some accounting error but Stephie's been over the books several times. They just don't add up. That's why we were looking for Esther's back-up files. Maybe they'd explain the discrepancy."

"How much is missing?"

"Several hundred thousand dollars. Enough that the project is insolvent. And if the feds got wind of this, I don't have to tell you…." Turner held both hands up in a surrender gesture.

"Who has access to these accounts?"

"Esther, of course. Myself." Turner took in a deep breath. "And Xander George."

※※※

Turner eased away from the red light in his silver Mercedes sedan, year-round tires gripping the snow like claws. He waved at that Malloy woman and her sidekick as he passed them standing in front of the restaurant, deep in conversation. They nodded.

That had gone well.

When he called them for the meet, it was to tell them about the missing funds. No one cares about missing files, it's only data, but lost treasure motivates people.

The problem is the files showed where the money had gone. And Turner needed to fix that. That's why he needed Maeve Malloy working on it.

Screw it. He should just pull up stakes now, grab Stephie, and get the hell out of this frozen wasteland. Go somewhere warm. Somewhere that didn't extradite. Start over.

The longer he stayed in Alaska, the more likely he'd get caught.

But there was money to be made here. You didn't even have to make it. They just throw it at you. Money pouring down from the federal government like manna from heaven. All you had to do was open your pockets and let the loot fall in.

If he could get the data, he could file the reports and get more money. And he could fix the books to cover up where the old money went. And then he could tell Maeve Malloy that it turned out just to be an accounting error. Sorry, Xander and Esther didn't rip off the corporation, just someone put some number in the wrong column. A big misunderstanding. No problem.

And if it all goes to hell, if the feds find out, it will look like Esther and Xander were the thieves.

Turner had thought about telling Malloy about the kickback he'd given Xander. If she thought Xander was demanding bribes, she'd start looking at him. She's a lawyer. People believe her. Then everyone else would start looking at Xander too. It would buy Turner more time.

The problem was, paying bribes is technically a crime, even if it was common business practice. Malloy wasn't his attorney. She could testify against him about anything he said. If the F.B.I. misconstrued the situation, he'd be screwed. After all, Turner was the victim here. He had to give Xander money to get the contract, the survival of his business depended on it.

But that's not how they saw it back in Boston.

Nothing he could do about it at this moment. Everything had been set into motion. Turner just needed to sit back, relax, and watch it all play out.

He checked his watch. Not even dinnertime. The evening was still young. He could sneak an extra hour and tell Stephie that he spent more time with the Malloy woman and her sidekick than he had anticipated. Bring home a bottle of wine, turn on the charm.

Come to think of it, he could pick up two bottles of wine. At the next light, he punched Ana's number into his cell phone. "Hey, baby, you busy?"

⚡⚡⚡

Ruth Berkowitz' home

Swathed in a purple paisley caftan, Ruth Berkowitz flowed into the living room, set a bone china teacup and saucer on the coffee table in front of Maeve, another on the side table for herself, then settled into a cream-colored silk club chair. Her bright orange bristle-cut hair swayed as she gathered the excess fabric around her body.

"So how are things?"

Maeve had to tell her. She'd do it quick, like ripping off a Band-Aid.

"Well, the state got sued for the Mataafa case. Then the state filed a bar complaint against me, trying to shift responsibility to minimize its own exposure. I know the woman who filed the suit, Irma Reyes. You were with me, in fact, when I went to make amends to her a while back. She said she had no idea that her attorney was filing suit and that she never agreed to it. I gave her statement to Arthur. He's working on a motion to dismiss the lawsuit. And once that goes away, maybe the bar thing will go away too."

"Holy crap, young lady! That's a lot on your plate!"

Maeve took a breath. One more tale to share.

"After the bar complaint came in, Tom and I took on a missing person investigation because I knew the mother of the woman who had disappeared. A few days after we started looking, she turned up dead in a snow bank."

"Oh, I'm sorry to hear that."

"She had a seven-year-old son, Evan," Maeve said. "I first met his grandmother, Cora, when I was working in Bethel and she brought him into the office when he was a baby. He's living in Anchorage now with Cora. Tom and I are trying to find out what happened."

"Isn't that a police matter?"

"The police didn't seem very motivated to help find her when it was just a missing person. Maybe they could have found her before she was killed. Maybe I could have found her in time, too, but I got on the case so late, who knows."

"You think you could have saved her so you're blaming yourself for her death."

Maeve froze, then caught herself, and reached for her tea. "It's not all about you" was one of Ruth's favorite themes. When Maeve first met with Ruth one afternoon last fall, the meeting had been much like this. Tea, canapés, and the problem with Maeve. It lasted well into the evening, and Ruth must have said "it's not all about you" twenty times. In the months since, Ruth had varied the language of the theme, but it always came back to the same refrain.

"Well, it doesn't look like they're doing anything to the family or to me. Given the police attitude when she disappeared, I somehow doubt they're suddenly motivated. It's Olafson all over again."

In the Olaf Olafson case, the police had rushed to judgment, wrongly charging Maeve's client with murder when a serial killer had been quietly and deftly exterminating the homeless population like they were vermin. Not until Maeve and Tom had dug in and discovered who the real culprit was did justice play out.

"The apathy of the authorities enabled that serial murderer for a long time," Maeve said. "Remember?"

"Like I'd forget? You kicked ass." Ruth motioned with the teapot. "Need your cup warmed up?"

"Please," Maeve said. Ruth was changing the subject. Perhaps Maeve had been a little too strident. Perhaps it was time to let go of the injustice done to homeless people, most of them Native Alaskans, by the indifference of an elite society evolved from a legion of racist carpetbaggers.

Or maybe someone needed to get angry.

It wasn't all about Maeve. This time it was all about Esther and Evan.

Ruth lowered her cup and saucer onto her lap. "How are things going with Tom?"

"We're not involved. I told you that. Besides, if I get disbarred, or even suspended, he'll have to go find work with someone else. This is probably our last case together. I won't ever see him again."

"You'll survive. What's the worst thing that could happen?"

"I could lose my license."

"And then what?"

"I wouldn't be a lawyer anymore."

"If Tom cares about you, he'll stick around."

"I don't know what you're talking about."

Ruth pressed on. "What would you be if you weren't a lawyer anymore?"

"No one."

"Of course, you'd be someone. Being a lawyer is a job. It's not who you are."

The dishwashing fantasy still sounded good, even if there was no Tom washing dishes next to her. But not quite good enough to say out loud. "I could sit it out, work as a paralegal for someone, and re-apply for admission when the suspension was over."

"Or?"

"There's nothing else I've ever wanted to do, Ruth. There aren't a lot of jobs that pay you to argue. All my life, that's all I've been good at. Fighting."

Maeve slumped into the sofa. She was silent for several

minutes. Ruth sipped her tea, watching her, waiting.

"I'd be a failure," Maeve said. She wouldn't be able to help people. There would be no reason for people to seek her out. She'd have no friends. She had no real friends now, no one who wanted to talk to her on the phone or hang out with her just to be with her. All her friends were at work. Tom, Arthur, maybe Sal. Their lives would go on without her.

Maeve's chest shuddered as she fought for air. Oh, look there, she discovered a third emotion. Sadness.

Ruth slipped Maeve's teacup out of her hands. "Let's get to work, shall we?"

⚘⚘⚘

Ana Olrun's condo

Turner caressed Ana's naked body from her shoulder on down, fascinated by her silky skin. She sighed and laid her head on his shoulder. Too romantic. He pinched her bottom. She squealed.

He reached for the wine glass on the nightstand and took another sip.

Her head turned toward him expectantly.

He put the glass down and checked his watch. "Sorry, baby, I got to head out."

She made a pouty face. Crap, how he hated that look.

He swatted her bottom. Her grimace was fleeting. She was trained to play along.

"No arguments. You know my situation. I never kept secrets from you. I've never lied to you. You know that."

Ana sat up, clutching the sheet over her small breasts.

Turner pushed out of the bed and looked for his socks. "There is something you can do for me, baby."

"What's that?" the tone in Ana's voice was apprehensive.

Turner reached for her neck, wrapped one hand around it and dragged her to him. He had her squatting on her knees. He thrust his tongue into her mouth, lolling it around until he could feel her muscles beneath his hand soften.

He let her go. She had that dreamy look in her eye. He turned to put his socks on. "That lawyer, Maeve Malloy. See if you can find out what she knows. Would you do that for me, baby?"

Ana didn't answer. He looked over his shoulder, saw she still had that dreamy look. He ran a thumb down her cheek but she didn't respond. He cocked his hand back for another slap.

Her eyes widened, pupils narrowed.

"For me, baby? Get that Malloy woman to tell you what she knows. Everything. About Xander, Neqa, Esther, me."

"When will I see you again?"

"Tomorrow night. Late. I expect a full report." Then he pinched her cheek.

CHAPTER SEVENTEEN

Thursday, January 17
Neqa Inc Parking Lot

M aeve peeled the lid off a paper cup. A mocha didn't taste like a mocha when it was covered. As she held the cup close to her face, steam warmed her nose. She sipped. Chocolate, warmth, and well-being glided down her throat.

Last night after Maeve had left Ruth's, she lay on her bed staring at the ceiling, listening to shrouded silence. Street sounds were dampened by heavy drifts of snow. The noisy ducks and geese that lived on the lake in the summer were long gone. There was no lovely loon call in a winter morning. Was this silence the peace and serenity she'd heard about in AA meetings? Or just big, empty, silent darkness.

Maeve took a slug of mocha. She was parked get-away style in the third row of a parking lot facing Neqa's designated slots listening to mournful Irish songs of love and war. If her vigil was a long one, she might regret the caffeine, need to find a ladies' room, and miss Xander's arrival. Or, worse yet, get caught coming out of the building with no reason to be there. But if she waited, the mocha would cool off.

Another slug.

Leaving Simon's yesterday, Maeve had seen Turner drive away in a silver Mercedes Benz sedan. That ruled him out as the mystery man Esther was meeting. Buddy Halcro's beat-up rig could in no way be mistaken for a big, shiny SUV. So Maeve had decided to stake out Xander George's parking spot, see what kind of car he drove.

There were just enough clues to be confusing. Missing files, missing money. Andrew Turner's hint the money had been taken by Xander George with Esther's help. Esther's unexplained money. But Xander had an alibi the night Esther disappeared.

Maeve had been waiting for seven minutes. It would have been more efficient to call Ana and find out when Xander came to work. That's probably what Tom would have done.

She hadn't heard from Tom yet that morning. When he disappeared like this, it usually meant a new girlfriend. The clues were easy enough to spot. A sudden increase in cell phone calls. A check of the caller I.D., call rejected, the phone stashed away without comment. Less time hanging around the office. Awkward responses when she called him at home.

It was none of her business.

Ruth was right. It wasn't all about Maeve.

A small Japanese sedan parked in front of her. Ana Olrun climbed out, swinging her long, dark hair away from her face as she straightened up. Maeve hadn't noticed before how much Ana looked like Esther, which was only logical since they came from the same remote area with a fairly isolated gene pool.

Maeve changed the C.D. to uplifting Irish fiddle tunes, mostly songs about drinking. This was her rich cultural heritage: lost love, lost wars, and booze. Maeve Artemis Malloy, a martyr to her people.

She chugged the mocha.

She had just tossed the empty paper cup in her back seat when a big shiny black SUV slotted into a Neqa parking slot.

※

Tom aimed a stream of cigarette smoke out the crack above the driver's side window and started the engine. He was parked in the fifth row.

Maeve had parked two rows in front of him without noticing his beige truck. That was the point, not being noticed. Still, you'd think she'd recognize it. She'd ridden in it at least a hundred times. And you'd think she'd be more aware of her surroundings. A babe in the woods.

What if Maeve got suspended from practice? Tom always landed on his feet, no problem. But how would she survive? She doesn't have any skills besides lawyering. Chances are Arthur would find something for her in his office, if she wasn't too proud to take his offer. Or she could get a job in a box store. A daycare. A fast food joint. But not even a burger joint will hire someone who is waiting around to get readmitted to the bar. Come to think of it, burger joints probably wouldn't want a lawyer working the window, afraid she might organize the workers. And, she probably would.

A black SUV cruised into the parking lot and slipped into a space just in front of Maeve. Xander George got out.

Tom snapped a photo.

⚘⚘⚘

Law Office of Maeve Malloy

When Maeve rounded into the corridor from the stairwell, Margaret Alexi was standing in front of her office door.

Surprise visits were never good.

"Is everything okay?" Maeve asked. "Buddy show up again?"

"Evan's school says it needs something saying Cora is his guardian. They don't think that custody order is good enough. It doesn't say Buddy can't have him. If they don't get guardianship papers, Buddy Poor Boy can still take him."

Maeve trudged through what little she remembered of probate law. Guardians, conservators, personal representatives, trusts. Esther was a single mother with a minor son. She owned a condo and a car. Alaska's permanent fund dividend check would come to her at the end of the year. The probate court could order a guardianship of Evan once the estate case was opened. Buddy would be the court's first pick for guardian unless...

"Did Esther leave a will?"

"Who thinks they're going to die at twenty-seven years old?" Margaret held up a large, stuffed manila envelope. "But I found this and thought you might need it."

After they settled in the office, Maeve at her desk, Margaret at the visitor's chair, Maeve examined the envelope marked *Important Papers* in a curly, round, juvenile hand. Inside was the title to Esther's home, the title to her car, Evan's birth certificate and a legal document several pages thick entitled *Settlement Agreement*. The parties to the settlement were Esther Fancyboy and Neqa Inc.

"What's this about?" Maeve held up the document.

"I've never seen it," Margaret said.

Maeve read. Neqa paid Esther two hundred and fifty thousand dollars in satisfaction of any claims she had or might have had arising from her employment. But there was no language specifying what the claims were.

"Did Esther say anything about suing Neqa? Or threatening to sue them?"

Margaret shook her head.

The settlement agreement was signed by Esther, Xander George, and Robert Edelson as Neqa's attorney, dated in June of last summer, about a month before Esther bought the condo and new car.

"Why'd they give her all that money?" Maeve asked.

"It had something to do with Xander," Margaret said. "Someone saw them together."

"Saw them, where? Doing what?"

"At their office. You know. What men and women do."

"They were a couple? But he was her boss. I thought he was married."

"She loved him. She thought he was going to leave his wife. But when they got caught, the Neqa Board said they couldn't work in the same office anymore. They gave her some money and sent her to Turner's office. That's all I know."

✯✯✯

After Margaret left, Maeve typed up a court order appointing Cora as Evan's legal guardian and sole custodian. She'd ask the judge to sign it at the hearing on Friday. It was almost lunchtime when Tom came into the office, the smell of baking bread from the Ten-Eighty below had turned into the smell of baking pizza.

"What's this?" he said when he noticed the envelope marked *Important Papers*.

"Take a look."

Tom threw his canvas coat and heavy gloves on the couch, took the visitor's chair, and opened the envelope. After he read the settlement agreement, he gave a long, low whistle. "Sure sounds like motive to me. If the Board caught Xander fooling around with Esther again, they'd fire him."

"You think he's the secret boyfriend?"

"He's got a black SUV." Tom leaned over to the couch, pulled a stack of photos from his coat pocket, and dropped it on her desk. "But you already knew that."

"How'd you find out?"

"I saw you."

Maeve picked up the stack. On top was a photo of Xander George next to his SUV. In the foreground was Maeve's Subaru. "I'm sorry. I didn't mean to do your job. I was just driving by there and thought I'd hang out for a while, see what turned up."

Maeve felt a stab in her right eye. Pressing her eyeball made the pain settle.

"Don't rub."

"It hurts."

"Go see an eye doctor."

A wave of nausea swept through her. "It's just a migraine, it'll pass."

"What's this?" Tom nudged an envelope toward her. It had

come in the morning mail while Maeve was typing. She needed to get the order filed as soon as possible before Buddy snatched Evan and before the bar jerked her license at which time there would be nothing she could do. So she'd ignored the morning mail.

"Something from the bar association."

"Maybe you should read it."

"I was about to, thank you." Maeve picked up the envelope. When she opened her eye, it felt like an ice pick was being driven through it. Nausea swelled again.

Maeve ripped the envelope apart. Covering her eye again, she read the letter. "It's a hearing date in front of the board of governors. January twenty-first."

"Five days. Not much time. You get the transcript of the Reyes interview?"

Maeve gave a small nod, trying not to aggravate the pain. "Arthur has it. He's drafting a motion to dismiss the lawsuit."

"Motions, cross motions, hearings, continuances, you don't have that kind of time, Counselor. Does Arthur know about the hearing date?"

"He should have gotten a copy of this notice too."

"You tell him about Royce? How he was representing Jones when Jones was a snitch? How he dumped the Mataafa case on you when he knew Jones was lying about the alibi?"

"I'm holding that back for now," Maeve said. "Think about it. We have Shaw dead to rights for filing a lawsuit without the party's permission. That's bad. But what's Arthur going to say about the Jones thing? Royce was just doing his job. And Bennett was just doing his job, too. They might be stepping on toes, but that's what happens in a small community."

"It's your toes that got stepped on. So he's going to say what you did was unethical, but Royce and Bennett setting you up is okay?"

"No, of course not. He's going to say that they didn't violate any rules, technically, and that complaining about what they did is not a good defense for my actions. So until I get a better idea for how we can use this information to its maximum advantage, I'm keeping it just between us."

"You're the captain of the ship. What about the bar association hearing?"

Maeve put the letter aside. "I need to get this order filed before I do anything else. Buddy could take Evan any minute and there'd be nothing we could do about it without a court order."

The pain in Maeve's eye infested her brain. She covered her face with both hands.

Tom stood, went to the wall switch, and turned off the lights. Then he came around Maeve's chair and gently laid his huge warm hands on her shoulders. He ran his thumbs up her tight neck lightly and then slowly added pressure until the muscles relaxed. The headache settled into something more bearable as he massaged.

Several minutes later, he bent next to her ear and spoke in a low tone. "Want me to drive you home?"

She shook her head.

He lifted the probate documents from Maeve's desk. "I'll get these filed. You wait for traffic to burn off. Home, dark room, forget about all this for a while."

No problem.

#⁣#⁣#

Maeve drove across town, wincing when headlights of oncoming cars stabbed her eyes. After Tom left, she had vomited in the trash can. Then she locked the office door, crawled under her desk, and cried. Her plans were evaporating before her eyes. Practicing law the way she wanted. Fighting for justice. Helping people who needed it, not just those who could afford it.

By the time she had calmed down, night had fallen. She crawled out from under the desk, shrugged on her coat, gloves, scarf, and hat, grabbed her briefcase and the now-stinking garbage bag, and locked the office door behind her.

Her cell phone chirped from the depths of her briefcase. Maeve put down the garbage bag and dug around for her phone.

"I need to talk," a woman said in a soft village accent.

Maeve's body shuddered when she inhaled, spent from crying. The voice sounded familiar but she couldn't place it. "How can I help you?"

"I'm still at work. He might hear me," the voice whispered.

"Ana?"

"Can you come to my condo in an hour?"

Maeve's head seared with pain. She touched an eyelid. It was hot and spongy. She must look hideous. If someone saw her, they'd know she'd been crying. She didn't want to fend off curiosity, and she certainly didn't want to tell the next stranger she met how her life was falling apart. "Can we make it ninety minutes?"

Ana agreed and gave Maeve directions.

Sixty minutes later, Maeve was on the road, showered and teeth brushed. The cool washcloth reduced the swelling to her eyes. Hopefully Ana was so involved in her own crisis, she wouldn't notice how bad Maeve looked.

Good thing Ana was ready to talk, Maeve had a lot of questions. Did Ana know about the Xander-Esther thing? Was it consensual? Had Xander and Esther still been seeing each other after the settlement? If anyone knew, it would be the receptionist who answered his phones. Even if he had a private line, her console would light up when he used it. Unless he had a private cell, but then she'd notice him sneaking away to make a call.

The townhouse-style condo was easy to find. Ana's little Japanese sedan was parked in the driveway. Maeve parked in the street. A sliver of light crept from the front door, which was slightly ajar. Tendrils of warm air escaped from inside, floating across the concrete stoop like wraiths.

Maeve paused at the door. "Ana?"

A rustling sound came from a distant room.

Maeve gently pushed the door open just enough to look

around. The foyer was empty. "Ana, it's Maeve Malloy," she called again and stepped inside.

More rustling, then quiet. The sound came from down the hall. It was followed by a popping sound, like a champagne cork, but too loud, then a thud.

"Ana, are you okay?" Maeve jogged down the hall. As she burst into the room, she saw Ana splayed across the couch.

A whirl of black crossed Maeve's peripheral vision.

Arm, face, foot. Maeve raised her arm. Her elbow snapped back into empty air. She stepped hard toward the blur, landing on someone's shoe. Underneath her foot, a sound like a twig snapping.

A loud crack rang between her ears. Then darkness.

CHAPTER EIGHTEEN

"**D**on't move," a man said in a cowboy twang. "You're under arrest."

Maeve came to, her vision blurred. The pain in her head made her clench her eyes.

Did I get drunk? Wreck my car? Hurt someone?

She was face down on the carpet with a man's weight crushing her. Her hands were wrenched behind her back and cold metal snapped across her wrists. The carpet made her face itch. Hands groped through her clothing, a little too thoroughly.

"Hey, watch it!" Maeve said, her speech muffled by the carpet into which her face was smashed.

"No weapon," Cowboy said.

"Any identification?" another man asked in a New York accent.

Footsteps approached from the hallway.

"Found a purse," Cowboy said. Maeve opened one eye. All she could see was a man's polished black dress shoe. "Driver's license says Maeve Malloy. And there's an I.D. card from the Alaska Bar Association."

"What?"

"Take a look for yourself."

A moment passed. One of them exhaled forcefully.

"Let her go," New York said.

When the handcuffs were unlocked, Maeve's arms dropped to the floor. She shook her hands to get feeling back in them.

"Here, let me help you." New York squatted beside her.

A strong hand wrapped around her upper arm and lifted her to a sit.

"You got a nasty bump on that head," he said. He guided her towards the wall and propped her up against it.

Maeve realized she could see only through one eye. She touched the closed eye. It was glued shut by something sticky.

"Careful, now," the man said. Cops? Of course, cops. Who else arrests people? Unless it was bad guys pretending to be cops. In Anchorage?

New York was still squatting next to her. He wore a dark blue suit and dress coat. His almost black hair was neatly clipped.

"What's going on?" Maeve asked.

"There was a shooting."

"Looks like he got away," Cowboy said. "Back door open. Footprints in the snow. Jones went after him."

"Ana?" Maeve asked.

"You know the resident?" New York asked.

"Who are you?"

"Could you please answer the question? Who is that woman over there?" He gestured toward Ana.

"Ana Olrun."

"You're an attorney, Ms. Malloy?"

Maeve inhaled sharply when she tried to nod. The inside of her head felt like chunks of broken glass were being tossed around. Her vision blurred. The room spun. She planted both hands on the floor and dry heaved.

New York adjusted his squat. "Everett, call an ambulance."

Maeve scanned the room. Ana was sprawled across the couch, her chestnut complexion drained to a chalky grey. Blood pooled beneath her. New York looked like a male model. Not your typical Anchorage patrol cop.

"Who are you guys?" Maeve asked.

※※※

Anchorage Hospital

Maeve rested in a dark cubicle following hours of examination by nurses and doctors and more nurses, wound cleaning, stitches, x-rays, a C.T. scan, and a merciful shot of pain medication.

"You decent?" Tom whispered as he rustled a curtain.

"Depends on your definition of decent." Her whisper didn't seem to escape her mouth.

Tom slipped through the curtains, arm extended, holding a paper cup, the acrid smell of burnt coffee reaching Maeve as Tom placed it on the nightstand.

"Thank you," Maeve mouthed. Her head was too heavy to lift off the pillow.

"It's the best I could do. The nurses kept me out when I first got here, so I took a hike."

"How did you know I was here?"

"You gave them my number when you came in."

Maeve didn't remember that. She couldn't remember coming to the hospital at all. The last thing she remembered was some man saying Ana was dead.

"Ms. Malloy?" A woman with spiky hair and no make-up wearing green scrubs and a white lab coat slipped inside the curtain.

Maeve nodded her head gently.

"Dr. Billingslea. I've been treating you since you arrived. How are you feeling?"

"Like roadkill."

The doctor took a hard look at Maeve. "You look worse, but you'll live. Your tests are back. No broken bones. A neurologist looked at your C.T. scan and says there isn't much to be concerned about. Looks like a routine concussion. Just to be on the safe side, we'll keep you for a few more hours for observation.

Do you have someone at home who can keep an eye on you?"

"I'll stay with her," Tom said.

"You are?"

"A friend."

"If that's alright with Ms. Malloy, we'll let you take her home. She'll need supervision for at least a couple of days, friend. We'll give you a sheet with the warning signs. And she needs to be taken to the neurologist for a follow-up."

Dr. Billingslea lifted a chart off the bed frame and made some notes. "Meanwhile, are you feeling up to talking? There's a couple of F.B.I. agents in the waiting room."

⚘⚘⚘

"I'm Special Agent Nathanial Forbes and this is Special Agent Everett," the cop with the New York accent said as he gestured to a freckly redheaded man hanging back. "Ms. Malloy, do you feel well enough to answer a few questions?"

Maeve pushed a button and the bed moved into an up-right position. Tom moved closer, blocking Forbes's approach. Forbes looped around to the other side of the bed. Everett turned up the lights.

The sudden light shot pain through Maeve like a bolt of electricity. She threw her arm up and groaned. Forbes gestured at Everett. The lights dimmed.

Agent Forbes handed Maeve two business cards. Heavy linen paper with a blue F.B.I. seal. Raised letterhead. Impressive. As nice as the cards from the Seattle lawyer.

"We found you at Ana Olrun's condominium this evening, do you recall that?" Forbes asked.

Maeve nodded delicately.

"Why were you there?"

"She called me."

"I thought you were staying in tonight," Tom said. "Migraine. I could have gone to talk to her."

"You made her nervous. I figured I'd get more information

from her alone."

"Can we get back to my interview?" Forbes asked. "Why did Ms. Olrun want to see you?"

"She wanted to talk about something, but not while she was at work. She didn't want to be overheard."

Everett scribbled away. Forbes paused, waiting for Everett to finish writing. Or waiting for Maeve to elaborate. Until Maeve knew what was going on, she'd answer the questions put to her, no more, no less. She wanted them to go away so she could sleep. She laid her head back and closed her eyes.

"Ms. Malloy, how did you know Ms. Olrun?"

"We met when we began looking for Esther Fancyboy." Maeve spoke without opening her eyes.

"We?"

Maeve gestured towards Tom.

"And you are?" Forbes asked Tom.

"Tom Sinclair. I work with Ms. Malloy. Cora Fancyboy asked us to look for daughter."

"When was that?"

"After the daughter disappeared," Tom said.

"What did you find out?"

"Not much." Tom was no fan of giving away information, either.

"What did Ana Olrun have to do with your investigation?"

"Esther worked for a joint venture involving Neqa Village Cooperative Inc," Maeve said. "Ana Olrun is, was, the receptionist at Neqa. We met her when we interviewed Xander George, the C.E.O."

"Get anything from him?"

"Saw nothing, knows nothing."

"So why was Ms. Olrun calling you earlier?"

"I have no idea. I never got to talk to her."

"See the shooter?"

"Just a blur. Bigger than me. I tried to block him but he was behind me so it didn't do much good. When I stepped on his shoe, I heard twigs snap. Maybe I broke the guy's foot."

"Scrappy of you."

Maeve opened her eyes just enough to see Forbes beyond the fringe of her lashes. "Tom showed me a few moves."

"You're lucky to be alive, Ms. Malloy. I suggest that you go back to your law practice and let the professionals handle this," Forbes said. "Meanwhile we need to exclude you as a suspect. You understand." He motioned to Everett, who beckoned to someone hidden behind the cubicle curtain. Another cop-looking guy came into the room carrying a small locker which he placed on Maeve's bedside table.

"Gunshot residue," Tom said.

"And fingerprints," Forbes said.

"Not a problem," Maeve said.

While the tech worked away under Forbes's supervision, Everett said, "What is it you do besides looking for missing persons, anyway? Divorce, or, what do they call it, personal injury?" He shot a judgmental look at Forbes. Forbes frowned at him.

What Everett meant was obvious to Maeve, that "they" called it "ambulance chasing."

"I practice criminal defense, Special Agent Everett," Maeve pushed herself up. "Are you telling me the F.B.I. is investigating the murder of Esther Fancyboy?"

"Sorry. I'm not at liberty to discuss what we are, or are not, investigating," Forbes interjected. "Surprised we haven't crossed paths before."

"I was at the state public defender's office. We didn't handle federal cases. Now I'm in private practice."

"Why did you leave the P.D.'s?"

"Does it matter?"

Forbes shrugged. "Were you investigating this case on the behalf of a client?"

"I wasn't hired in my capacity as a criminal defense attorney." We had already told him that Cora had asked for help, Maeve thought. Twice. "Cora is Esther's mother. She wanted us to find Esther because Anchorage police weren't doing anything. We're helping her out. Pro bono."

"Pro bono?" Forbes asked.

"For free," Tom interjected.

"Lawyers working for free?" Everett asked.

"It's good for the soul," Maeve said. "You should give it a try sometime, Special Agent."

"Can we get back on track?" Forbes shot Everett a warning look. "Ana Olrun wanted to talk to you at her condo so as not to be overheard?"

"That's right."

"Who was she keeping secrets from?"

"Xander George."

≉≉≉

Friday, January 18
Nesbett Courthouse

Maeve sat at counsel's table, head throbbing. Cora sat at her side as Evan waited in the hallway with Margaret. Despite Maeve's warning, Cora wanted Evan there, so Tom kept them company, just in case Buddy showed up.

The hearing had been set for eleven a.m. The court clerk entered the courtroom with Judge Rhys behind her at five minutes after. Maeve stood and motioned to Cora to stand. The judge, a round woman with glasses and a pony tail, waved them to sit.

She settled behind the bench and opened the file in front of her. "We're on the record in the matter of Evan Fancyboy. The petitioner, Cora Fancyboy, is present in the courtroom with her attorney, Maeve Malloy." The judge scanned the room. "Ms. Malloy, do you know if any other parties will be present?"

"Evan's natural father, Buddy Halcro, was notified of the time and place of this hearing, but I haven't heard from him, Your Honor."

"Very well. We shall proceed. Ms. Malloy, you may begin."

The courtroom door crashed open and Buddy Halcro

stumbled inside. He reached for a pew to steady himself. His frayed jacket was stained with motor oil, his jeans looked as if he'd slept in them, and he was sporting a fresh black eye. The sour odor of yesterday's booze enveloped him.

"Sir? May I have your name?" The judge asked.

Buddy looked around the courtroom until he found the judge. "Buddy Halcro. I'm Evan's father."

"Very well, Mr. Halcro. Please come forward and take a seat at the respondent's table, then we can proceed."

As he stepped forward, Buddy banged into the table. "He's my son. I'm his father. I'm on the birth certificate. A boy needs his father." He placed both hands on the table to steady himself.

"You'll have your opportunity to address the court, Mr. Halcro. But first I'd like to hear from petitioner's counsel."

Buddy fell into a chair with a grunt and wheeled around to watch Maeve.

Maeve stood. "Your Honor, the facts are set forth in the petition. Evan Fancyboy is a seven-year-old boy. His mother, Esther Fancyboy, was murdered on January seventh. Cora Fancyboy, my client and the petitioner, is his maternal grandmother. She has served as *in loco parentis* since he was born, having raised him from infancy in the village of St. Innocent's while Esther pursued her education in Anchorage. She's happy to answer any questions from the Court."

Maeve sat down.

"Mr. Halcro," the judge said. "Is that true? Has Mrs. Fancyboy raised Evan since birth."

Buddy shrugged.

"I'm sorry, Mr. Halcro, you'll need to answer audibly."

"Yeah, sure. I was...I don't live in the village."

Maeve had attached copies of Buddy's arrests and convictions so Judge Rhys, who was known to read the file before she came into the courtroom, knew exactly why Buddy wasn't around. He had been in jail.

"How much contact have you had with Evan, Mr. Halcro?"

"Esther didn't let me see him."

Maeve began to stand. The judge waved her down.

"Mr. Halcro," the judge continued, "is it true Evan lived with Cora before his mother's death?"

"Guess so."

"And he's lived with her since his mother died?"

"Yeah."

"Is it true you were recently released from jail for a probation violation?"

Buddy nodded.

"Let the record show Mr. Halcro nodded in the affirmative," the judge said. "Mr. Halcro, is it also true that you have a conviction for counterfeiting, another conviction for assault and two convictions for driving while under the influence?"

Buddy threw his hands in the air.

"Tell me this, Mr. Halcro, what is your son's shoe size?"

"What?"

"Your son's shoe size. When was the last time you bought him a pair of shoes?"

"I don't. Cora handles all that stuff."

"Very well, Mr. Halcro. The court is ruling that it is in the best interests of the minor child to remain in the custody of Cora Fancyboy." Judge Rhys signed a document. "You may be excused. Ms. Malloy, you may pick up the order at the clerk's office."

The judge gathered her file and exited the room through the side door, the court clerk following close behind her. Maeve heard the deadbolt slide into place that prevented disgruntled parties from following the judge.

Maeve hesitated. In family disputes, it's better to let one party leave the courtroom first while the other hangs back, avoiding a confrontation. She hoped Buddy would leave first. Buddy didn't move.

"A boy needs his father," Buddy muttered to himself.

Maeve escorted Cora out of the courtroom. As the door closed, Buddy yelled, "I'm not done with you yet! You can't take my boy away from me!"

Tom hustled Maeve, Cora, Margaret, and Evan toward the elevator. He punched the button and watched the lights above the door as if he could will the elevator's arrival. They weren't moving. He punched the button again.

The courtroom door slammed open.

"He's my son!" Buddy wiped tears from his face with a dirty sleeve. "You can't take my boy."

CHAPTER NINETEEN

5:30 PM
Nelson & Associates

"Thank you for coming in, Ryan," Arthur said as he showed Ryan Shaw into his office where Maeve and Tom were waiting.

Shaw arrived ten minutes early for the meeting, and Arthur had let him sit in the firm's lobby. Arthur, Maeve, and Tom passed the time, talking about the weather, snow predicted again, and weekend plans, finding out who killed Esther Fancyboy. At the appointed time, Arthur had personally gone to the waiting room to escort Shaw to his office.

Tom lowered his voice. "You feeling okay?"

Stiffness had set in all over her body but the screaming head pain had dialed down to a mere whine. "Better," Maeve said.

She imagined Shaw sitting in the impressive paneled lobby, sinking into the leather sofa, gazing at photos of Arthur Nelson on the wall with the current governor, the last governor, the governor before him, and Senator Ted Stevens. Maybe Ryan imagined another picture on that wall, one of Arthur and himself, trotting down the Supreme Courthouse steps. Shaw was just the kind of guy to make that leap of faith. And then the mighty man himself, Arthur Nelson, had come out personally to greet him.

Must have felt good.

Shaw's voice bubbled in conversation as he and Arthur

walked toward Arthur's office. Once inside, he saw Maeve and Tom and stopped short. He turned to Arthur with a frown of confusion. Arthur closed the door and gestured to the third empty chair. "Have a seat, Ryan. I think you know my other guests."

Shaw obeyed, dragging his chair a few feet away from where Maeve and Tom sat.

Shaw faced Arthur, turning his shoulder to Maeve. "What's this about, Mr. Nelson?"

Arthur produced a copy of the Irma Reyes interview transcript from his desk drawer and slid it across the desk to Shaw. "You might want to look at this before we talk, Ryan."

Shaw didn't move.

Arthur sat back in his chair, his hands clasped loosely on his lap.

The sound of traffic died away as the last of the downtown office workers drove home. Maeve took a long deep breath in and a long deep breath out, slowing down her heartbeat.

Shaw picked up the thin transcript. Ten minutes of interview on eight pages. He read it and then set it back down again.

"She's been talking to my client?" Shaw gestured at Maeve with a thumb.

Arthur smiled. "An interesting point, Ryan, because technically Irma Reyes is not your client in this case. She never agreed to you representing her against the state and Ms. Malloy. So, no, Ms. Malloy didn't talk to your client."

Shaw looked over at Maeve. She waved at him.

"Hearsay," Shaw said.

"Let's not play games here, Ryan. Mr. Sinclair sat in on the interview. He's prepared to testify about Mrs. Reyes's statements."

Shaw stole a look at Tom. Tom jerked his head in acknowledgment.

"Let's get to the point," Arthur said with a smile, "the real import of Mrs. Reyes's statement. She never agreed to this lawsuit, which means you have a serious problem."

"I have a fee agreement."

Arthur selected a copy of the fee agreement from his desktop and slid that over to Shaw. "As do we. There is nothing in that agreement that authorized this lawsuit. I know you're eager to make your place in this world. So many young attorneys in your position go astray, overstepping the boundaries because they don't know any better."

"Mr. Nelson, I think there's a misunderstanding..."

Arthur held up his hand, stopping Shaw. "There is another problem, Ryan. The manner in which you obtained the information about the perjured alibi that is the basis of your complaint. You heard it from Mr. Jones himself. Your client. There is no other way. And the bar association takes a very dim view of attorneys using confidential information for personal gain."

"I didn't sue Jones. I sued the state."

"The state was your employer. You obtained the information by virtue of your position as an assistant public defender. The term for such behavior is 'abuse of office.' Of course, in no way should you infer that I am threatening you with criminal prosecution in order to leverage a civil compromise. That would be highly unethical. But you do need to understand that in my role as Ms. Malloy's attorney, I will be filing a motion to dismiss, outlining these events. Once this motion hits the court system, we no longer have control over who uses this information, or how. Judges have been known to refer disciplinary matters to the bar association."

Arthur slid a third set of documents to Shaw, the motion to dismiss he had drafted.

"And that's why I called you in, Ryan. I know that youth and inexperience can result in misjudgment but there's no reason why you should be punished so early in your career when a simple fix is all that's needed."

Shaw rolled the papers into a bat and beat it against his leg. "What did you have in mind? I'd be happy to convey any settlement offers to my client."

Tom snorted. Maeve swallowed the urge to laugh.

"Money settlement is not what we had in mind, Ryan," Arthur said as he stood. "Take the weekend to think about it. I'm sure you can come up with a solution to our problem."

Arthur showed Ryan out the door.

While he was gone, Tom said, "You okay with this? Letting Shaw off the hook?"

Maeve nodded. She didn't want revenge. She just wanted to be left alone.

"He'll be back, you know. You just showed him up. In his head, it's you against him. Sooner or later, he'll come at you again."

"Let him."

Arthur returned.

"You sure this is going to work?" Tom asked.

Arthur unbuttoned his gray suit jacket, smoothed his silver silk tie, and slid into his leather chair. "You bet your ass it will."

※※※

After Tom took Maeve home, he came back to the office, parked his truck behind the building, and walked across the street to the nearly empty district attorney's parking lot.

There wasn't a lot of time left. Maeve had insisted that she didn't want to unearth the Jones-Royce-Bennett thing yet, not until she was certain what Shaw would do. But the bar hearing was on Tuesday. She needed to act fast. If she wasn't going to do something, Tom would.

Tom leaned against a shiny new pickup and the cold metal bit through his jeans. He zipped his jacket shut, dug out a pack of cigarettes, and lit one.

The temperature dropped fast as cloud cover turned from light gray to dark gray, never quite becoming black. Blue-white L.E.D. light from street lamps bounced between the snow-covered ground and low gray clouds so that nighttime Anchorage was one long eerie twilight until the next day.

Across the street, the lights of the Ten-Eighty winked out. A couple of ravens pecking around the dumpsters squabbled and flapped their wings, rising into the air a few feet then settling on the ground again.

Sal's van waddled over the rutted alleyway, flustering the birds again. Tom cupped his cigarette so the ember wouldn't draw attention. He didn't want to spook the man he was waiting for. One guy lying in wait would be a surprise. A guy lying in wait talking to a retired cop could be socially awkward.

Tom watched Sal pull onto the street and drive away. He crushed the cigarette out with his boot and had just grabbed the cigarette pack again when Jefferson Bennett rounded the building.

"You mind? That's a new paint job," Bennett said as he approached.

Tom pulled away from the truck. "Need a word."

Bennett pointedly checked his watch.

"I wouldn't be freezing my ass off if it wasn't important," Tom said. "It's about Maeve."

Bennett unlocked the driver's door and tossed his briefcase inside.

"Your pal Addison Royce snitched her out to the bar association about the Mataafa thing. You and I both know that ain't right. Deals were going down and you knew about them. You were in the background, but you sure as hell knew. You own a piece of this cluster fuck as much as anyone."

Bennett leaned into the truck, started the engine, and closed the door again. He ran a hand across his mouth then shoved both hands into his pockets. The expression on his face was neither hostile nor agreeable, just tired.

Tom put the pack of cigarettes back in his pocket. "Do the right thing, Bennett."

≢≢≢

Saturday January 19

Law Office of Maeve Malloy

Tom found her sleeping on the office couch under her coat. He pulled the coat up under her chin and draped his own coat over her legs. She stirred, opened her eyes, saw Tom, and frowned.

"I thought you were home," he said.

Maeve pushed herself up, threw the coats onto the floor. "Crap, what time is it? Am I late for court?"

"Relax, Counselor, it's Saturday. The last time I saw you, I was dropping you off at your house Friday night. What are you doing in the office?"

"Geez, it's freezing." Maeve reached for her coat and pulled it on.

"Landlord turns off the heat on the weekends."

"I was working. What are you doing here?"

"Just driving by. Come on, Counselor, I'll buy you breakfast."

≢≢≢

Pipeline Diner
Anchorage, Alaska

Maeve followed Tom to a red upholstered booth in a back corner. Regulars Maeve had seen before were already seated at their favorite booths. Two brothers were perched on bar stools. In their fifties, they were big working men with square heads, rough hands, and clipped hair. A cheerful husband and wife in their sixties were in one of the booths near the kitchen, where they could chat with the cook. Every time Maeve saw them, she wondered if they had married late in life or if they were one of those rare couples who still liked each other after forty years.

The booth was so deep and the table so high that it nearly reached Maeve's chin. The Pipeline had been built in the seventies, catering to the big appetites of the big men who had built

Alaska. Tom flipped through the boothside jukebox menu.

"You just don't see these anymore." He said that every time they came in.

"Jukebox is broke," the waitress said. She said that every time, too. Maeve could never remember her name. She set a coffee carafe on the table. "What're we having?"

"Waffles, sausage, eggs over easy, orange juice," Tom said. "Thanks, Betty."

Betty turned to Maeve. "And I expect you'll be wanting the egg white omelet, no cheese, just veggies, dry toast, and coffee?"

Maeve couldn't remember Betty's name but Betty could remember Maeve's order. If she had been a client or witness, her name would have been engraved in Maeve's head. But it wasn't. There was something wrong with that. And in the very near future, Maeve could well have enough time to figure out what that was.

"Thanks, Betty. Sounds perfect."

After the waitress had gone to check on the happily married couple, Tom picked up a couple of sugar packets and tore the ends off them both in one expert movement. "You didn't answer my question, Counselor. Why were you freezing your butt off in the office?"

"I couldn't sleep and I didn't want to wait until Sunday to copy my exhibits for Monday's hearing. I kept thinking I'd run out of toner or paper or the copier feeder would jam."

"Isn't Nelson handling that?"

"I forgot to give him Jones's criminal files showing the trail between Royce and Jones when I was there on Friday. His staff doesn't come in on the weekend and I don't want to dump a bunch of paper on them Monday so figured I'd do it myself."

"Just asking." Tom poured coffee for Maeve. "Here, drink this. It'll make you feel better."

Maeve drank. The coffee was weak and metallic. Without a doubt, the worst coffee in town.

"Worried you're going to lose the hearing?" Tom asked.

"Let's change the subject." Maeve waved down Betty. "Can I get some hot water for tea?"

"Sure, honey, be right with you."

"Any news out of Buddy?" Tom asked.

"Nope. It's been less than twenty-four hours since the hearing. I'd say he's still drunk or sleeping it off."

"Good guess."

"Esther," Maeve said.

"Esther," Tom repeated.

"What do we know?"

"She was last seen talking to some guy driving a black SUV at Starring."

"Then she turned up days later in a snow bank, beaten to death. No sign of sexual assault."

"But she'd apparently had consensual sex."

"Right."

"And she'd been meeting some guy in a black SUV behind the bars downtown."

"We don't know if she met him there more than once. Could have been just that one time."

"Does it make a difference how long it was going on? New boyfriend, old boyfriend. He was a secret boyfriend at any rate."

Betty appeared at their table with two plates held by towels. "Watch it, now. They're hot." She placed Maeve's meal on the table, then Tom's. "Anything else I can get you?"

"Hot water and some tea bags?"

"Sorry, honey, I'll be right back."

"And she had that key to Neqa's suite," Tom said while he carved up his waffle.

"She could have been escorting some out-of-town VIP."

"Uh-huh," Tom said with a mouthful of food. He didn't sound convinced.

"You think she was still seeing Xander."

"Why would he dip his quill in the company ink, get caught, and then do it again? Don't make sense. Sure, if he couldn't keep his hands off her and if she was going to snitch him out, he might kill her in a fit of rage, but I just don't see him doing it. The guy is calm and cool. And, if they did hook up again after they got caught the first time, he must have really cared for her. Besides, he's got an alibi."

"Did you notice how much Esther and Ana looked alike?"

"Figures. They're from the same part of Alaska. Probably related somehow."

"Maybe Esther wasn't the target in the first place. Maybe it was mistaken identity and Ana was the target all along." Maeve sniffed at the coffee. It didn't smell any better than it'd tasted. "I'm never getting that tea."

"Looks like you're not."

Maeve picked up Tom's orange juice and took a slug. "Sorry, got to get that taste out of my mouth."

"Take it," Tom said.

"Turner said Xander and Esther were ripping off the corporation. He might have killed her if he was afraid she was going to tell."

"I am telling you he was in love with the girl. He's in mourning, you can tell by looking at him. I don't think they were ripping off Neqa. At least she wasn't. She didn't have any unexplained money. That settlement she got was enough to buy the condo and the car. After that, she was living on her salary. Besides, why would Xander kill Ana?"

"You're assuming the same person killed Anna and Esther."

"Isn't everyone?"

⚡⚡⚡

Sunday, January 19
Esther Fancyboy's Condominium

Maeve followed Margaret as they each carried mugs of tea to the dining room. Margaret set a mug in front of Cora, then one in front of Tom. Maeve put down mugs for Margaret and herself. A box of juice sat in front of Evan, which he ignored.

Evan scratched at his chapped thumbs as he had on the day at the medical examiner's when Esther's body had been found.

"Just got off the phone with the cops," Tom said. "Buddy's in jail. He won't be back for a while."

Margaret looked at Maeve. "What's next?"

"You know, I've never seen your room, Evan," Maeve said brightly, then tossed a warning frown to Tom. Kids shouldn't listen to discussions like this. They soak up stress and guilt, burdens not theirs to carry.

Saturday night, Buddy Halcro had shown up at the condo, drunk, and beat on Cora's door demanding to see Evan. Margaret called Maeve and Maeve called the cops. By the time Maeve and Tom had pulled up, the police were already there with Buddy in custody.

Blue and red lights flashed against an upstairs window. As each color burst faded, Maeve saw Evan watching his father being led to a patrol car, hands cuffed behind his back. When Evan spotted Maeve, he had dropped the curtain into place.

Maeve stood. "Is it okay if Evan shows me his room?"

Cora looked at Evan. Something unsaid passed between them.

Evan rose from his seat. Maeve followed him up the stairs.

Evan's room was painted dark blue. Over his headboard was a large poster of a superhero with a cape. His neatly made bed had a superhero comforter on it. The room was as spotless as the rest of the house. No clothes on the floor. No piles of homework thrown about. On the dresser was the framed photo of Evan and Esther just like the one in Esther's office at Turner International.

Evan sat on the bed and looked up at Maeve expectantly.

"May I sit down?" Maeve asked.

Evan scooted aside to make room for her. She sat beside him.

"How are you doing, Evan?"

He shrugged his thin shoulders.

"The police coming to your house must have been scary."

He pulled his knees to his chin and wrapped his arms around them.

The muffled voices of the adults downstairs floated up to Evan's room in wisps, a phrase here, a phrase there: "bail.... visitation rights.... judge." Maeve looked around the room for inspiration, something to talk about that would divert Evan's attention.

He clenched his face as tears bloomed, buried his head in the cocoon he'd created, and shook.

Maeve lightly put a hand on his shoulder. He paid no notice. She wanted to say something soothing, but the right words wouldn't come. She lightly stroked his back. The little bones of his spine felt like a stack of marbles under his t-shirt.

Evan leaned into Maeve. She wrapped her arms around him and rocked.

ΨΨΨ

Monday January 21
Law Office of Maeve Malloy

The fax was waiting for Maeve when she opened the office. Ryan Shaw had sent it, a notice of dismissal of the case of Reyes v. State of Alaska and Maeve Artemis Malloy.

The darkness outside her window no longer seemed to smother her.

The next item on the agenda was to get the bar hearing canceled. She had told Tom there was no chance, but secretly hoped Arthur could prevail upon the bar association not to waste its time. She'd lied to Tom so he wouldn't dwell on how they could make it go away. A man of action, he was always looking for some way to fix things, but there was nothing they could do. If the bar association canceled the hearing, it was because Arthur had spoken to the right people and the right people had listened.

There were too many variables to predict the outcome if the bar complaint went to a hearing. The board of governors was like a super jury with fifteen different experiences and biases. And not least of those unpredictable variables was Addison Royce's testimony. Somehow, she didn't think he'd step up to take responsibility. It wasn't his style.

To hell with what Arthur said. She had to talk to Royce.

She had lifted the receiver when the office door opened. The sound of two people shuffling into the reception room drifted towards her. Maeve hung up and rose to greet them.

Margaret Alexi was standing in the office with a young Native man. He was as tall and thin as Margaret was short and round. His skin was darker, his shiny black hair was bristle-short and his eyes were so narrow, they looked solid black. He carried himself with an easy grace. She'd never seen him before.

Maeve reached out her hand. "I'm Maeve Malloy."

"Gordi Alexi," the young man said.

"Our cousin," Margaret said. "He has something to tell you. It's about Esther."

Maeve led them into her office and gestured for them to sit on the couch. She drug her desk chair over to sit opposite.

"I talked to Esther when we were at fish camp," Gordi said, "about the water system they had just installed in the village."

Gordi paused. Just when Maeve was beginning to think he was finished, he said, "I looked inside the tank."

She waited again. He didn't continue. "What did you find?"

"Nothing. There was nothing in the tank except water. No filter system."

"What happened to it?"

"Looks like it never got installed."

Margaret interjected, "The water that is being pumped into homes is coming from the river without being sanitized. They might as well drink straight from the river."

"What made you look?" Maeve asked Gordi.

"The reason we had tanks installed, to clean the water so people wouldn't get sick, but they still were getting sick. I was home on summer vacation from engineering school in Fairbanks, and I was interested in how the water filter system worked. Esther had been talking about it for a long time and I told her I wanted to know more. I wanted to help install the system, but Turner said no. He said it had to be their people because of licensing and insurance and things."

"Something's fishy," Margaret said. "No one said there was a problem. The Turner people and Xander all acted like everything was fine."

"Did you tell Esther the filter was missing, Gordi?"

"I told her. She said she didn't know what happened, that she'd find out."

"Then what?"

"I don't know. I never talked to her after that."

CHAPTER TWENTY

Neqa Inc
Conference Room

"**W**ere you aware that the filter system is not in place?" Maeve asked Xander George. She, Tom and Xander were seated around the conference table.

"Who said that?"

Maeve weighed her answer. On one hand, she hadn't promised Gordi anonymity. On the other hand, the Yup'iks carried grudges for generations. When she was in Bethel, she'd heard stories from the locals about family feuds that had endured for centuries.

"I'm not at liberty to say."

Xander rose from his chair. "Someone will look into it." He left the room without a goodbye.

And, without a limp.

"Wasn't him," Maeve said.

"Wasn't who?" Tom asked.

"The guy who killed Ana and attacked me. I stepped hard on his foot and I heard bones break. He should be in a cast."

"Come on, Xander didn't do it," Tom said. "Natives don't commit premeditated murder. If someone gets killed, it's an accident or a barroom brawl."

Right. In Bethel and Anchorage, Maeve had defended Natives accused of all kinds of atrocities when they were drinking, but never a deliberately plotted murder when sober. Not even between feuding families. Then again, even twenty years ago,

Natives didn't wear expensive suits and work in posh offices either.

"Maybe it wasn't premeditated. Maybe whoever killed Ana was surprised when I walked in and over-reacted."

⚘⚘⚘

Turner International

Thirty minutes later, Jerri ushered Maeve and Tom to Andrew Turner's office. She lingered to bat her eyes at Tom. He hesitated before sitting, just to show Jerri he'd noticed but was trying to be inconspicuous. Maeve pointedly turned her head to watch him sit down.

Tom threw his hands up in a universal gesture of "what?" Maeve ignored him.

She turned to face Turner. "We understand the water filter system wasn't installed."

"How do you come by that information?" Turner stood, resting his fingertips on the desktop.

"It's confidential. Can you explain what happened?"

"How is that relevant?"

"Anything Esther was working on at the time of her disappearance could be relevant."

"That's quite a leap, Ms. Malloy." He paused, considering her through narrowed eyes. "There's no great mystery," he said slowly. "The filter malfunctioned so we removed it. We had to send it to the Lower Forty-Eight for repairs. It's a custom piece of equipment."

"Shouldn't Xander George have known about it, Mr. Turner?"

"Of course, he knew. Esther was in very close communication with him about that very issue."

"He acted as if he didn't."

"Perhaps he thought it was none of your business." Turner gestured toward the door. "Now, if you don't mind, I'm very busy."

Maeve settled back into her chair. She wasn't leaving until she had answers. "What reason does he have to lie when we're trying to help?"

"You'd have to ask him that, Ms. Malloy," Turner said coldly. He appeared to reconsider and then added a little more sociably, "You know Xander. He plays his hand close to his chest. I have no way of knowing why he does what he does."

That was all the answer Maeve needed. Turner was playing a shell game, trying to hide the truth with sleight-of-hand, and Maeve had caught on. Xander didn't know about the filter issue because Turner had withheld that information from him, hoping to get it fixed before anyone discovered there was a problem. But someone had found out. Esther.

As Maeve and Tom stood, Jerri the receptionist rushed into the room as fast as her stilettos could carry her. "Andrew, there's...."

Two men in suits and overcoats stepped through the door. It was the two F.B.I. agents that had arrested Maeve at Ana's home.

"Mr. Turner? Special Agent Forbes and Special Agent Everett," said Forbes, scanning the room. "F.B.I."

Forbes' eyes rested on Maeve. "May we have a word privately?"

Leaving Everett with Turner and Jerri, Forbes followed Maeve and Tom down the hall to the empty reception area.

Maeve asked, "What can we do for you, Special Agent?"

"I recall advising you to stay out of the investigation."

"You refused to tell me what you're investigating, so I don't know how to stay out of your way. In fact, I don't know what you were doing at Ana Olrun's condo."

"Very possibly saving your life, Counselor."

Forbes looked at Maeve with his wait-it-out-for-the-next-guy-to-move look he had used in the hospital.

Maeve stared back. His eyes were clear blue, like a child's marble. He was bent over her so that his eyes dominated her field of vision. She was vaguely aware of someone in her peripheral vision, Tom closing in.

Tom's voice was unusually deep. "Anything else, Forbes?"

"Let me make myself clear, Mr. Sinclair." Forbes drew himself to his full height, without taking his eyes off Maeve. "This is a federal investigation. If you do anything which compromises it, you could be charged with obstruction."

"Understood." Stepping between Maeve and Forbes, Tom took her elbow and steered her out the door.

As they made their way down the hall, Tom said, "Turner didn't get up. Wonder how that foot is feeling."

≹≹

Law Office of Maeve Malloy

"Smells good," said a man standing behind Maeve.

She jumped at the unexpected voice, raising her arm in a block before she realized she was moving. The fresh grounds she had been pouring into the coffeemaker scattered across the machine and the table.

"Sorry, didn't mean to scare you," Agent Forbes said.

"You didn't. I was just thinking." That wasn't quite true. She was watching the endless loop of Ana's murder that ran through her mind over and over again when she let her concentration relax. The curling mist from the open front door. The long hallway. The scuffling sounds from another room. Pop, thud. Ana, arm raised. A blast of light. Pop, thud again. Struggling with someone larger than her. The bones breaking beneath her foot like twigs snapping. The light inside her head when the pistol smashed into her head. Her brain smashing back and forth inside her skull. The curling mist...

Maeve reached for the carafe of water to pour into the machine. Her hands shook so hard, the carafe seemed it was trying to jump out of her grasp.

Forbes gently took the carafe. "Here, let me help." He

poured the water into the brewer, ground new beans, cleaned up the table, and hit the power button while Maeve watched. She'd never seen a man make coffee before.

While it brewed, Forbes wandered into Maeve's inner office and examined Maeve's certificates on the wall.

With Forbes in her inner office, Maeve turned her back to him so that he wouldn't see that her hands were still shaking. Maeve brought his mug first, holding it with both hands. She had learned that trick in rehab. Two shaking hands on either side of a cup seemed to cancel each other out.

"Where's your sidekick?" Forbes asked.

"Picking up lunch."

Forbes smiled to himself, one of those condescending male smiles. He had obviously concluded that Tom was an errand boy. He didn't need to know that the tension between Maeve and Tom had grown intolerable during their drive back from Turner's office.

Tom was being even more taciturn than usual and by the time they got back to the office, the tension in the truck was stifling. Maeve wanted to fix it but didn't know how. Tom left, with as few words as possible, to pick up lunch over an hour ago. He could be back soon. Or not at all.

She slipped behind her desk. "Special Agent Forbes, I just saw you at Turner International. What brings you in here?"

After sipping his coffee, Forbes carefully placed the cup on her desk. "I need to talk with you and Turner's office wasn't the best place. Thought you'd like to know Esther Fancyboy's vehicle was found. Her purse was inside. None of the credit cards were missing. There was even some cash in the wallet."

"Where?"

"In a towing yard. It had been parked on Fourth Avenue and had accumulated several parking tickets."

"When did the tickets start?"

"January ninth."

"Not the day before?"

"No ma'am."

Why hadn't we thought of tow yards? Would it have mattered?
Cora and Evan first came into the office on January ninth. Esther's remains were found the night of January tenth. She was probably already dead when Cora had asked Maeve for help. There was nothing Maeve could have done. Maybe.

Maeve sank into her chair. "Are you sure there were no tickets on the eighth? It was a weekday."

"Yes, it was. And the parking authority was on duty. Tickets were issued on Fourth Avenue on January eighth, but none to this vehicle."

"Someone drove it there late on the eighth or the ninth and then left it?"

"So it appears."

"Esther disappeared on the seventh. Either she was still alive a day or two later and left her car there or someone else moved it, trying to cover their tracks."

"Do you have any idea who that might have been, Ms. Malloy?"

"Murder is usually motivated by love or money, right?"

"Love, money, concealing another crime, opportunistic killings, power, domination, revenge, thrills."

"Esther was beaten to death. Does that suggest premeditation to you?"

"More likely, someone lost their temper in the heat of the moment. We found greeting cards in the glove box. The mushy kind, all hearts and flowers. Unsigned. But dated." Forbes flipped open a small stenopad, like the one Tom kept. "The dates were from last year, starting with Valentine's Day and running up to Christmas."

"There were flowers in Esther's office," Maeve said.

"When was that?"

"I didn't see them. Jerri, Turner's secretary, said she had thrown them out so it had to have been after Esther disappeared. No one goes through another person's office unless they don't expect them to come back. It's a violation of privacy." At first, Maeve's theory had been Turner knew Esther wouldn't be back, and that's why he had Jerri toss the flowers. But now she knew Turner had Jerri search the office for the thumb drive, not knowing whether Esther would return.

Maeve said, "The ex-boyfriend, Buddy Halcro, admitted he was trying to resume their relationship. But she was done with him. The cards and the flowers could have been from him. Or maybe Xander George. He once had a relationship with her and nearly lost his job over it. He drives a black SUV like the one someone saw at Starring, so maybe she made plans to meet Xander somewhere later that evening."

"A date?"

"Maybe," Maeve said. "Has anyone had forensics done?"

"Sure, the usual. We're collecting DNA samples from the family to eliminate them. The steering wheel was wiped, no prints. Unlikely we'll obtain anything useful from the vehicle."

"Was there any blood?"

"None. She must have been killed somewhere else."

"So why are you interested in Esther's murder, Agent Forbes? Does it have something to do with why you were at Ana's condo?"

"Nice try, Counselor, but like I've said, I'm not at liberty to discuss our investigation."

Maeve stood. "More coffee?"

"You haven't drunk any of yours."

"I'm up. Want me to warm your cup?"

"Sure."

As Maeve took the cup from Forbes's hand, their fingers brushed. He smiled. She felt herself blushing.

When she returned, she placed the full cup in front of him and sat down again. "Agent Forbes, are you using me?"

"I beg your pardon, Ms. Malloy?" Forbes said, poker-faced.

"You say you can't tell me anything, but you freely disclosed the discovery of Esther's car and its contents."

"We're obligated to notify the vehicle owner. That's all. We were hoping you could let Cora Fancyboy know the car had been located."

"Then why not call Cora directly?"

"It's something that should be told in person. We don't have the time to drive out to her place and thought it might be better coming from you."

"Okay, just one more question," Maeve said. "Did you find a thumb drive?"

"What thumb drive?"

No thumb drive then. Maeve saw a single paperclip on her desktop. She opened the drawer and slid it in with the blade of her hand. "Then, without disclosing your investigation, can you tell me whether you think Ana's murder is related to Esther's murder?"

"That's two questions," Forbes said. The hard line of his mouth softened.

"C'mon, just one tiny question. Is there a connection?"

"Without disclosing our investigation, Ms. Malloy, I can tell you I think there is no such thing as coincidence. Especially when it comes to murder."

Maeve twirled the hurricane pen caddy. Red and black pens whirled around the glass' edge creating a void in its center. The dark hole blurred before her eyes. Who wanted to kill both Esther and Ana? Someone who knew them both. Someone they both knew. Someone who felt threatened by both.

"There's another reason I dropped by," Forbes said as he reached into his suit jacket. He produced a neatly folded paper, opened it up, and placed it on her desk so that she could read it. "I have a search warrant to take Esther Fancyboy's laptop."

¥¥¥

Esther Fancyboy's Condominium

When Maeve and Tom walked in, they saw shards that had once been a plate scattered across the carpet. Cora and Margaret were on their hands and knees picking up clumps of fiberfill and foam from the gutted couch and shoving them into garbage bags.

Maeve fell to her knees and began to help. Broken feathers from Esther's dance fans floated in air currents every time someone moved.

Tom stood to the side, looking awkward. "When did this happen?"

"When Cora and I were out arranging Esther's celebration of life," Margaret said.

"In broad daylight?" Maeve asked. "Did anyone call the cops?"

Margaret nodded. "They took a report. They said there's nothing they can do."

"What about upstairs?" Maeve asked.

"The beds are ripped apart," Margaret said. "Dressers turned over. Clothes everywhere."

Tom trotted up the stairs and came back down a few minutes later. "It looks like a big chinook tore through."

Tom's reference quieted the room. It was a chinook wind that had melted the snow a few days ago, revealing Esther's body. Maeve shot Tom a warning look. He looked back at her with a confused expression.

"Anything missing?" Maeve asked.

"Esther's box of papers," Margaret said. "You know, receipts and things like that, stuff for taxes. I was going to bring them to your office tomorrow for the estate, in case you needed them."

"How'd the burglars get in?" Maeve asked.

Margaret shook her head. "No sign of forced entry, the police said. Not like last time, after fish camp when they smashed a window. But they didn't take anything last time."

Fish camp had been when everything changed. It was at fish camp that Gordi had told Esther about the missing filter system, and she said she'd handle it. When Esther came back to town, she distanced herself from Ana. She would have said something to someone about the filters. After that, there had been a break-in, but nothing was taken.

Then all was quiet until Starring when Esther disappeared and was murdered.

Tom went to the front door, jiggled the handle, and came back. "These box-store locks are pretty easy to pick."

"Or he had a key," Maeve said. Whoever drove Esther's car downtown had her keys and her purse. They'd know where she lived and have the means to enter. And whoever that was could come in here, anytime, and do anything they wanted to the people who lived here.

"Where's Evan?"

"School," Margaret said.

"Is there any way Esther might have given a key to a boyfriend?" Tom asked as he watched the women clean.

Margaret stopped working and sat on her heels.

"What is it?" Maeve asked.

"It was supposed to be a secret," Margaret said. "She made me promise not to tell."

Maeve pushed her hair out of her face so she could look Margaret in the eye. "Cora and Evan could be in danger. We need to know everything,"

Maeve paused to give Margaret time to volunteer the information.

Margaret's thin lips pressed together.

Maeve said, "Now would be good."

"Esther was still with Xander. I'm sorry, Cora, she was afraid to tell you."

Cora went on stuffing the garbage bags as if she hadn't heard.

"It's not like they said," Margaret said to Maeve. "He wasn't bothering her. Esther loved Xander. He was going to marry her. But then they got caught and everything got screwed up."

The love cards from a secret boyfriend. Of course, it was Xander. Not only was his marriage a reason for secrecy, they'd both lose their cushy jobs if they were found out again. And, it explained the key to the Neqa suite at Inlet Towers. It was their love nest.

"Did Esther see Xander the night she disappeared?" Maeve asked.

"She stopped off at the Neqa office to talk to Xander before she picked up Cora and Evan. That's why she was late."

CHAPTER TWENTY-ONE

6 p.m.
Public Defender Building

I t was now or never.

The bar hearing was less than twenty-four hours away. If Maeve was going to convince Royce to drop the charges, she needed to catch him alone tonight. Tom came along for moral support, amongst other reasons.

They stood outside the door of Royce's private unmarked office door, the one he used when he didn't want to get caught in the reception room by disgruntled clients. Royce had told Maeve once that he couldn't stand the smell of a room filled with criminals.

But that wasn't the only reason he avoided clients. The ones who lingered in the reception room were electric with anxiety. They were angry their lives had been disrupted by an arrest. They were angry their attorneys didn't return their multiple phone calls per day. They were afraid of what was going to happen. And they took it out on the first human beings they met, ironically the people who were trying to help them, the P.D. staff.

Receptionists never stayed for long. It was an entry-level job, and one that no one wanted. The people who took it were there only for the state benefits. As soon as they found another job in another department, they were gone.

The office had been locked up at 4:30 p.m., the close of the state government's day. The secretaries and paralegals promptly clocked out and poured from the building like fleeing rats. The attorneys straggled out not long after.

Royce stayed late at the office. One reason was to avoid any resourceful unhappy clients who hung around the building waiting for an attorney to come out. And once business officially shut down for the day, the power brokers had time to talk to each other on the phone without interruption.

Maeve and Tom had staked out their position a little after five. Late enough they wouldn't be seen by P.D. office staff, but early enough to catch Royce sneaking out.

Maeve pressed her ear to Royce's private door. He was talking. The other voice was on speaker, loud but the words were muffled. Maeve pictured him leaning back in his chair, his feet on the desk. Then she heard him start his winding-up salutation, the notes in his voice climbing just a couple of steps, his responses shortening. He would be leaning forward now, both elbows on the desktop, his hand resting on the phone's kill button.

Royce said, "Let's get lunch next time you're in town."

The caller must have been the governor. He was the only person Royce would be seen with in public.

"Yes, sir," Royce said, and laughed. Everyone in Alaska referred to the governor by his first name, Todd. Alaska was that kind of place, small enough that everyone was separated by two degrees at most. Shades of the frontier spirit, us against the world, infused all relationships. But Royce was formal with the governor even in private, acknowledging how far they had both come from shooting hoops together at West High.

The governor made a garbled response. Maeve heard static, then quiet. Royce would have punched the kill button with his left forefinger, wearing a self-pleased smile. He would stand, stretch, take his suit jacket from the door hanger, shrug into it, reach into his pants pocket, jingling the car keys to make sure they were there, and then...

Maeve leapt back. Tom straightened. The door opened.

Royce filled the threshold and stopped. "What are you

doing here?" Royce asked in a way that was more accusatory than inquisitive.

"A word?" Maeve asked. She sounded more sinister than solicitous.

Royce sized up Tom, then glared at Maeve in a poor imitation of a judge provoked.

Maeve forced herself not to laugh. Royce looked like a little boy playing dress up in his father's clothes. She felt a shift in Tom. He'd seen the charade too. She dared not make eye contact with Tom lest they break out laughing. She needed to make Royce feel like a power player if only for a bit longer for her gambit to work.

"Here in the hall," Maeve said, dramatically craning her neck in one direction and then another. "Or in your office."

She paused to give him a moment to consider, then for the sake of stoking his fragile ego, she added politely, "Your call."

She'd let Royce feel like he would be making the decisions, just as Arthur had made Shaw feel like he had come up with a solution, even if Arthur had boxed him in.

Royce looked at Tom again. She could see the wheels turning in his head. He knew why Tom had come, as witness to what was said and not said.

But Tom was there for more. Royce could dismiss Maeve's argument as conjecture. He couldn't dismiss the evidence uncovered by Tom. This was no longer a spat between ex-lovers. It was two lawyers leveraging each other.

For a moment, she thought Royce would refuse.

Royce backed into his office. Maeve entered and Tom followed. Royce shut the door and gave it an extra push, making sure it clacked into place. He didn't offer them seats. Instead, he looked at his watch, then jerked his head impatiently at Maeve.

She knew that gesture. It said, the sooner you start talking, the sooner we can get out of here. She'd seen it several times in the last days of their romance. At the time, he had blamed his impatience on the press of work.

A pain stabbed Maeve's heart. It wasn't his workload that

had kept him from her. He had dumped her for another woman. She was so busy with her own cases that she hadn't noticed.

"The bar hearing is tomorrow," Maeve said. "You're a witness."

Royce jerked his head again as if to say, not just a witness, *the* key witness.

"I'm not here to find out what you're going to say. I can figure that out for myself. I'm also not here to ask you to change or soften your testimony."

"Then what are you here for?" Royce's stare bore into Maeve. It was the stare of someone examining the bottom of his shoe.

The stab deepened. Then, without warning, it vanished. There was only so much rejection, humiliation, guilt, and shame one person could tolerate. She felt nothing but calm.

"To fill in, for your benefit, the other evidence we expect to hear tomorrow," Maeve said.

Something flared deep inside Royce's eyes.

"After I transferred from the Bethel office to Anchorage, you and I began working together." Maeve paused. "Closely. Some might even say very closely. At cocktail parties, bar functions, you'd introduce me as your protégé, the hot new trial attorney, someone you were grooming for chief of the felony unit."

She let that sink in. She knew that Royce feared that she would mention their affair in front of Tom. She hadn't. And she wouldn't. Not here, at least, because if she did, if their secret was in the open, he would deal with it, lie probably, and then her leverage, his fear of exposure, would have evaporated.

She could see him thinking about it. He would have to live with his fear instead.

"When Filippo Mataafa was charged with the gas station robbery, you personally assigned the case to me. You told me that it was a slam dunk. Another victory for my win-loss tally. You were so, so very sure that the case was winnable."

"You did win," Royce said.

Maeve gave an unamused laugh. "Well, here's the thing, see. You told me that Mataafa's alibi was genuine. You told me that Enrique Jones was a reliable witness. You know you did. I had no reason to doubt you. I assumed you knew something I didn't know. And you know what? You did."

Royce's posture settled into the waiting-for-this-to-be-over stance.

"And Tom found out something very interesting. Or actually, I should say, Tom found *someone* very interesting."

Royce's back stiffened.

"I got a witness," Tom said, staring down at Royce. "She told me what really happened with the gas station robbery. Jones wasn't with Mataafa that night because he was somewhere else doing a drug deal with an undercover cop. He wasn't just an ordinary snitch. He was working with the cops setting up drug deals and getting folks busted. It don't take a lot of smarts to figure out he was using the cops to get rid of his competition."

Maeve picked up the story. "At the time of the gas station robbery, Jones was under indictment in a previous drug case. You knew that because *you* were his attorney. *You* set him up to work as a snitch. *You* got a good deal for your client. It made *you* look good to the D.A. and the cops, for whatever that's worth. But most importantly, *you* knew that Jones was lying about the gas station alibi. But you vouched for his credibility anyway when you handed the case off to me."

Tom spoke again. "And you told me not to work the case."

Royce spoke for the first time. "That's not true."

"Oh, pal, it is true," Tom said. "You took me into your office, told me you were sending me to Bethel on another case and ordered me not to work the case. It wasn't until the night before Jones took the stand that you authorized four lousy hours, figuring I couldn't find anything in that amount of time. Except I did." Tom's baritone dropped. "And you shipped me out to Bethel before I could get a chance to tell Maeve."

"You set me up," Maeve said. She had been dancing around the idea for a while. Speaking those words made it real. He had used her and thrown her away. He had arranged it so that if anyone had ever found out about Jones's perjured alibi, her career would be destroyed and Royce would be rid of her. Like she was trash.

"The bar association might ask itself, why would you set me up to take the fall on the eve of your marriage to the governor's sister?"

Without actually mentioning their affair, she had spun back to it. Without threatening exposure out loud, she had implied it. Political careers had been destroyed by less.

Royce crossed his arms. "Okay, okay, I see where you're going with this. Look, as it happens, the civil case was dismissed this morning. I'll see what I can do."

It was too easy, Maeve thought. No argument. No wheedling. Too good to be true.

"I'll call risk management tomorrow, get their okay," Royce said. "It shouldn't be a big deal. Then I'll call the bar association, tell them we're withdrawing the complaint." Royce looked at his watch again. "Seriously, Maeve, that's the best I can do. No one is answering their phones this late, even if they're still in their offices."

It would have to do.

❀❀❀

8 p.m.
Buddy Halcro's trailer

The humming sound stopped after Tom pounded on the door.

When Buddy answered, he had one hand on a vacuum cleaner. Draped across his shoulder was a dirty towel.

"What the..." Tom let the sentence drop off.

"It's freezing out there," Buddy said. "Hurry up."

Buddy moved aside and Tom stepped up into the trailer. The spicy-green smell of growing pot was gone, replaced by a chemical lemon stink. The sofa and recliner were pulled away from the wall.

"You can't sit down," Buddy said. "I just steam-cleaned the furniture."

The trailer was dark. The paneling absorbed the kitchen's overhead fixture's glow, but Buddy had taken the shades off the fluted amber glass lamps. The increased lighting revealed the brown shag carpet's bald spots and stains. The place would look better in the dark.

Tom looked at Buddy again. The puffiness in his face was gone, leaving a hang-dog look. The piss-yellow color of his eyes was paler. The black circles underneath were fading. He was sober. By the looks of it, he had been sober for a couple of days, probably ever since he got busted at Esther's condo Saturday night for disorderly conduct.

"I'm getting my kid back," Buddy said. "I talked to a lawyer. He said the court has to give me parent's preference. As long as I stay out of trouble, they have to give me my kid back. What are you doing here?"

Tom had nearly forgotten the reason for his visit, the images in front of him momentarily disrupting his sense of reality. Maeve had said she was pretty sure Esther's secret lover was Xander George, but she wanted Tom to see how Buddy reacted to the love letters. If he had been stalking her, he could have sent them.

"The cops got Esther's car. They found some lovey-dovey cards she'd been hiding in there. You know anything about that?"

"I'm not the cards and flowers type."

"Just checking." Tom scanned the room again.

"It's got to be that sugar daddy of hers," Buddy said. "I told you about him. Saw her sneaking into the alley to meet some guy in a SUV."

"You never said that."

"You didn't ask."

"Followed them where, when?"

"You're not going to tell anyone, are you? They're going to think I was harassing her."

Buddy *had* been stalking her but Tom didn't need to argue the point. "What did you see?"

"I happened to be driving by where she worked," Buddy said.

Translation: he was parked outside her office building.

"And I seen her get into her car and drive the wrong way. I know it was the wrong way 'cause she has to turn right to go home, but she turned left instead. I happened to be driving in that direction, like I said."

Translation: he followed her. "I'm listening."

"So she pulls into the Inlet Towers parking lot. I know it was that guy's rig because she kissed her fingertips and then touched the hood of the car," Buddy said, then demonstrated with a big smooch to his fingers and then pressing them to the kitchen counter. He paused for a moment, looking at the countertop. "Weird little thing she did. She used to do it with my car."

"And then?"

"And then she goes inside. Comes out a couple of hours later. It don't take a rocket scientist to figure out why she'd go into a hotel and come out two hours later."

Translation: Buddy sat in his car watching and waiting the whole time.

"You ever see the guy?" Tom asked.

"No, I didn't hang around after that. I'm telling you, the woman was screwing some sugar daddy like some cheap bimbo when she should have been home taking care of my kid. What kind of mother does that?"

CHAPTER TWENTY-TWO

Tuesday, January 21
Law Office of Maeve Malloy

M aeve watched as Andrew Turner paced, his cashmere coat flapping in his wake. "I don't know what to do."

"Have a seat," Maeve said. "Coffee?"

He waved a dismissal. "The F.B.I. was at my office. All afternoon. You saw them. They came in when you were leaving. With search warrants! Why did they have search warrants? You're a lawyer. What's going on? Am I in some sort of trouble?"

"Well, I suppose—"

"They locked me up in the conference room. Kept me out of my own office. And they kept asking me questions." He ran his hand through his hair.

"What kind of—"

"Nothing like this has happened before." He stopped in his tracks. "Stephie is beside herself. We had a late lunch date and they kept her out of the office. And Jerri, you met Jerri. She quit. Walked out on me the minute they let her go. Traitor."

"Mr. Turner—"

"What could they possibly be looking for?" He collapsed into the visitor's chair. One knee bounced erratically.

"Did they give you an inventory when they left?"

Turner patted his suit jacket. "It's here somewhere." He stood, dug in his pants pockets, found a piece of paper, and handed it to her.

Maeve examined the document. "It's a valid search warrant."

"Search warrant, smirch warrant. What is it, fruit of the poisonous tree? Can't you get the evidence suppressed? You're a lawyer, for chrissake. You're supposed to know this stuff."

"Whoa, slow down, Mr. Turner. Do you expect you'll be prosecuted?"

Turner sat down again. He crossed his legs, stilling the bouncing knee but his foot agitated in the air erratically. "For what?"

"That's my question, Mr. Turner. Is there any reason you could be prosecuted?"

Turner squinted out the window. Not as if he was looking for the answer written on the clouds. More like he was cooking up a reply. He cleared his throat. "There was a problem back east. Before we moved to Alaska."

"What kind of problem?"

"I had this engineering firm. There was a surprise audit. Accounting irregularities, they called it. I'm afraid my partner wasn't very good with books." He scoffed. "He went to jail. We went bankrupt. I had no idea what was going on, of course. I was out in the field most of the time, so the feds couldn't get me. Not that they didn't want to. I was the target, of course."

"Why you?"

"My first wife's father was a politician. A very important one. They were looking for some sort of insider-stuff, preferential treatment. To get at him. Turns out he and my partner were doing some shady stuff behind my back."

"Shady stuff," Maeve repeated.

"Gratuities, whatever you call it. In kind, not money, the lawyer said. We did some free work on the gazebo of his summer home, designed it, got it built. And since we were working on some projects he'd gotten funded by congress, the feds acted as if we were bribing him, which was just ridiculous. We were doing a favor for a friend, a family member. The feds hauled me in, interviewed me for hours and ransacked the office. Did I tell you we ended up bankrupt over it? For doing a favor for my father-in-law?"

He stood and began to pace again. "When the F.B.I. showed up, it brought that all back. You know what? I think they're still after me for the corruption angle, still trying to get at me."

"Did you tell the F.B.I. about the missing money from the Neqa account?"

"No way. I have a right to remain silent, don't I? Just like them to show up without notice so I wouldn't have an attorney sitting there in the office. You were there, but you left. That's why Esther's files are so important."

"You haven't found them?"

"We looked everywhere. Say, you found her laptop. Maybe we could get some computer genius to look at it?"

"Feds took it."

"What?" He froze. "Why didn't someone tell me?"

"Should we have?"

"Trade secrets. I have a proprietary interest. It might be her laptop, but the information on it belongs to me. Hell, yes, I should have been told."

"I'm telling you now."

"Sure, sure, of course." He sat down again, crossed his legs again, uncrossed them. "I need an attorney. That's why I'm here. You already know so much about the case."

"Sorry, Mr. Turner. As I explained to you last time, I'm working for Evan Fancyboy."

"Is he a suspect?" Turner asked.

"Hardly." Maeve smiled. "But my duty of loyalty is to him. I suggest you call the bar association. They should steer you to someone who can help." She wrote the telephone number on a sticky and handed it to him.

Turner held the note gingerly. "They'd probably want to get paid."

"I imagine." Maeve stood. "Sorry I couldn't be more help to you."

"For what it's worth," Turner said, more to himself than to Maeve. He stood, slipped the note in his pocket, and strode out the door.

≢≢≢

Tom answered on the sixth ring, groggy. He never was a morning person. Not that it was morning. It was practically lunch time. The Ten-Eighty's ovens had been baking for a couple of hours already, filling the office with the aroma of fresh baked bread.

"You'll never guess!" Maeve said. "Jerri walked out on Turner just as the F.B.I. searched his office Saturday."

She could hear the wheels turning in his head. Why would Maeve wake him up just to spread some office gossip?

"Guess that little romance is over," Tom said.

"What romance?" Did he mean Jerri and Turner? Had Tom flirted with Jerri in front of Turner, just to tweak Turner's nose? Getting back at him about the Rolex? Or did Tom just flirt with any leggy blonde with cascading tresses? "You know something I don't know?"

"Just a vibe I picked up, that's all," Tom said, his voice thick with sleep. "Is this important?"

If Tom's flirtations weren't important to him, they shouldn't be important to Maeve. It was none of her business. It wasn't like they were intimate.

"Turner thinks it has something to do with political corruption," Maeve said. "The F.B.I. has jurisdiction over federal funding so they might have found out about the missing money and suspected it was embezzled. Murder is not usually federal jurisdiction. It's state jurisdiction unless the murder was wrapped up in some conspiracy to violate federal law, like embezzling federal funds."

"Nah, Esther? Hard-working village girl, gets a college degree, single mother? She doesn't strike me as the thief type."

"Really?" Maeve hadn't gotten a payoff when Royce booted her to the curb. She hadn't made a claim because she didn't feel like she was harassed. She was a grown woman in full possession of her faculties who had gotten involved with her boss and it turned out badly. Or so she'd thought at the time. Now, she realized that even if she felt like a consenting adult, his power over her job gave him all the control. They never were equal partners.

Lesson learned.

Esther hadn't made a claim either. Someone had found out about her affair with Xander and told the board of directors. They handled "the problem" by giving her money and a promotion, a sophisticated strategy for people who had only just been introduced to the American legal system. In fact, it was the kind of machination only a lawyer would think up. A lawyer like Robert Edelson, who had been hanging around Neqa a lot lately.

"If the feds thought Esther took the money, why are they still investigating?" Tom asked. "She's dead. There's no one to prosecute."

Maeve considered Tom's argument. "They knew she was dead when they searched Turner's office and then came to my office for the laptop. So, it's safe to assume the feds are investigating embezzlement, and their suspect is still very much alive."

"Yeah, so?"

"Yeah, so, they had search warrants. They don't just type those things up themselves. A magistrate signs them after they convince him they have probable cause. They needed to convince him a crime was being committed and that the evidence was on the laptop and in Turner's office. The feds needed some evidence upon which to base that belief."

"Like what?"

"Like, there's got to be a snitch."

❦❦❦

Polaris I.T. Office

Tom pulled his truck up to a run-down office building in an industrial area. Rusty stains streamed down cream stucco walls. Blistered brown paint peeled from the doors and window trim. The only window was painted black.

"You sure this is the correct address?" Maeve asked. "There's no sign."

"It's what I got from Josh."

Tom tried the knob. Locked.

Maeve pointed to a bell. Tom pushed the button and a loud ugly buzz came from inside. After a few moments, the door opened.

"Sorry," Josh said. "We try to keep it low key around here. With all the computers we have, we could get ripped off pretty bad."

Inside, colorless outdoor carpet smelled of mildew. Cheap paneling covered the walls. Computer guts were stacked neatly on shelves of industrial-style bookcases on one wall. A fully assembled computer hummed on a workbench as indecipherable letters and numbers crawled across the monitor. On the back wall, a dingy once-white door hung open revealing a toilet and sink. The acrid smell of burnt coffee wafted from a stained carafe on a burner.

"It's home," Josh said, shrugging.

There was only one chair. "You probably don't get a lot of visitors," Maeve said.

"Mostly I work on site. I'm in the middle of something." Josh gestured to the humming computer. "What do you need?"

"The F.B.I. searched Turner International's office and its computers," Maeve said.

Josh's eyelids fluttered. His face paled.

"You've been talking to the feds," Maeve said.

Josh squinted at her. "How did you know?"

"Who else could have led them to Turner's database? And who else could have led them to my office for Esther's laptop?"

"You think Turner knows?" Josh jammed his hands into his jeans pockets.

"For all he knows, the F.B.I. is on a fishing expedition. Why were you talking to them in the first place?"

"They said I had to. They said I could go to jail for obstruction of justice if I didn't."

"But how'd they get on to you?"

"Esther."

Maeve cocked her head. She wondered how cops keep their cool while they waited for a suspect to answer. She focused on her breath. Breath in, breath out.

Josh shuffled his feel. "I promised not to tell."

Maeve resumed counting breaths.

Josh pulled his hands from his pockets, crossing his arms. "A week or so before she disappeared, I found a locked file on the server. I tried all the passwords Mr. Turner had given me but I couldn't get it open. It was a little bit after five and Mr. Turner was gone for the day so I asked Esther."

"And?"

"Then she warned me that Turner was up to something and I should cover my you-know-what. She made a big deal out of it. Told me not to let Turner know I saw the file. Just forget what I saw, she said, it wasn't my problem."

Josh fidgeted. "After that, she turns up dead. Man, I didn't know what to think. You know, it could have just been a coincidence."

He looked at Maeve, waiting for her to ask the right question.

"So what did you do?"

"Hacked in," Josh's words were almost a whisper. He scanned Maeve and Tom for a reaction.

Maeve forced her face to remain still, muscles relaxed, but she could feel her breathing speed up. She was sure her pupils would have flashed. She didn't have to look at Tom to know he was wearing his poker face.

Josh tightened the cross of his arms, shoulders hitched almost to his ears.

"Then the F.B.I. showed up here." Josh nodded at the door. "They said Esther had told them about me. So I told them what

I saw. I mean, they're the feds. I can't withhold information from the F.B.I. Or maybe I should have demanded a lawyer? Did I screw up?"

"Josh, this is really important. I need to know what you told them."

"About the money. About all the money Turner gave to Acme Inc."

*⁣⁣⁣⁣⁣⁣⁣⁣

F.B.I. Office

"Thank you for coming in," Forbes said as he gestured to two chairs opposite his desk.

While Maeve would have preferred to spend the afternoon searching Esther's condo for a thumb drive, it was hard to decline an invitation from the feds. Impossible, even.

Maeve took a seat in one chair. Tom settled into the other. Everett leaned against the wall, poised to take notes.

The office was cramped. Maeve could almost hear the F.B.I. hive's grating whine. Agents hidden away, furiously trying to boost their careers with another solve, hoping to retire and get the hell out of Alaska before they died of heart attack.

A few agents came to Alaska late in their career to retire, the fishing and hunting enthusiasts. But most believed they had been marooned in outer Siberia, taking the assignment only to work their way up the ladder to a better job. A better place. Somewhere that wasn't freezing all the time. A place you could get to without flying in planes the size of large mosquitoes. A place with indoor toilets.

Everett was that kind of agent. Perpetual discomfort emanated from him. He was on his way out of here the first chance he got.

Maeve wasn't sure about Forbes. He might stick around. On the far wall of his office hung one photo that told all. A happy Forbes stood on a dock next to an enormous halibut two feet taller than him. It was the only personal photo on all four walls.

Otherwise, Forbes' small office was neat and spare. A desk, his chair, two visitor's chairs, a bookcase and a few certificates on the wall. The certificates and photo were hung perfectly square. There was nothing on his desk other than the telephone and his nameplate.

Maeve examined Forbes' certificates. College degree. F.B.I. academy. Law degree. "Did you practice law before joining the agency, Agent Forbes?"

Forbes adjusted his tie. "Assistant prosecutor in New York. White collar crime, mostly."

Maeve smiled to herself. Finally, she had gotten an answer out of him.

Everett cleared his throat, then tapped his notepad a couple of times.

Forbes squinted at Everett, obviously irritated.

"How can we be of assistance?" Maeve asked.

"We understand you were called to the Fancyboy residence following a break-in."

"We were called. How did you learn about it?"

"The F.B.I. doesn't answer questions, Ms. Malloy. I thought I made that clear earlier," Forbes said.

Right.

"What did you observe?" Forbes asked.

"A lot of damage. Plates and glasses broken. Things torn off walls. Upholstery slashed."

"Anything taken?"

"Didn't the police give you their report?" Maeve asked.

"Regardless, I'd like to hear it from you."

"All of Esther's paperwork was taken. Cora didn't know what documents were included. She'd boxed it up to bring in to my office because I'm handling the estate but she hadn't brought it in yet."

"Television, electronics?"

"Nothing like that," Maeve said.

"Any sign of a break-in?"

Tom said, "None, but those locks are easy enough to pick."

"Anyone else have a key?" Forbes asked.

Maeve said, "Just the guy who had the keys to her car as far as we know. That's the guy who probably killed her, don't you think?" Maeve watched Forbes, his expression impenetrable. "Did you find out anything about who had the car after she disappeared?"

"Nice try, Ms. Malloy, but I'm still not answering your questions." He stood. "Thank you for coming in. And a reminder. Don't obstruct our investigation." His tone was hard.

Maeve and Tom stood.

"If we still don't know what you're investigating, how can we stay out of your way?" Maeve asked.

Forbes opened the door for Maeve without answering. She halted in front of him and looked up. She could feel the pressure of Tom crowding into her space.

Forbes softened his expression when their eyes met. "Please, Ms. Malloy, watch your back."

Forbes led them to the building exit with Everett bringing up the rear. Maeve looked for open doors to peek into, for klatches of employees gathered in the hallway, but saw no one. As they progressed through beige corridors intersecting with more beige corridors, Maeve noticed a fragrance. Gardenia, the cloying scent Jerri, Turner's secretary, wore.

When they were on the street, Maeve looked over her shoulder to make sure Forbes and Everett were truly gone, then said to Tom, "They have two informants."

CHAPTER TWENTY-THREE

Law Office of Maeve Malloy

W ho, other than Saturday morning cartoons, names their
business "Acme"?

Maeve stared at the computer screen incredulously as she
surfed through page after page of Acme companies. A lot of
people, that's who.

To one particular person who wanted his corporation
hidden in the internet's super-highway, Acme looked like just
another small-sized gray sedan in the flow of urban rush hour
traffic.

After hours of internet surfing, Maeve found the Acme
company Josh had told her about, incorporated in Delaware.
The president and sole shareholder was Andrew Turner.

Shift. Print.

Half an hour later, Maeve had found the name of Andrew
Turner's former father-in-law, Senator Theodore Roberts, and
Boston news site stories about the corruption scandal. Little
was said about Andrew Turner himself, a mere footnote in the
drama. Having not been charged, the news sites wouldn't name
him, even tangentially, concerned with libel exposure.

But even the most careful editors would identify the accused with the liberal use of the word "alleged." Turner's former
partner in Boston, Randolph Thorndike, was so named. Now
that Maeve had his name, she jumped onto the federal court system's database and found the case.

The indictment recited a laundry list of acts attributed to

the conspiracy to commit mail fraud. The easiest way to get any kind of theft crime into federal court was to plead mail fraud. As long as there was some kind of fraud perpetuated by telephone, cell phone, internet or the mail, there was mail fraud, and, ergo, federal jurisdiction. Otherwise all those same acts gave rise to theft crimes in state jurisdictions. Why the U.S. Attorneys wanted to pursue one case rather than another in federal court was usually a mystery, but, as a general rule, they could be counted on to prosecute a senator.

Andrew Turner's father-in-law was one such senator.

The indictment alleged that Senator Roberts and Randolph Thorndike had conspired to bilk a federal contract for bogus fees and services. Thorndike got the contracts. Senator Roberts got the kickbacks.

While the indictment printed, Maeve cruised through the index for telltale signs of a defendant copping a deal. In a multiple defendant case, the U.S. Attorney didn't disclose the fact that one defendant was turning on another until the last possible minute before trial, but the evidence was there if you knew what to look for.

Ex parte hearings. "Ex parte" meant "one-sided," meant not everyone was invited. Indeed, there was one such hearing in the case of *United States vs. Roberts and Thorndike.*

Defendant number two, Thorndike, was in an ex parte hearing two weeks before the scheduled trial date. Defendant number one, Senator Roberts, had a change of plea hearing scheduled for the day before trial, but it never took place. Instead, Roberts' hearing was mysteriously canceled on the same day that the charges were dismissed.

Turner had said that Thorndike went to jail. But he couldn't have because the court file said the case had been dismissed.

She searched the internet for Randolph Thorndike. That was when she found the obituary. The cause of death wasn't specified, but the obit said he'd died at home. Suicide? Sure sounded like it.

⚜⚜⚜

Five p.m.
Alaska Bar Association

Maeve and Tom sat in the hallway outside the conference room like pigeons on a telephone line. Wearing her black skirted suit and cream silk blouse, Maeve sat with her knees glued together and hands folded in her lap. Her inner thighs ached from so much propriety.

The bar hadn't called to cancel the hearing, so Maeve had no idea if Royce had done as he promised and dropped the complaint. She couldn't ask Arthur because he didn't know about the meeting with Royce. So here they sat.

Tom gnawed on a toothpick. He took it out, flicked it into a nearby trash can, and before it tinkled out of sight, he had a new toothpick jabbed into his mouth.

The conference room door opened. Arthur stepped out. He snapped the drape of his silver-gray suit jacket into place, then slipped one button closed. "They're ready for us."

Maeve stood. She looked around for her briefcase. It wasn't there. She'd intentionally left it at the office. She wasn't the advocate today, she was the accused. Her hands fluttered uselessly at her side.

She looked at Tom. This could be the end. She could go into that room a lawyer and come out a no-one with nothing to do and no reason to get up in the morning. With no reason to call Tom and get him out of bed.

"One day at a time, Counselor," Tom said, as if reading her thoughts.

She inhaled deeply and stepped past Arthur into a room filled by an immense conference table. All the seats but three were taken by men and women in suits, a neat stack of papers before each.

Maeve didn't recognize anyone. The bar association's

board was made up of big firm attorneys she hadn't met, and non-attorney citizens she didn't know, all appointed by the governor. The only citizens she knew were defendants, witnesses, and alcoholics. It suddenly struck Maeve that she had a limited social life.

She tasted metal as adrenalin flooded her system and her heart raced. Fight or flight? Neither, she told herself. Sit through it and take the beating.

Arthur led Maeve to an open chair and sat beside her. A third vacant chair was across from them. The witness stand.

Maeve settled, folding her hands in her lap as the nuns had taught her ladies should do. She crossed her legs at the ankle.

"We're on record in the case of Maeve Artemis Malloy, attorney licensed in the state of Alaska." The stocky middle-aged man at the head of the table identified himself as the chair and then continued.

Maeve's ears buzzed so loudly she didn't catch his name.

"The members have a copy of the allegations. Briefly, Ms. Malloy is accused of violating Alaska Rule of Professional Conduct 3.3(b), to wit: A lawyer who represents a client in an adjudicative proceeding and who knows that a person, including the lawyer's client, intends to engage, is engaging, or has engaged in criminal or fraudulent conduct related to the proceeding shall take reasonable and timely remedial measures, including, if necessary, disclosure to the tribunal."

The chair paused and took a sip of water. "The allegations are that Ms. Malloy was representing one Filippo Mataafa in a criminal trial when her investigator learned that his alibi witness was untruthful. Her investigator had placed a note in Ms. Malloy's file to inform her of such. Ms. Malloy claims she did not see the note before putting the witness on the stand whose testimony resulted in an acquittal.

"Following the acquittal, Ms. Malloy discovered the note and failed to inform the court of what she had learned. For our non-attorney members, I should point out that double jeopardy had attached and the defendant, having been acquitted, could not be retried. Regardless, it is the bar's position that in the discharge of Ms. Malloy's ethical obligations, she should have notified the court of the note when she discovered it."

As the chair read the charges, Maeve scanned the room again. Most of the faces looking back at her were set in veils of tension, but there were a few pairs of sympathetic eyes and one weak smile.

Maeve stole a look at Arthur. He smiled and patted her on the shoulder. It was the exact same act of reassurance she performed for all her clients in court, the ones who went free as well as the ones who went to jail, the innocent and the guilty alike.

The chair turned the page he read over, nodded to a secretary seated away from the table stationed by the door. "Our first witness is Addison Royce, the public defender for the state of Alaska."

The secretary stood, opened the door and beckoned. Royce stepped inside, broad-shouldered in a navy blazer, his fine, blond hair neatly trimmed and combed.

"The formal rules of court do not apply to this proceeding, Mr. Royce," the chair said, "so please explain to us the facts as you know them."

"Thank you, Mr. Chair." Royce avoided eye contact with Maeve. Instead, he turned ever so slightly away from Maeve as he spoke. Why was he testifying when he promised to drop the complaint? All he had to do was not show up. The bar wouldn't have gone forward without him.

Because he was still trying to run her out of town, that's why.

"Ms. Malloy was one of my trial attorneys and had been with the office for quite a while. Last year, she was assigned to defend Filippo Mataafa, a man accused of armed robbery arising from a gas station hold-up. Mataafa claimed he had an alibi and produced a witness, Enrique Jones. Both Mataafa and Jones testified at trial establishing the alibi and Mataafa was acquitted.

"Ms. Malloy's investigator, Thomas Sinclair, discovered

the alibi was perjured and left a note clipped to the top of the file where she could see it the morning before she put Mr. Mataafa and Mr. Jones on the stand."

"Why didn't he tell her personally, Mr. Royce?" asked a young male attorney. Red-haired and cleanly shaven, he wore a pinstripe suit and yellow tie, the big firm uniform.

"He only discovered the truth the night before and was on his way out to Bethel on another case," Royce answered. "So he clipped the note where it could be seen in plain sight."

"Didn't he try to call her?" he asked.

"Her phone was turned off."

"Did anyone make any effort at all to alert her to the note?" The question came from a suited female who looked like a teenager. Very straight brown hair was chopped off at her chin line and held away from her face with a tortoise shell barrette. The frown she wore looked like a mask affected to give herself an air of gravitas.

"I'm not aware of any efforts," Royce said.

"What exactly did the note say?" Barrette Woman asked.

The chair cleared his throat. "You'll find the note in your packet attached as exhibit one."

The suits rummaged through their packets. No one spoke as they settled on the page.

Arthur ignored the documents in front of him. He had seen the note often enough preparing for the hearing, as had Maeve, and they didn't need to look at it again.

"I can't read this," said an older woman in a dowdy brown suit. Behind rimless glasses were heavy bags under red-rimmed eyes.

Several mumbled in assent. A few shook their heads.

"If I may," Royce said. "The note reads 'alibi N.G.'"

"That's it?" the woman asked.

"That's it."

"And it's your belief that this undated, unsigned, vague note scrawled and stuck in a file should have alerted Ms. Malloy that the defendant and his witness were untruthful," Dowdy

Brown Suit said.

Arthur leaned back in his chair.

Royce's neck twitched. "That note should have alerted Ms. Malloy that there was a problem with the alibi evidence. However, unbeknownst to me at the time, Ms. Malloy was suffering from a drinking problem, so she didn't review the file closely. She entered alcohol rehabilitation a few days after the Mataafa trial concluded."

"Objection," Maeve heard in her head. She looked around. No one else had heard it. Had this been a criminal trial, that evidence would have been inadmissible and worth fighting. Maeve looked at Arthur. He was placid, serene even. This wasn't a criminal trial. Everything and anything was admissible.

Every word Royce had spoken was true. But it wasn't the whole truth. He had left out the part where he knew the alibi was perjured when he assigned the case to Maeve.

There was a perceptible shift in the room's energy. Those who had been challenging Royce sagged into their chairs. No longer were there sympathetic looks or even weak smiles. Every man and woman in the room refused eye contact with Maeve.

She forced back her tears, but her nose began to run. A dead giveaway that she was on the verge of crying, that runny nose of hers. If she sniffed, they'd know she was emotional. If she didn't sniff, it would drip on her blouse. She wiped her nose in a delicate move, trying not to attract attention.

Maeve hadn't told Arthur about the Jones snitch deal. Arthur knew nothing about Royce's participation in it, so he didn't have that material to cross-examine Royce. He might not have used it anyway because the evidence was thin and circumstantial. Royce could deny it and it would look like a baseless attempt to smear the complaining witness. Never a good strategy.

"If there are no more questions for Mr. Royce, he may be excused," the chair said. "Our next witness is Assistant District Attorney Jefferson Bennett."

Bennett? Bennett had been her adversary in half her trials.

It was he who unjustly prosecuted Ollie Olafson, a trial she won just a few months ago despite having only three weeks to prepare. She had convinced the jury Bennett's investigation was sloppy. Not only that, she had caught him hiding evidence and when she brought this to the judge's attention, Bennett had been found in contempt of court.

Bennett shouldered past Royce without acknowledgement.

Arthur flicked a piece of lint off the file on the conference table.

"Mr. Bennett," the chair said, "was the prosecutor in the case of *State vs. Filippo Mataafa* and he's agreed to speak with us. Could you explain to the board, Mr. Bennett, when you first learned that Mr. Mataafa's alibi was untruthful testimony."

"I always knew."

The clatter inside Maeve's head was like a car crash. From the corner of her eye, she saw a flurry of motion down the table as the suits threw down pens and adjusted their positions.

"We're not all criminal attorneys, Mr. Bennett," said the chair. "In fact, several board members are non-lawyers from the community. Please explain to us the process by which you learned the alibi testimony was untruthful."

Bennett turned to the board just as Royce had, just like any trained witness would. "When a defendant in a criminal case claims he has an alibi, his attorney is required to give the prosecution written notice. Ms. Malloy filed and served her written alibi notice timely as required by the rules. When I received the notice, I assigned a member of the Anchorage police department to investigate the facts alleged in the alibi and the witness involved. Well before the trial, I learned the alibi was untruthful and the alibi witness was in fact in another place with other people at the time of the gas station robbery."

"Did you disclose this information to Ms. Malloy?" the chair asked.

"I did not."

"Why not?"

"I'm not at liberty to disclose prosecutorial deliberations."

"What's that mean?" a previously quiet man asked. "I'm not a lawyer, I don't understand."

"There are certain things which the district attorney of the state of Alaska is privileged from disclosing at any time to any person, due to the sensitivity of the information," Bennett responded. "Disclosure can endanger ongoing investigations or persons."

The car crash in Maeve's head settled. She scrawled a note on the legal pad in front of her and slid it over to Arthur. It said: *snitch.*

Arthur read the note and nodded.

"Mr. Bennett," Arthur said. "Was the alibi witness, Enrique Jones, cooperating with the state in any way?"

"I'm not at liberty to discuss that."

"Is that not something you were obliged to disclose to Ms. Malloy during the course of the Mataafa case?"

"That is not my interpretation of the law."

"That may be, Mr. Bennett, but you can agree that the United States Supreme Court ruled in *Davis vs. Alaska* that evidence of a witness' relationship with the prosecution's office must be disclosed as it may affect the witness' bias."

"That case was a different set of facts."

"Mr. Bennett, did you cross-examine Mr. Jones?"

"I did not."

Maeve had never understood why Bennett waived cross-examination of Jones until today. Now it made sense. He hadn't wanted to blow Jones's cover.

"And you failed to cross-examine Mr. Jones because you were concerned he might blurt out his relationship with the state?"

"As I said, I'm unable to disclose whether he had a relationship with the state, so I cannot answer your question."

"Your silence speaks volumes, Mr. Bennett," Arthur said. "I think we all understand what's going on here. One more question. In the course of your ethical obligation to the court, did you at any time disclose to the court or counsel that you knew the alibi testimony was untruthful?"

Bennett took a beat before answering. His voice was deep and strong when he did. "No, sir, I did not."

"The bar association has no further witnesses," the chair said. "Does Ms. Malloy wish to call any?"

"No, thank you, Mr. Chair, we do not," Arthur said.

Maeve was expecting Arthur to call Tom. As did Tom, which is why he had dressed up and why he was sitting in the hallway outside. With Bennett's testimony, Tom had nothing new or different to add in the way of information. And in terms of endearing himself or Maeve to the board members, Tom would not be useful. Charming he was not. Just as well Arthur had decided not to call him.

"In that case, the evidence is closed," the chair said. "I don't need to repeat the allegations. I think the board members understand the case. Mr. Nelson, is there something you wish to say?"

"Yes, indeed, Mr. Chair, thank you for the opportunity," Arthur said in his famous baritone. "Ladies and gentlemen, I had the honor of mentoring Maeve Malloy this past year and it is with firm conviction that I tell you that she is a gifted and devoted criminal defense attorney. Last year, she accepted representation in a murder case merely three weeks before it went to trial following the unfortunate demise of the defendant's previous attorney, Frank Delgado."

Arthur paused while the board members called into memory Frank's suicide. He had been a drunk, not a recovering alcoholic, and had continued to drink despite warnings from the same board she was facing now. Once a familiar face in the bars after hours, he had started coming to court inebriated. Then, he quit showing up altogether. Instead, he'd call from his home, drunk. Then, one day, he didn't call. He had shot himself in the head.

There but for the grace of God go I, Maeve thought.

"Ms. Malloy performed an exemplary job defending Mr. Olafson. Not just exemplary, but stellar. In the course of three short weeks, she was ready for trial and was ultimately successful in persuading the judge to dismiss the case mid-trial. A Herculean feat, let me assure you. She not only uncovered the evidence of her client's innocence, but she found the true murderer and he was arrested. Because of her, an innocent man went free. Because of her, society is protected from further violence at the hands of a serial murderer.

"The misjudgment of which she is accused was a minor transgression. Had she disclosed the untruthful testimony when she learned of it after the acquittal, nothing could have, or would have, been done. Mataafa could not have been retried because of double jeopardy. Jones would not have been brought to justice because the state could not prosecute either Mataafa or Jones for perjury without revealing Jones' role as a confidential informant.

Arthur's voice rose. "But that is not all I wish you to focus upon. Ms. Malloy is accused of violating her duty to the court because she didn't disclose the untruthful testimony after she learned of it, after the acquittal, after nothing could have been done. However, Jefferson Bennett, the D.A. who prosecuted the case, is not so charged despite the fact he knew before Jones took the stand that his testimony would be untruthful and he chose not to cross-examine in order to protect Jones' status as a confidential informant.

"I urge you to consider what is just and fair as you contemplate Ms. Malloy's future. Thank you."

Maeve felt surge of another new emotion. She must be up to five, no six, emotions now: fear, anger, happy, sad, shame, and what? This was what it felt like when someone believed in you. This was what it felt like when someone fought for you.

Maeve had never had a champion growing up. Her parents, absorbed in their own pursuits, treated her like a little adult. Her mother abandoned the family, expecting Maeve to take care of her father. And her father was too crippled by his own alcoholism to be the parent.

The emotion she was feeling towards Art was gratitude. She wiped her eyes with the palm of her hand.

"Thank you, Mr. Nelson," the chair said. "We'll take the matter under advisement."

❦❦❦

"What happened?" Tom spun around as Maeve and Arthur stepped out of the conference room.

"They will deliberate and mail out a written decision," Arthur said. "The process can take a few days or a few weeks. It's late. Maeve, will you be alright going home?"

"She's riding with me," Tom said.

"In that case, I'll bid you a good night." Arthur kissed Maeve on the top of the head and headed for the elevators.

"Bennett practically admitted Enrique Jones was a snitch," Maeve said.

Tom put on a blank face. He wasn't telling everything he knew.

Maeve stared at him, trying to telepathically tap into his mind. All she got back was what she already knew. Enrique Jones was a snitch and had lied about Mataafa's alibi. Someone murdered Ana Olrun. Someone murdered Esther Fancyboy. Esther was a whistle-blower. Everyone was looking for the missing data.

Maeve checked her watch. If she found the thumb drive, she'd find out why it was so important. It was too late to drop in on Cora to search her home. And she didn't want Evan distressed any more than he already was.

Another thing she knew was that everyone who was looking for that thumb drive had an alibi, just like Filippo Mataafa had.

"We need to double check everyone's stories for the night Esther Fancyboy disappeared. Someone's lying."

CHAPTER TWENTY-FOUR

8 p.m.
Xander George's home

X ander George's home was ordinary, surprisingly so. On the drive through dark, snowy streets, Maeve had envisioned a house as impressive as his office. Instead, she stood in front of an ordinary split entry with a sagging roof exactly like hundreds of houses that had been thrown up during the 1970's oil boom.

Maeve rang the bell. She was alone. When they left the hearing, she and Tom agreed to split up so as to cover more territory faster.

A teenage boy opened the door. He was a younger, taller version of Xander in baggy t-shirt and jeans. Fog billowed around Maeve as warm air rushed out of the house.

"Yeah?"

"I'd like to speak with Xander George," Maeve said.

"Dad, there's some white lady at the door for you," the kid yelled over his shoulder.

Having come straight from the bar association, Maeve was still dressed in a suit and dress coat, stylish but not warm. Freezing air worked its way up her skirt.

The kid watched Maeve, unaffected by the temperature.

Xander appeared at the door. The kid staked a position just behind him. Xander and the kid stared at her.

"Mr. George, you said that after Starring, you came home with your family."

"Yes."

"What's going on, Dad?" the kid asked.

Xander raised a hand to quiet him.

"I need to speak to your wife to corroborate that information, if I may."

Xander turned to his son and gestured. The kid disappeared and came back a few moments later with a short thin Yup'ik woman. She blinked at Xander.

"Are you Mrs. George?" Maeve asked.

"This is my wife," Xander answered.

"Mrs. George, can you tell us if Mr. George came home with you after Starring and stayed the whole night here?"

Mrs. George looked up at her husband as he stared at Maeve. Mrs. George shrugged.

Xander said, "Her answer is yes." With that, he closed the door.

⚡⚡⚡

Aurora Bingo Parlor

"Dude!" Igor said as Tom approached.

"Tom."

"Whatever. Playing bingo tonight?"

Tom shook his head.

"Wanna buy some pull-tabs?"

Tom shook his head again.

A middle-aged man who looked like he didn't have money to spare laid a twenty-dollar bill on the countertop and dug through a jar of pull-tabs. He dug out four small cardboard slips, ripped them open one at a time, threw them on the counter, and shuffled away.

"Bummer," Igor called after him. "Better luck next time."

Tom waited as the loser wandered out of earshot.

"About Buddy," Tom said.

"What about Buddy?"

"Remember you said you were with him the night Esther Fancyboy disappeared?"

"Yeah, *Magic of Merlin* at the comic book store. What of it?"

"Is there any way you can corroborate that?"

"Like how?"

"Like did you buy anything that night? Or did you stop off to buy cigarettes somewhere? Or did either of you talk to someone on the phone?"

Igor's face scrunched as he appeared to search his memory. "No, man, nada. You know how it is when you get to playing. Next thing you know it's two in the morning."

Magic of Merlin? Tom had no idea what that was, but he knew what it was like to stay up all night playing poker. Your entire universe is the table. You don't notice people coming and going. Night becomes morning and if you're lucky, you have enough money left for breakfast.

"Give me a call if you think of something."

"Sure thing, dude."

⚡⚡⚡

Wednesday morning January 22
Law Office of Maeve Malloy

Jerri sprawled cat-like in the visitor's chair across the desk from Maeve. When she crossed her legs, the side-split skirt opened, revealing a well-toned bronze thigh.

Tom, standing in the doorway, noticed. When Maeve caught his eye, he threw his hands up.

Jerri's gardenia perfume dominated the room. The same perfume she had worn when they met her at Turner International. The same perfume that had lingered at the F.B.I. office.

"Thanks so much for agreeing to meet with us, Jerri," Maeve said. "How's the job hunt coming along?"

"Not worried, really. I can find a job when I want one."

Jerri shook out her blond hair.

"It's come to our attention you've been talking to the F.B.I.," Maeve said.

"Who told you?"

"It doesn't matter. What matters is that you have information that might be helpful to us."

"I thought you were looking for Esther Fancyboy. You found her. What could you possibly need from me?"

"For openers, what can you tell us about Andrew Turner?"

"Andy?" Jerri's face bloomed into a toothpaste-ad smile. It was a smile that had been practiced in a mirror, eyes wide as her lips drew back to reveal gleaming white teeth.

She did have amazing teeth. They must have cost a fortune.

"Andy is not what he seems," Jerri continued. "Nice clothes, expensive haircut, expensive car. And he's broke."

"He mentioned having cash flow difficulties when problems arose with the Neqa water project."

"Oh, no, he was broke long before that. His business back east went bankrupt, his partner went to prison, and Andy's first wife took whatever was left in the divorce. He was living on credit cards when he came up here. You saw the business. No employees, just me. Nothing happening. The only phone calls are from creditors."

"He told you that the partner went to prison?"

"That's what I said."

"What do you know about his problems back east?" Maeve asked.

"His ex-father-in-law was a big politician. There was some corruption scandal but Andy skated out of it because he didn't handle the books. His partner did all the bookkeeping. Very smart of Andy. When the feds raided the business, good old Andy wasn't where he was supposed to be. He'd told everyone he was out on a job, but he was really in some fancy hotel room with Stephie." Jerri paused. "You know, Stephie? The new wife?"

"Where'd she come from?"

"She was his receptionist!"

It was then Maeve realized how much Jerri resembled Stephie. The long blonde hair, the tight-fitting clothes, the legs-up-to-here, the stiletto heels, the eyelashes. Only Jerri was slightly younger and firmer. Andrew Turner was attracted to a certain type of woman not often seen in Alaska, glamorous blondes.

Maeve softened her voice. "Did Andy make you any promises?"

"He said Stephie was a shrew." Jerri whipped her hair back. "Well, he was right about that. And he said he'd divorce her, he was just waiting for the right time."

"When was the right time?"

"That's what I wanted to know. It was always some excuse. Work, the holidays, whatever. So I started reading his mail."

Maeve felt her eyebrows rise.

"I'm the receptionist, you know. I open all the mail. That's how I found out he's broke. Then the creditors started calling."

"Do you have any idea what happened to the money?"

"All I know is he hasn't paid any of his bills. The Mercedes is leased. The dealership kept calling, they wanted it back. He's behind in the office rent and his credit cards. Lying bastard."

"One more question. Were you talking to the F.B.I. before they searched Turner International?"

Jerri stood, shrugged on a full length ivory-colored wool coat, and paused on her way out the door. "I just want everyone to know I had nothing to do with what's going on."

A long moment passed in silence as Jerri's perfume dissipated.

Tom flopped in the chair Jerri had vacated. "Man, the first rule is don't dip your quill in the company ink. The second rule, don't tell your darkest secrets to the woman you're lying to. Hell hath no fury..." Tom started the quote before he noticed the expression on Maeve's face.

He pulled himself upright. "What's next, Counselor?"

⚜⚜⚜

A split-second of white screen as the monitor refreshed. An index of federal cases sharpened into view.

"Got it."

The aroma of baking pizza filled the office from the restaurant downstairs.

"You hungry yet?" Tom asked.

"It's not even eleven," Maeve responded without shifting her eyes from the computer monitor. If she did lose her practice, the upside would be salvation from the constant allure of pizza.

George W. Phillips. Maeve wrote down the name of the attorney who represented Randolph Thorndike in the Boston case. She found his phone number on line and called it. Her stomach began to rumble while the phone rang.

"Law office," a man answered, sounding irritated by the interruption.

"Mr. Phillips, this is Maeve Malloy. I'm an attorney in Anchorage, Alaska, working on a case involving Andrew Turner. Can I put you on speaker?"

Maeve explained why Andrew Turner was interesting to her, adding, "I found Randolph Thorndike's obituary. The newspaper didn't give a cause of death, which made me think it might have been suicide."

"Suicide? No way. He didn't have any reason to feel guilty. Sure, he lost everything he had but he could have started over. My client wouldn't have been caught up in that whole mess if it hadn't been for Andrew Turner. Turner's smart, you got to give him that. He made sure he wasn't around when the senator's gazebo was built and he stuck Randy with managing the project. Randy had no choice but to take a deal and cooperate."

"He was going to testify against Turner."

"You betcha," Phillips said. "But he died just before the trial. Someone broke into his home and shot him to death."

✻✻✻

Turner International

A thick blanket of silence greeted Maeve and Tom when they entered Turner's reception area. Jerri's desk was vacant.

Andrew Turner waved to them from down the hall, standing in the threshold of his office door. "Thanks for calling ahead," he said. "I'm up to my ears in paperwork and might not have—"

"No receptionist yet?" Maeve asked.

"I have an agency working on it. We start interviewing next week."

Josh the I.T. guy came out of the server room pulling on an oversized parka. "Mr. Turner?

"Did you find them?" Turner asked.

"Sorry, Mr. Turner, I've been all through the files again."

"The corporate reports must be in there somewhere. Where else could Esther have kept them?"

"Did she have a personal computer?" Josh asked, innocently enough.

Turner stumbled for a response. He knew the feds had it, but apparently wasn't willing to let Josh know that he was being investigated.

Josh stole a look at Maeve.

Maeve caught his glance. When she and Tom had met with Josh, they'd agreed to keep up his charade. "We found a laptop at her house, but it had a virus. All the information is gone."

"Then she must have kept a backup. A thumb drive. It's got to be somewhere and it's not in the office." Turner's tone was accusatory. "Maybe she hid it in her condo."

"Someone burglarized Esther's home," Maeve said. "If it was there before, it's gone now."

Josh handed Turner a clipboard. "Can you sign this?"

Turner examined the invoice. "I'm supposed to pay you for finding nothing?"

"I get paid by the hour, Mr. Turner," Josh said. "I'll bill you." He collected his clipboard and side-stepped past Maeve and Tom as he exited.

"I have a question about that case back east you told us about," Maeve said.

Turner ran his hand through his hair. "What's that?"

"I wasn't aware that your partner died before the case came to trial."

"Tragic. Suicide, they said. You can imagine that I don't like to talk about it."

The office phone rang. Turner held up one finger, strode back to his desk and picked it up. "Stephie. I have some visitors here. Ms. Malloy and her investigator. You remember them?" He covered the mouthpiece. "Stephie says hello."

"Great timing, Mr. Turner," Maeve said. "We'd like to speak with Mrs. Turner as well."

Turner looked quizzical, then shrugged. "Did you hear that, darling? Is it alright if I put you on speaker?" He listened again, then punched a button on the console. "Still there?"

"Yes, I am," Stephie said in a throaty Hollywood vixen voice.

"We're double checking everyone's whereabouts on the night Esther Fancyboy disappeared. Do you remember that night, Mrs. Turner?" Maeve said in a voice loud enough to be heard through the console's microphone.

"I wouldn't normally, but we've been asked so many times, I do now. It was a Tuesday."

"Yes, that's right."

"Andy came home as he usually does around seven. We had dinner and then spent the evening together."

"Was he home all night?"

"Oh, yes, Ms. Malloy. When Andy comes home, I make sure he has no chance to leave again."

"Pardon?"

"We're newlyweds, Ms. Malloy. Must I explain?"

CHAPTER TWENTY-FIVE

The Comic Book Store

T om skidded across the icy parking lot in front of a former carwash recently remodeled into a comic book store.

Inside, he stopped and scanned his surroundings. Stuff everywhere. Running all the way to the back of the shop were display racks. A grown man in a superhero costume thumbed through a comic book display, deep in thought.

To the left was the checkout counter. To the right, display racks on a wall. From floor to ceiling there were comic books, boxed games, and action figures. Above the counter, what appeared to be genuine Japanese swords. What Japanese swords had to do with comic books, Tom didn't know.

Behind the counter a skinny young man with a serious look and a peach fuzz beard covering acne tabulated something.

Tom edged around the center display rack and planted himself before the kid, who kept staring at the papers in front of him.

Tom rapped his knuckles on the glass top.

Peach Fuzz looked up, frown intact. "Need something?"

"Need to find out about these games you guys play here," Tom said.

Peach Fuzz pointed to a rack on the counter, keeping his other hand splayed across his paperwork. "Schedule's over there." He went back to his task.

Tom slipped a sheet of paper from the rack and examined it. Mondays: comic book trading. Tuesdays: card trading. Wednesdays: new comic day. Thursdays: *Magic of Merlin*.

"Wait," Tom said. Peach Fuzz's head jerked up, his frown deepening.

"Is this the schedule you had since New Year's?" Tom asked.

"Winter schedule, dude," Peach Fuzz said. "Says so on top. We've had that schedule since Labor Day."

"What's this card trading on Tuesdays? That got anything to do with *Magic of Merlin*?"

The kid huffed. Tom was showing his age and extreme uncoolness. "Nothing, dude. Two whole different things."

"You seen a guy named Buddy Halcro come in here on Tuesday nights?"

The kid looked blank.

"Scrawny, five ten or so, reeks of beer."

The kid still looked blank.

"What about Igor? You can't miss him."

"Cards not his thing. He's strictly *M.O.M.* Thursdays. He only comes in on Thursdays."

ŧŧŧ

4 p.m.
Esther Fancyboy's condo

"What time does Evan come home from school?" Maeve asked as she hung her coat on a peg by the front door.

"Soon," Cora answered.

The condo smelled of freshly baked chocolate chip cookies. From the foyer, Maeve spied a plate cooling on the kitchen counter. It had been a long, long time since she ate a chocolate chip cookie.

Cora noticed Maeve looking at them. "For Evan," Cora said.

Maeve followed Cora to the living room. She had been sitting in her favorite spot on the couch, sewing, the basket at her feet. Maeve scanned the room.

235

Cora looked up at her expectantly.

If the thumb drive had been in that room after the burglary, they would have found it when they were cleaning up. If Esther was hiding a thumb drive in her home, she most likely hid it in some place she didn't expect a lot of people to access. "Do you mind if I look at her room again?"

Cora shrugged and led the way upstairs.

It was just as Maeve had found it before. Bed neatly made. Earring rack with long beaded earrings.

Cora stood in the doorway.

Maeve ran her hands under the mattress. She opened drawers, looked behind them, under them. She scooted the dresser away from the wall, found nothing hidden behind that. She took everything out of the closet, clothes, shoes, shoe boxes. As she put the items back, she looked inside boxes, felt inside the shoes, felt inside pockets.

Forty-five minutes later, the room was put back into order.

"It's got to be here," Maeve said. "Somewhere. Maybe we missed something downstairs."

In the living room, Cora's sewing supplies were in a basket next to the mittens Esther had started. Maeve picked up the basket and mittens to move them so she could search under the sofa. The cuff of one mitten drooped from Maeve's hand as if it was weighted. She fingered the fur trim and found something inside, something hard.

≵≵≵

4:15 p.m.
East Anchorage

Evan shoved his hands into his pockets. Snowflakes had started falling when the bus left his school. By the time it had dropped him off, the flurry had thickened. He couldn't see beyond a few houses when he stepped off the bus.

Evan stood on the sidewalk as the bus edged away. Big flakes landed on his face and stuck to his eyelashes. He flipped up his parka hood and leaned into the wind.

He began the three blocks towards home where he knew Cora waited for him with warm cookies. Evan had chocolate chip cookies for the first time when he started school in Anchorage, and when his grandmother found out he liked them, she learned how to make them. Every day since his mother disappeared, Cora had warm cookies waiting for him.

He'd walked past a few houses when a vehicle drew up beside him and slowed. With his head tucked into his hood, he could only see the tires and body of the car idling slowly beside him.

Evan felt his heart speed up. Last month, a police officer had talked to his class about strangers. You should never get into a car with a stranger. You should have a secret password only known to your parents. If someone said your mother sent him, he needed to know the password.

The vehicle stopped and a window rolled down.

"Waqaa!" the man said.

❦❦❦

With a seam ripper, Cora tore out the stitches sewn into the mitten's lining and the hide. She slipped a thin forefinger inside, dug around, stopped, and frowned. She manipulated the mitten until something small and black squeezed out of the hole she'd made. A thumb drive.

Cora handed it to Maeve.

"Is it okay if I take this?" Maeve asked. "It may be important."

Cora didn't respond. She didn't seem to understand, or care, about the little plastic box. Maeve slipped the thumb drive into her jeans pocket.

Cora stood, went to the window by the front door and

pushed the curtain aside.

"What is it?" Maeve asked.

"Evan is late."

"Maybe he stopped off at another kid's house. Does he walk home with anyone?"

"The girl across the street."

Maeve went out of the house, forgetting her coat and trotted to the house Cora had pointed to, slipping and nearly falling. She rang the bell, huddling to keep warm. The door was opened by a young woman in a t-shirt and pajama bottoms. She looked at Maeve, incredulous to find someone standing on her doorstep coatless in freezing temperatures. "Can I help you?"

"I'm a friend of Cora Fancyboy. Is Evan over here?"

"No, sorry. My little girl stayed home sick from school today."

"Do you know anyone else he might have gone home with?"

"Sorry, it's just those two. Is there something wrong?"

Maeve shuffled as fast as she dared back across the street. Snow crusted on her back and arms. Cora held the door open. As Maeve stepped inside, the cell phone in her coat pocket rang. She shook her head to Cora, Evan wasn't across the street, and answered the call.

"Buddy's alibi fell apart," Tom said.

"Evan's missing. He didn't come home from school. Buddy must've taken him. I'll meet you at his place."

Maeve grabbed her coat and said, "I'll call you as soon as I know something."

As she climbed in her Subaru, the image of Cora in the doorway burned into her mind.

She looked small.

※※※

Tom banged on Buddy's door with his fist. "Open up!"

He turned around to look at the SUV in the driveway. It

was covered in snow, hood included, meaning the engine was cold. That rig hadn't been driven in hours.

Tom pounded on the door again and yelled louder. "Open up!"

The path from the sidewalk to the door was unshoveled, with no fresh prints in the snow. No one had come to the front door in at least a couple of hours.

Maeve's Subaru slid around the corner and stuck in the snow bank in front of the trailer. She got out and shuffle-ran to the stoop while Tom beat on the door.

The door opened. Buddy held a vacuum cleaner in his hand.

"Sorry, man, didn't hear you. I was vacuuming."

"Again?" Tom asked.

Tom was inside the trailer in one giant step. Maeve followed. They were smacked in the face by the stifling heat. Maeve unzipped her coat. Tom stalked down the hall, following the cord, opening doors.

"Hey! What do you think you're doing?"

"Where's Evan?" Maeve demanded.

"With Cora." He jabbed a finger at Maeve's face. "You made sure of that. But my lawyer's getting my kid back."

Maeve's phone rang. She answered.

"You got something I want. And I got something, too, or should I say someone," Andrew Turner said. "Photo coming to you now."

The phone clunked, signaling a text message. Maeve opened it up and saw a photo of Evan still in his parka. He was sitting in the passenger seat of a car, looking up at the driver. He didn't look scared. He looked confused.

Just then, Tom came out of a back bedroom carrying a women's black leather jacket.

※

In nearly zero visibility, Maeve dodged cars sliding out of control as she sped to her office to meet Andrew Turner. Tom followed just close enough to keep in sight.

"How do we know he'll bring Evan?" Tom's voice came across the cell phone Maeve held in one hand as she drove with the other.

"Got a better idea?" Maeve yelled back.

A repeating loop of information circled through Maeve's mind as she wished herself a few minutes into a future where Evan was safe.

Esther was murdered. Ana was murdered. Turner's former partner was murdered. Turner had reason to want his partner dead. He was about to testify. Turner stole Neqa's money. Turner had Evan. How far would Turner go?

Maeve sped up as the stoplight turned from yellow to red. The car next to her stopped. The car behind crashed into it and fished tailed across the road. Maeve stared in the rearview mirror, willing Tom to avoid the accident. Tom drove his truck onto the median and around the second car now spinning out of control.

Maeve lost traction, sliding as she approached the next intersection. She was halfway through when a sporty economy car came from the right. The eyes of the driver, a teenage girl, were wide as she braced her arms.

The impact lifted the Subaru onto the left tires. It hung in the air soundlessly. Maeve watched the earth fall away as if she was on a Ferris wheel ride.

The Subaru slammed back to earth and bounced on the road several times before it stopped.

The crash caved in the passenger door. Bits of shattered glass pelted Maeve's face. Maeve squeezed her eyes shut and held on tighter.

Maeve heard Tom's voice. "Are you okay?" She looked at her left hand, where the cell had been, now wrapped tightly around the steering wheel, knuckles white. The cell was gone.

"Are you okay?" she heard again. Tom was at the driver window. She must have lost time. She didn't see him get out of his truck.

Maeve pushed the seatbelt release and jerked the strap. It was jammed. "I can't get out." She heard panic in her own voice.

Tom wrenched the door open. He pulled a hunting knife out of his jeans pocket, and he cut the straps as she leaned away from the blade.

When her feet hit the ground, her knees gave way. Tom caught her.

"I'm okay," Maeve said.

Across the street, the teenager was out of her car, crying. Her passenger, another crying teenage girl, tried to dial a cell phone with shaky hands.

The Subaru lay on its belly with tires splayed apart. "Axle's broke. Ain't going nowhere," Tom said.

He steered Maeve to his truck and opened the passenger door. "Get in."

"Hey, wait a minute, she can't leave!" one of the teenagers yelled.

He pulled his business card out of his wallet and strode over to her so fast that she jumped back. He handed the girl his card. "Cops. Call them. Now."

The girl's mouth hung open as she stared at him.

"Now!" Tom shouted.

CHAPTER TWENTY-SIX

There were no cars in the parking lot behind Maeve's office. As they'd planned on the way over, Maeve went straight into the office building while Tom parked in back and circled the block on foot.

The building's front door swung open easily. Maeve took the steps two at a time, her lungs starved for oxygen. There was pain in her side.

Her office door was locked, as she expected. There was no way Turner could have gotten a set of keys to the office and nowhere did she see breaking and entering in his resume. Her hands shaking, she dug a key out of her jeans pocket and unlocked the door.

As she stepped inside, she saw Turner and Evan standing in her inner office. Turner gripped Evan's shoulders, keeping him from running to Maeve.

A dark figure came from behind the door with an arm rising towards Maeve. Maeve stepped in and smashed the arm upwards. She snapped her elbow into the intruder's face then smashed her foot down on the instep.

A scream split the air. The intruder grabbed Maeve's hair and jerked her head back. Maeve dropped her chin down and stepped away. The fist let go. Maeve grabbed the attacker's hand, turned it upwards, grinding the wrist bones. Something metallic fell from the hand, bouncing off Maeve's outstretched arm, and clattered to the floor.

Her opponent twisted but Maeve held on. Maeve smashed the other's face into the wall. She tore the black balaclava off and a river of blonde hair cascaded into her face, threatening to smother her. She wrenched the arm up the attacker's back, feeling tendons tear as she did, then pressed her knee into the spine and gripped the flying blonde hair in her other hand as they fell to the floor.

A moment passed in stunned silence.

The blonde writhed under Maeve. "Get off me, bitch."

The door slammed open and Tom slid in. He looked at Maeve straddling a snarling Stephie Turner. "What the...?"

Turner let Evan go and tried to rush past Tom. Tom turned, his shoulders blocking the doorway. "Don't even."

Turner backed off, looking around the room for another escape route. There was none.

Tom pointed to Maeve's arm. "You're bleeding."

Red streams trickled from several nicks on Maeve's forearm where the knife had bounced. She didn't feel pain from the cuts, only warmth oozing down her arm. She nodded at the knife.

Tom picked it up, closed the blade, and dropped it in his pocket.

≀≀≀

As the sun crested the Chugach mountain range, the mirrored siding of the D.A.'s building across the street turned amber and the sky behind it lightened to violet blue.

Maeve's mind was still for the first time in days as she watched the building and sky change hue. Her swivel chair was pushed away from her desk. Her hands were wrapped around a mug of coffee.

One needle of light suddenly flared as it struck the amber glass and bounced, making the frosty web on Maeve's window glow.

"Knock, knock," Special Agent Forbes said from her threshold.

Maeve stared at the window's frost crystals a moment

243

longer, trying to memorize the pattern. The flare disappeared. And the frost became ordinary again.

Maeve sighed. The pain in her side felt like a knife.

She turned to Forbes. He was standing patiently, watching her, waiting until she was ready. Everett lingered behind his shoulder, looking twitchy.

"Come in, gentlemen," Maeve said.

"Did you go home at all last night?" Forbes asked.

Maeve shook her head. After the police had arrested Turner and interviewed all the witnesses, there was no point.

Despite the leaden feeling in her gut, she was wound up all night. She and Tom had stayed in the office after Margaret and Cora had picked up Evan. One moment she was pacing around the office, moving stacks of paper from one place to another and back again. The next moment, she collapsed on the couch.

A couple of hours later, the jabbing pain in her side woke her. She was lying under a pile of coats, hers and Tom's. He must have covered her up after she fell asleep. He was sleeping in her swivel chair, feet on her desk, head dropped back. His snores sounded like a lion's purrs.

She turned over to sleep some more. The second time she woke, it was to the smell of brewing coffee. When she pushed herself up, she found Tom sitting at her desk, watching her. He scrubbed his face with his hands. "How's the side feeling?"

"Fine, probably just a strain," Maeve said. "It'll go away by itself."

"Yeah, well, if it doesn't, I'm taking you to the emergency room."

Tom was on a bagel run when Forbes and Everett arrived. Maeve looked at Forbes for an explanation, too tired for Maeve-questions-Forbes-doesn't-answer game.

"Got a statement out of Turner," Forbes said. "He folded like a deck of cards. According to Turner, he never meant to hurt Evan. It wasn't like kidnapping, he says, he was just giving Evan a ride home."

Maeve said, "Turner picked Evan up a block from his

house, drove him halfway across town to give him a lift home and then broke into my office? How did he think he'd get away with it?"

"He says he was as surprised as anyone when Stephie attacked you. If things had gone as planned, no one would have found out about them breaking in. They'd read about the Eli Coffer attack last fall. My guess is they figured Coffer would get blamed when your body was found."

"Huge coincidence that he lured me here with a photo of Evan."

"But they would have never gotten caught if Stephie had won that fight. She'd have gotten the thumb drive and Turner would have taken Evan home with a big apology for worrying Cora."

"But Evan saw the whole thing, he could have told everyone what happened."

"According to Turner, that wasn't supposed to happen."

"If I lost the fight, what would they have done to Evan?"

All three fell silent thinking the scenario through. If Maeve had lost the fight, they would have gotten the thumb drive and Evan would have been a witness who needed to be eliminated.

Forbes returned to his story. "Turner suspected Esther was the whistle-blower. He knew she backed up all the files and the thumb drive had to be somewhere. He admitted Stephie broke into Esther's condo twice, searching for it. He swore he had nothing to do with Ana's death. He reneged on Stephie's alibi for the night Ana was killed and he's been doling out hints that he has evidence she killed his partner back in Boston. He's already cut a deal with the U.S. attorney and he's testifying against her."

"Charming guy. So, that was you guys in the black SUV, in the alley and at Starring? Esther was your snitch?"

"Cooperating witness is the term we prefer," Forbes said. "She was supposed to hand over the thumb drive at Starring. When we got there, she said she didn't have time to retrieve it from her hiding place in the condo so she had to go back home. We agreed to meet behind the Last Frontier but she never showed. Apparently, Buddy got her into his car in the parking lot after we left."

Esther hadn't had time to unsew the mitten and dig out the thumb drive because she had stopped at Neqa on the way home. Probably to ask Xander if he had anything to do with the disappearance of the money before she handed the evidence over to the feds, and they ended up making love. Maeve wondered if Esther had ever gotten an answer to her question, or if she had intentionally left the thumb drive at home and never intended to meet the agents later that night because she thought she was protecting Xander.

"So why were you guys staking out Ana's house?"

Forbes looked at her with his not-answering face.

"What? Like I'm supposed to believe a bunch of F.B.I. guys happened to be driving by a residential neighborhood in the early evening in the middle of winter and heard gunshot through the raised windows of their sedan with the heater blowing on high and then hustled over? Of course, you were staking her out."

"We knew Ana was Esther's friend. We spotted her visiting Turner's office after Esther disappeared. As far as we could tell, there wasn't any reason for her to visit Turner unless she was in the middle of something she shouldn't have been. So we kept an eye on her. We didn't see Stephie Turner, she must have hopped over the back fence to break into Ana's condo. That was the way she left. She must have had Andrew's key. Andrew and Ana had a thing going. The rest you know."

CHAPTER TWENTY-SEVEN

February 7th
Holy Ascension Russian Orthodox Church

The church's gold onion dome glowed in the long rays of the setting sun. Men, women, and children, about twenty of them, stood in loose clumps in a field behind the church. A pit had been cleared and enclosed with large rocks. When Maeve and Tom arrived, two large men were filling the pit with tree branches.

Maeve and Tom found Cora and Evan. Evan was wearing Esther's black leather jacket, the one Tom had found in Buddy's trailer. The sleeves were so long they draped off his arms. He hung close to Cora, from time to time burying his face in her kuspuk.

Maeve and Tom drew closer to say hello. The family was standing around a shrunken old lady sitting in a lawnchair wrapped in a fur parka. She wore the mittens Esther had made. "This is my mother, Agatha. She came in from St. Innocent's," Cora said.

"Waqaa," Maeve said. It felt inadequate, but nothing else came to mind.

"Waqaa," the old lady replied.

The family looked at Maeve, waiting for her to say something.

They all smiled and nodded. The moment felt awkward. It seemed they would be more comfortable if she wasn't there. Not that she had offended them, more like they didn't know how to treat her.

Maeve waved to them, nodded at Tom to follow her, and they drifted to the outer circle of the mourners. The men went back to building the kindling as Evan, Cora and Margaret looked on.

As the crowd gathered around the pit, Maeve noticed Sal lumbering in their direction. "How's that rib, Bella?"

She still had a stabbing pain when she inhaled. "Improving," she said. A few days after Andrew and Stephie Turner were arrested, Tom took Maeve to emergency room for the once-over. The doctors found a broken rib, probably from the car wreck.

"So, what's happening here?" Sal asked.

"It's tradition in Cora's village to burn the deceased's clothing thirty days after the death," Maeve said.

"Makes sense, in case of disease," Sal said.

"And avoids arguments over who gets what," Tom said.

Men lit the fire.

"Saw the news the other night," Sal said. "Buddy Halcro got indicted."

"He confessed," Maeve said. "Esther's coat was in Buddy's trailer. He must have killed her there. The police think he confronted Esther in the parking lot outside Starring as she was getting into her car. The F.B.I. had come by the hospital earlier to get the thumb drive from her but she hadn't had time to get it. She told them she'd meet them behind the Last Frontier, their usual meeting place. Buddy had once seen her talking to a man in the dark SUV behind the bar. He saw them talking again at Starring. He figured she was making a date."

"What was he doing in the parking lot?"

"Stalking her," Maeve answered. "Apparently she got into his car to appease him and he took her to his trailer. Forensics prove she was there when she died. She would have taken her coat off the minute she walked in because he kept the trailer so hot for the pot growing operation. The cops found lights and leaf litter in one of the bedrooms. He must have taken it down after Tom visited him the first time. The night Evan was abducted, he was trying to clean up. When we showed up, he was vacuuming."

Tom picked up the story. "So Halcro dumped her body in a snow bank, figuring she wouldn't turn up until break-up. Then he got his buddy, Igor, to help him move the car downtown on Thursday night to make it look like she hooked up with some guy in a bar."

"The mother of his son and this is how he treats her," Sal said.

The flames shot up, crackled and spat out embers. The flash illuminated Evan hiding in the folds of Cora's parka as he gazed into the blaze. One of the men went inside the church and came out carrying a basket of clothes.

"Heard anything from the bar association?" Tom asked.

Maeve slipped her hand into her coat pocket. She pulled an opened envelope out and handed it to Tom.

Maeve stared at the fire while he read. He wrapped one arm around her and hugged her tightly, smashing her face into his bony sternum.

"How long have you known?" he asked.

"A few days."

Margaret picked up a dress from one of the baskets and tossed it onto the flames. The fire devoured it. Gordi threw another dress into the fire. Evan stood apart from Cora now. He looked like a little man, wise beyond his years and utterly alone.

"What's going on?" Sal asked.

"Okay if he reads it?" Tom said, gesturing with the letter.

Maeve nodded.

Evan slipped out of Esther's jacket. He swung the jacket up and let go. The jacket hung in the heated air momentarily. Then, the sleeves inflated and waved as it fluttered down into the fire.

Gordi stepped next to Evan and put a hand on his shoulder.

"Suspended? How is this fair?" Sal said, looking up from the letter. "They set you up. Royce knew about it. Bennett knew about it. Why aren't they getting busted?"

"I was the one in the court room," Maeve said.

"You're not just going to take this, are you?" Sal asked. "Can't you do some lawyer thing like file for reconsideration, or appeal? Something?"

"They make the rules. They interpret the rules. They enforce the rules. If they say I broke the rules, then they're right."

Maeve wrapped both arms around Tom and hugged him hard. It made her rib ache but the warmth felt good. "It's not the end of the world."

Tom leaned back to look into her face. "You sure, Counselor?"

"We're here for you, you know that," Sal said, patting her on the back.

The pain in Maeve's side deepened as Tom pressed her close. She touched her face and found it was wet. What was the name of this emotion? She was a little happy, a little sad, a little tired, a little joyful, and in the middle of that was calm.

Serenity, Maeve decided. This is what serenity feels like.

"Door closes, window opens, guys. Everything is going to be okay."

The group standing around Agatha had stilled. She was speaking. Each man, woman, and child paid close attention. Evan was sitting on Cora's lap.

Maeve disentangled herself from Tom. With one hand, she took his hand and with the other she took Sal's. "Now, shush, I want to hear this," she said as she led them back to the circle.

As Maeve, Tom and Sal grew closer, Agatha switched from speaking Yup'ik to English. She was telling a story.

"A long time ago, the world was covered in darkness. A magician had captured all the light and hidden it in a cedar box in his home. One day, Raven was flying overhead when he saw a stream of light shoot up through the smoke-hole. He flew close and saw the magician's daughter playing with the light. Raven wanted it.

"Raven waited outside the house until the magician's daughter went to the river to collect water. Then he turned himself into a hemlock needle and dropped into her water basket. When the daughter drank the water, she swallowed the hemlock needle. And Raven turned himself into a baby inside the daughter.

"When the baby was born, the magician and his daughter loved him very much. But the baby cried all of the time. He wanted to play with the light inside the box. The magician gave up. He opened the box, took out the ball of light and gave it to the baby Raven.

"Raven turned himself back into a bird and flew straight out the smoke-hole with the light. While he was playing, he dropped the ball and it shattered into one big piece and lots of tiny bits. That is why we have the sun and the stars."

The dying fire crackled and sparks floated on smoke plumes into the night air. Evan, with his family gathered around him, looked peaceful. Maeve remembered something Evan had said to her, that when his mother smiled, it made his heart feel happy. She understood now how he felt.

The End

DEFINITIONS

Akutaq: "Eskimo ice cream." The recipe varies depending on the availability of ingredients in different localities. Traditionally it is made from whale fat, seal oil, and blueberries, and beaten to the consistency of whipped cream.

Break-up: Spring in Alaska. The name comes from the breaking of river ice as it thaws.

Cheechako: Newcomer to Alaska. The term is believed to have evolved during the Gold Rush and is a corruption of "Chicago."

Chinook: "Big." Chinook salmon are king salmon. Chinook winds are fast, hot winds that come over the Chugach range in the winter time.

Kuspuk: A hooded thigh-length coat. Summer kuspuks are made of calico printed cotton and sometimes trimmed in fur and bric-a-brac. Winter kuspuks are lined with down-filled material. The outer material is often velvet and it is also trimmed in fur and bric-a-brac.

Ulu: a crescent shaped knife mounted on a bone handle.

Waqaa: "Hello" in Yup'ik.

AUTHOR'S NOTE

On July 15, 1733, a landing party from the Russian ship *Sv. Pavel* stepped ashore on Prince of Wales island in southeast Alaska and are believed to be the first Europeans to step foot on Alaskan soil. By the time British Capt. James Cook explored Alaska fifty years later in 1778, the Russians had already established a number of colonies up and down the west coast of North America and in Hawaii.

The Russian Empire conferred upon the Russian-American company a monopoly on North America in 1799, the purpose of which was to obtain furs by trading with Native Americans. With the same stroke of a pen, rights were granted to the Russian Orthodox Church. The church had already been established in Alaska and was converting Native Alaskans to orthodox Christianity. The first Natives to be converted were the Aleuts.

In 1840, the first bishop of Alaska, Innocent, was appointed. He was sainted by the Orthodox Church in 1977 and is known as "Enlightener of the Aleuts and Apostle to the Americas."

By the 1850's, sea otters were nearly extinct in Alaska and Russia had just lost the Crimean War to England. Emperor Alexander II decided to sell Russia's interest because of dwindling resources, the difficulty of maintaining colonies at such a distance from Russia and concern that the territory would be lost to England if another war broke out between the two countries. Both the United States and England were approached. England turned down the offer flatly. Negotiations with the United States were delayed by the American Civil War.

In 1867, the United States purchased Alaska from Russia, an event that was ridiculed as "Seward's Folly." Little did those critics know that Alaska had large deposits of gold and oil. By the time of the sale, most of the colonies outside of Alaska had been abandoned by Russia. Although the Russian-American company departed when their interests were sold, the Russian Orthodox religion remained.

The Russian influence can still be detected throughout Alaska in place names, now Anglicized, such as Kodiak, St. Paul, St. George, Diomede Islands, and Andreanof Islands. Russian family names are common, such as Alexie, George, Gregory, Ivanoff, Melovidov, Merculief, Nicolai, Rukovishnikoff, and Stepetin. It is not unusual to meet Native Alaskans who have inherited blonde hair and blue eyes from their Russian ancestors.

Modernly, the Diocese of Alaska of the Orthodox Church of America has churches in rural towns and villages as well as in Anchorage, Alaska's urban hub, where many Native Alaskans, including Yup'ik Eskimos, Alutiiq Eskimos, Aleuts and Tlingits, have relocated.

The Orthodox religion celebrates Christmas on January 7th. In rural Alaska, villagers go from house to house, caroling as they spin large colorful stars. In Anchorage, practitioners gather at the Alaska Native Medical Center to celebrate Starring, a scene which is described in chapter one of this book.

ACKNOWLEDGEMENTS

Thanks to my editor, Francesca Coltrera.

All writers owe so much to their beta readers, who selflessly give of their time and energy. I am humbly grateful to my beta readers, the input of whom was invaluable: Elizabeth Amann, Jean Clarkin, and Jennie LeGate.

And a big thanks to the Spenard Literary Society who suffered with me through the umpteen drafts: Stan Jones, Mary Katzke, Chris Lundgren, and Mary Wasche.

Thanks, too, to the IT guru and author, Glen Klinkhart.

Thanks to the authors who have encouraged and inspired me: Louise Penny, Hank Phillippi Ryan, Hallie Ephron, David Corbett, Charles and Caroline Todd, Cynthia Kuhn, and Ellen Byron.

And thanks to fellow blogging partners at Mysteristas: Peg Brantley, Kait Carson, Becky Clark, Barb Howe, Mia Manansala, Liz Milliron, Pamela Oberg, and Sue Star.

In 2014, I learned about the William F. Deeck-Malice Domestic Grant and applied. The grant is given to an unpublished writer to encourage that person's advancement. The following year, the grant was awarded to Cynthia Kuhn and myself. Receiving the grant was the moment when my dream of seeing this book published became a reality. If you look at the list of recipients on the Malice Domestic website, you recognize the names of many writers who went on to publish. My sincerest thanks to Malice Domestic Board of Directors, the Grants Chair Harriette Sackler, and the grants committee, and my Malice buddies, Bill Starck, and Adolph Falcon.

The Book Passages Mystery Writers Conference in Corte Madera, California, was the most valuable writing conference I've attended, and I want to thank the writers who took the time to mentor me there including Rhys Bowen, David Corbett, Hallie Ephron and Tim Maleeny. A big thanks to the organizers of the conference, Kathryn Petrocelli, Cara Black and David Corbett.

And to Level Best Books, Harriette Sackler, Verena Rose, Shawn Reilly Simmons, I owe gratitude beyond measure.

Lastly, I want to thank my family, Rory and Hardy Bryant, for their support. Without them, I would not be here.

Born in Roswell, New Mexico, several years after certain out-of-towners visited, Keenan Powell, the daughter of an Air Force pilot, grew up moving from base to base.

The family ultimately settled in northern California where she obtained a Bachelor's of Arts in Broadcast Communication Arts from San Francisco State University and a Juris Doctorate from McGeorge School of Law. One summer during law school, she visited a friend in Anchorage, Alaska. Upon stepping off the plane, she picked the next place to go. The day after graduation, she moved to Anchorage.

Her first artistic endeavor was drawing, which led to illustrating the original *Dungeons and Dragons* (known as *Original Dungeons and Dragons*) when still in high school.
A past winner of the William F. Deeck-Malice Domestic Grant, her publications include "Criminal Law 101" in the June 2015 issue of *The Writer* magazine and several short stories. She is currently writing the legal column, "Ipso Facto" for the Guppies' newsletter, *First Draft*, and blogging with the Mysteristas.

She still lives, and practices law, in Anchorage. When not writing or lawyering, she can be found riding her bike, hanging out with her Irish Wolfhound, studying the concert harp, or dinking around with oil paints.

A NOTE FROM THE AUTHOR

For more information about Maeve Malloy series, visit my website, www.keenanpowellauthor.com, where you can find more information about my inspirations, Alaska, and sign up for my newsletter. I always love to hear from readers. You can e-mail me directly at keenan@gci.net.

Made in the USA
Lexington, KY
07 November 2019